I0563769

The
Glass Factory

The Glass Factory

A FILOMENA BUSCARSELA MYSTERY

k. j. a. Wishnia

A DUTTON BOOK

DUTTON
Published by the Penguin Group
Penguin Putnam Inc., 375 Hudson Street, New York, New York 10014, U.S.A.
Penguin Books Ltd, 27 Wrights Lane, London W8 5TZ, England
Penguin Books Australia Ltd, Ringwood, Victoria, Australia
Penguin Books Canada Ltd, 10 Alcorn Avenue, Toronto, Ontario, Canada M4V 3B2
Penguin Books (N.Z.) Ltd, 182–190 Wairau Road, Auckland 10, New Zealand

Penguin Books Ltd, Registered Offices: Harmondsworth, Middlesex, England

First published by Dutton, a member of Penguin Putnam Inc.

First Printing, June, 2000
10 9 8 7 6 5 4 3 2 1

REGISTERED TRADEMARK—MARCA REGISTRADA

LIBRARY OF CONGRESS CATALOGING-IN-PUBLICATION DATA

Wishnia, k. j. a.
   The glass factory : a Filomena Buscarsela mystery / k. j. a. Wishnia.
      p. cm.
   ISBN 0-525-94545-8
   1. Buscarsela, Filomena (Fictitious character)—Fiction. 2. Policewomen—New York
(State)—New York—Fiction. 3. Hispanic Americans—Fiction. 4. Glass factories—Corrupt
practices—Fiction. 5. Hazardous wastes—Fiction. I. Title.
PS3573.I875 G58 2000
813'.54—dc21   99-087740

Printed in the United States of America
Set in Minion
Designed by Leonard Telesca

PUBLISHER'S NOTE
This is a work of fiction. Names, characters, places, and incidents are either the products of the author's
imagination or are used fictitiously, and any resemblance to actual persons, living or dead, business
establishments, events, or locales is entirely coincidental.

This book is printed on acid-free paper. ∞

To the real Katherina Minola

Do not go gentle into that good night.
Rage, rage against the dying of the light.
—DYLAN THOMAS

Prologue

It's too hot for me here, man."

"Relax, Abie. They're gonna send you to Venezuela."

Black shoes polished to gleaming bite into the plush evergreen rug in the shadow of the grandfather clock, leaving the tufted arabesques of a flock of seagulls taking flight.

"Of course, it'd be cheaper just to rub you out."

"Wha—?"

Blam! Flecks of red spatter the green.

They dump him on the pool table and go. They do not see. He's still alive. Still breathing. He scratches a word in the soft, green felt.

Then the tips of his nose hairs curl hotly with the unmistakable sharp scent—the slicing, acrid fingers of burning gasoline.

No.

I

The call came late. I hadn't heard from Detective "Van" Snyder in months.

"Yo, Filgirl! What you been up to? Puke in anybody's van lately?"

"I made it to the sidewalk."

"Not completely, baby."

"Sorry. That was a long, long time ago."

"Yeah. In dog years, maybe. So what are you up to?"

"Job hunting and trying to be a better parent than mine were."

"Another job search? Jeezus, you're all over the place, Fil—"

"Listen, Van, it's late. Why are you calling?"

"Late? It's not even eleven-thirty. I even know where my children are!"

"Well, mine's in bed, which is where I should be because she's going to get up in about six hours."

"Jeezus, Fil, why do you put up with that shit?"

"Because she's there."

"Yeah: her and Mount Everest both. Kids sure tie you down—"

"So what's up?"

"Remember your old friend Mr. Samuel Morse?"

"Every time I have to spray for roaches. Even a whiff of second-hand cigarette smoke still makes me feel like I'm gagging on a spiny sea urchin."

"Sounds bad, Fil. Anyway, I suppose you heard Morse has contracts in the works to add Kim Tungsten to that financial empire he's building out on the Island."

"I don't need this kind of torment, Van."

"Just thought you'd be interested."

"If I want to see two vipers fucking I'll watch *National Geographic,* okay? Speaking of reptiles, how's the lieutenant?"

"He's still the lieutenant. But hey, every year he stays a lieutenant is another year we don't gotta deal with him as a freakin' captain! You don't know him like I do, Fil. You see, underneath that rough exterior, lies a heart of *pure shit.*"

That makes me laugh. Good. If a detective sergeant can still make me laugh there's hope for me yet.

"Why don't you come around some time?" he asks me.

I tell him sure.

I don't think much more about it until one morning three weeks later when I start coughing up blood.

Shit.

And three months without a decent job or a health plan that considers my eyes and teeth to be part of my body. But it was better than nothing. Now I'm pulling in $6.75 an hour—no benefits— for extracting clogged data from the jaws of aging computers with red-hot pliers. And now this.

I decide I'd better not let it wait. For about forty dollars in U.S. currency I can get a "free" checkup at this Medicaid mill across the Harlem River and deep into the darkest Bronx.

Antonia asks me, "What's the matter, Mommy?" I tell her I'm coughing. She says, "Did you take that medicine to make you cough?"

"You mean 'cough medicine,' Tonia?"

"Yes. Because every time you take it, you always coughing after."

I'm trying to tie a bow in her shoes and I start laughing. "That's great," I tell her. She always sees me coughing when I take the medicine. Therefore, I must be taking medicine that makes me cough. Some detective she'd make. "Do you have to make pee-pee before we go?"

Of course she does. Now I have to undo everything I just did and put her on the toilet. Turns out she has a great deal of business to attend to. When she's finished, she insists on flushing the toilet. She once had a fit when I absentmindedly flushed it myself.

"Bye-bye, caca," she says, as it starts to go down. I shake my head at the kid things I would never think of (*I* sure didn't teach her this stuff), the natural Dadaist wonderland kids inhabit, like when she finds the stairs *up* to the library more interesting than anything *in* the library. "Daddy calls it 'shit,' " she tells me.

And I'm going to have to talk to Daddy, a.k.a. Raúl (that bum). Only sees her three hours a week but still manages to fuck up the kid's speech. (See? He's even got me doing it.) So we walk down four flights with me explaining how Mommy calls it "caca" because "shit" is a bad word and that we're not supposed to use bad words. Fine. Then we get outside, walk over to West 207th and Broadway just in time to hear two angry young dudes heat the air with swears:

"So the motherfucker tells me the fucking place won't haul without thirty-five *porciento* deposit *after* the twenty they've already done me for—"

"Damn!"

"I told 'em I don't take that shit."

And before I can stop her Antonia jerks herself loose and turns to one of the guys, who towers over her, big and dark against the sky: "Ooh, you said a bad word!" she says.

I've already thought up five different ways of saving my child's life when the big guy cracks a smile and starts laughing like a kid himself. "Your mama teach you that?" he says, eyeing me from top to bottom. "That's good. Your mama's all right. You listen to her."

Like I said: Kid things. We get to the corner and the light's against us. I lean out to see if the bus is coming and Antonia tells me, "Be careful," with the *exact* same intonation I use on her. I don't know which is more jarring: When she comes up with something completely original, which proves she's already a thinking individual, or when she says something that is such a perfect replica of my words that the implications are frightening. And only three. What's it going to be like when she's thirteen?

I give some change to the homeless panhandler standing on the corner like the messenger of some dark anonymous gods. Given our mission today, I need to appease them with some sacrifice.

The lights change and we cross the street, and suddenly the crosswalk is transformed into a glittering runway as I hear some guy singing, "There she goes, Miss America" at me, which I think is kind of cute until I see he's waiting at the bus stop. So now Tonia and I have to stand for ten minutes next to a guy who doesn't just imagine he's hosting the Miss America Pageant—no, that would be normal—he imagines he's *rehearsing* the Miss America Pageant: He keeps raising an arm to women crossing the street to C Town and singing and re-singing, "There she goes—There—There she goes, Miss A-*mer*-ica" as if he's testing the acoustics of the hall. Tonia thinks it's funny. I think he should be coming with us.

Halfway through the swimsuit competition the bus finally comes and I have to hold the kerchief that I keep in my pocket at all times to my nose and mouth because it's an old diesel that spews more smoke than a coal-burning Andean bus using mashed bananas for motor oil. We sit down by a window so Antonia can point out every third object all the way to Fordham Road. And she does, too. Then we transfer and wait for the long ride south.

Somebody's filming a movie two blocks down. We get to see a stuntman earn his pay by doing a one-and-a-half gainer headfirst out a six-storey window into the Grand Concourse with nothing but an "invisible" bungee cord tied to his ankle. Then they set up an "after" shot and drag a dummy corpse out onto the spot. Like there aren't enough real ones around.

"What's he doing?" asks Antonia.

I tell her they're making a movie.

"But why is he jumping?"

I tell her they're making a *stupid* movie.

"Why?"

Try explaining *that* to a kid.

I do the best I can before the bus comes and we grab a seat with today's paper left on it. After I install her by the window with an apple and a cracker she lets me open the paper and I learn that a three-mile oil slick with Day-Glo orange clumps floating in it was stopped with glorified sponges just one-and-a-half miles upriver from Manitock Inlet, a major fishing ground, source of maybe thirty thousand year-round jobs, half of the tourist dollars for Eastern Suffolk County and food for a few million people up and down the eastern seaboard. No one knows who dumped the stuff.

But I have my own problems. I get a sudden cough attack and I'm not quick enough with the kerchief. Blood comes up. Antonia asks what's wrong and I tell her that's why we're going to the doctor. She wants to know if the doctor is going to hurt me. I tell her no, as if I know anything.

The elderly black woman sitting across from us takes a sandwich wrapped in wax paper out of a brown paper bag, lays it across her knee and says silent grace over it. She may not know it, but I join her in it.

The glycerin suppositories feel like depth charges on the way in, then I've got to waddle to a seat around a guy in sandals and a Yankees jacket who seems to think he's directing helicopter traffic in the outpatient waiting area.

The medical staff think it's an ulcer or something digestive, so they ask me about a million questions about my diet even though I tried to tell them I think it's my lungs. They ignore me. So now I've got to dance and cringe on line for the one working bathroom on the floor because the depth charges have gone off without warning. It's actually enlightening how painful this is.

A test tube brush dipped in lye would have been smoother, but not as thorough. In the wink of an eye (or about four hours in real time) they take me into a four-person examination room so they can ram me with an anoscope—or whatever the hell they call it—which feels like a cheese grater going in and an ocean liner backing out. Antonia is getting very upset because I can't hide my pain.

Forty-five minutes later the kid has begun to split into three personalities on me and they come back to report that everything's fine with me. *Now* will they look at my lungs?

"X ray's closed. Come back tomorrow," I am told. I look at them like they're not getting rid of me that easy. "Unless you want to go to Emergency."

"Yeah."

Fortunately the ER has enough rubber gloves that can be blown up into five-fingered balloons, tongue depressors and other toys for the amusement of tots that Antonia adjusts to another two hours' worth of waiting a lot better than I do. I'm thinking, three months since I've had a decent job and all my pay goes to day care. I might as well be back in Ecuador. I mean, I've been thinking about heading back sometime ever since I came here more than a dozen years ago. I'd have a hard time surviving there, too, but at least I'd be with family. Warmth, love: These are good things. Tonia would love it, and besides, I think I've been away long enough to put up with the pain of trying to patch up and reorder the mess I left behind nearly half a lifetime ago. It can't be worse than this.

By the time someone comes to see me and I see that he's a first-year intern I'm too deep-fried into submission to ask for someone with more experience. I tell him the whole story: Heavy ex-smoker, ex-beat cop breathing in truck exhaust for five years, but the kicker is the time a man named Morse tried to kill me by locking me in a room with enough methyl isocyanate to take out a city of a hundred thousand.

He looks at me like that's only the third weirdest thing he's heard today. I told you this was a tough neighborhood. He decides to take a peek down my throat, makes me cough, then signs me up for an X ray. There's only a three-hour wait. If drama is real life with the dull parts cut out, then this must be where they send all the dull parts they don't use; so let's just say it's almost midnight when the intern comes back and tells me that the lung damage I suffered in an attempt on my life years before has developed into cancer, and that when it spreads to the rest of my body, I will die.

I know it's a cliché, but I'm under a lot of pressure here: I ask him how much time I've got.

He says, "Not much. Three to four months."

"*Whaaaaat?*"

"Maybe six to eight."

I guess I go a little nuts. I grab the X ray. It's got my name on it, all right.

No.

"No, wait," I begin to say, and he cuts me off.

"Look, pictures don't lie. I got twenty-seven more people waiting."

No.

I feel it. Burning in my chest. Hot, deep in the heart of me, eating its way out.

Of me . . .

DAMMIT! NO! NO! NO!

"Mommy?"

NO!

"Mommy?"

NO!

"Mommy! Mommy! Mommy!"

So that's it. Sickness. Loneliness. Death. Only good deeds will get you through it, or so they tell me. And then, gaseous expansion and decomposition. I shudder. A *cold* shudder. Not one of those nice ones like your lover's caress, partway between a tickle and a shiver. Not like that. A real *nasty* one.

"Mommy?"

"Yes, gorgeous?"

And yet there is continuing. My child, long and lanky, full of energy, full of life, full of questions, with her dark *canela* coloring, kinky raven hair and headstrong disposition. I'd better make sure Antonia doesn't get left with nothing, that there's something for her . . . not to follow—I mean, why should she follow me or anyone else's flawed example? But something . . . to guide her on . . . I shake my head. I don't know. . . . This isn't happening.

I hug her to me.

I pick up the phone and dial Van Snyder. He's not at the precinct house but they give me his beeper number without the usual sniggers. Maybe it's something in my voice.

I'm really glad when the phone rings. I'd open my soul to a direct mail solicitor right now.

It's Van. I tell him I want a warrant issued for Samuel Morse's arrest.

"Great! What's the charge?"

"Murder One."

"That was fast: Who's he killed?"

"Me."

"Fil, I'm on a short break, here—"

"I know you've got a stack of violations on him that are stickier than the floor of a porno theater."

"Oh, those. It'll take years to bring charges."

"I don't *have* years."

"Huh?"

"Well, maybe. I'm getting a second opinion."

"Fil. . . . What's wrong now?"

I tell him pretty much everything. For some reason I've always been that way with him. I even ask him how his wife is, who hated me so much.

"Fine," he says. Then: "Jeezus, Fil, I didn't expect—"

"I didn't expect either. Now will you help me?"

"Help you what? You want to go digging, go ahead. You want me to bail your ass out when you get caught, it's not my jurisdiction."

"Since when?"

"Didn't I tell you Morse is on the island? You know, that 'hospitable economic climate' they got out there?"

"Where?"

"He's got two big plants out in Carthage. What are you thinking of doing?"

"Nothing. Yet."

"I like the first part. Keep it that way, will ya?"

"Sure."

"And Fil—Jeez, I don't know what to say to you. If there's anything I can do . . ."

"Yeah. Thanks."

I think about that bastard Morse. What he did to me and what he's doing to others. Hundreds, probably thousands of workers dying a slow death from carcinogenic chemicals, insufficient workplace safety and his squash-anything-that-gets-in-my-way personality. It got him controlling interest in nine companies worth between $55 million and $2.3 billion *each*. But this all happened so long ago that if it weren't for the scarred lung tissue, it would have long since faded into memory. Then last year he had the balls to threaten my kid. Sometimes, I really wish I hadn't dropped my gun down that hole in the ice.

Antonia wants to play but my mind's too bent out of shape to stay at it for more than fifteen minutes. So I turn on the TV and hug her to me. I bury my nose in her hair. They've got a rerun of *Spartacus* on channel 9. Now *there's* a guy with problems. And I get a kick out of seeing how he deals with them, too. No "It'll take years to bring charges" for him. And you know, even in ghosting black and white, that scene where the trainer paints Kirk Douglas's bare, glistening torso just makes me melt. I'm not really happy about Antonia watching this, but she won't go to bed and I really want to see what happens. Try explaining Imperial Rome and slavery to a three-and-a-half-year-old sometime! Finally the first rebellion comes; guards get knifed, throttled—I'll never eat tomato soup again—and when they fall into a pool, Tonia says to me, "They're going to get wet."

I laugh. Such innocence. I almost wish she'd never lose it. But of course she will—she must—to survive. Oh, Lord. . . . Why? Why?

I read her to sleep, then pick up the phone to call—who? Jen? Beto? Betty's on vacation. I even think of calling Mr. Wang, for Christ's sake! I've got to try to sort this out. This isn't happening. . . . Okay, Antonia's got to come first. So I think of Rowena and George:

She teaches Africana studies at Bronx Community College, he's a jet-black cricketeer from Trinidad who plays hardball gloveless. We've cared for each other's kids through the babysitting co-op—and that's about as close a relationship as I've got in the 'hood and, yes, I really do have their phone number on the inside of a matchbook.

And of course it's too late at night to call someone with kids.

I get about as much sleep as any infantrywoman gets the night before battle, so I'm fresh as a sun-dried Dumpster daisy when I get George on the phone and arrange to meet at the playground. I try to put Antonia in a T-shirt and jeans since she always wants to design cities in the sandbox, but she insists on a dress. Where does she get this urge for femininity from? Must be TV. Not from me.

It's one of those spring days that's sunny enough to fool you until a cloud passes and the temperature drops twenty degrees. Antonia runs free to join the kids on the jungle gym. George is cleaning up some trash from last night's adult playground users.

"Hey, Trini-dude-man, what's up?"

"They say people are drinking less hard alcohol," he says, dropping an armful of cans and bottles into the recycling pail. "Obviously not around here."

We spend about fifteen minutes shooting the breeze because neither of our cultures considers it polite to get directly to an issue. Also, how do you ask someone if he's willing to make sure your kid gets back to your family safely just in case you happen to die in the next couple of weeks? Stumped you? Well, keep thinking. Turns out he's got bad news of his own. The coffee plant, jewel of Hoboken and biggest employer on the Jersey-side waterfront, is closing. We agree that the local economy is becoming indistinguishable from those "Third World" economies we both fled to come here. Eventually I get around to telling him that I need a couple to act as godparents, just in case.

He says, "How 'bout Raúl?"

"No."

"He is Toni's father."

"Don't remind me."

"You've gotta stop being such a lone wolf, Filomena. You can't take on something like this alone. Think of Antonia."

"I am: Her father sold all our stuff to pay the rent on that cocaine castle in the air he was living in and you want me to go to *him* for help?"

"That was three years ago."

"Okay, last year he stole my tax refund check, forged my endorsement and bought himself a new car stereo with it."

"Yeah, well this is different. He's the girl's father, and you need him. You might as well admit it."

This is *not* what I wanted to hear.

I watch Antonia swinging upside down, her dress falling down over her face and laughing.

I curse.

And agree with him.

"Yo, where's the party at?"

"Why do you always answer the phone like that?" I thought it was cute, once.

"Filomena! *¡Mamita! ¿Como vás muchachita?*"

"Like shit, Raúl. I need your help."

"*¡Que milagro!* You *must* be doing like shit if you want *my* help."

"Don't make this any harder. Can I come over?"

"*Ah, por fín te recuerdas que nadie te lo da como yo—*"

"Make me heave, all right? I've got a problem. A *real* one."

"Baby, if it's your problem—"

"Raúl, never be indifferent when people need you."

"Yes, ma'am. What's in it for me?"

"No jail time and you can keep the car stereo, too."

"You still pissed off about that? Because let me tell you, *chiquitína—*"

"Raúl, will you shut the fuck up and listen to me?! I'm—I'm sick."

"So take a aspirin."

"No, I mean—Boy it all comes back so quick with you. We always had *real* communication problems."

"Funny, you never said anything about it to me. . . ."

"Could you turn the music down for a second? This is serious. It's about Antonia." *That* gets him.

"My little sugarplum? What about her?"

"I'm worried. I don't think she should stay in the *barrio* any longer."

"Why not?"

"It's not healthy for her. I have to tell her *never* to touch the needles she sees in front of the building."

"Hmm. *¿Y qué entonces?*"

I realize that we have switched to Spanish without me noticing it. That's not like me. I mean, my survival usually depends on me noticing things. "I'm thinking of maybe taking her back to Ecuador with me. But I don't have the money. These last three months have really scraped me to the bone."

"Back to Ecuador? With my kid? Fuck that. She can come live with me!"

"You just agreed she should move out of the city."

"Oh, yeah. Well she can stay with my sister."

"Oh, terrific. This is the woman who has never seen her niece? No thanks."

"Hey: You've never seen her kids neither. Least they've got a backyard."

"Where's that?"

"Minoa."

"Where's *that?*"

"Long Island."

You can just about hear me go *ding!* "Is that anywhere near Carthage?"

"How the fuck should I know? Get a fuckin' map! No, wait—now that you mention it, yeah—I think it's like about five, maybe ten miles west of there: The big steel-and-glass place, right?"

"Computer casings."

"Yeah, sure, that's the place. Yeah, five miles, tops."

"What's her number?"

"You serious?"

"Yeah."

"Hey, great! Does this mean we—?"

"Make me heave, all right?"

Raúl gives me his sister Colomba's number and I scramble for a map of Long Island. Antonia wants to see where all her friends live, which I'm usually more than willing to show her—maps are supposed to be educational, right?—but I'm trying to dial someone who hates me, look up Minoa and Carthage on a map of Suffolk County and Antonia keeps wanting to turn back to the page with New York City on it.

"Mommy!"

"Later, Toni."

"Mommy!"

"Not now, dear. Mommy has to kill someone."

2

It is my belief, Watson, founded upon my experience, that the lowest and vilest alleys in London do not present a more dreadful record of sin than does the smiling and beautiful countryside . . . Think of the deeds of hellish cruelty, the hidden wickedness which may go on, year in, year out, in such places, and none the wiser.
— SHERLOCK HOLMES in "The Copper Beeches"

I've been told that true heroes do not set out on quests, they are forced into action by circumstances. But Heracles, Samson, and our own defiant Incan leader Atahualpa never had to ride an LIRR train that smells like last month's sewage. The stop is called Nequonsett, and it looks close to Minoa on the map, but five miles is a long freaking way when you're hauling a menagerie with you. I should have known better.

Aeneas-like, I enter the new world lugging my past on my back and my kid by one hand. Plus a cat carrier with our orange tabby, Puchungo. Don't ask. Last night after cramming our lives into storage crates, mailing books off to South America, letting the landlord know he was going to have to suck someone *else's* blood for a while and quitting my job (notice?—Ha!), the kid decided to lose contact with reality regarding our need to give the cat away and by a quarter to midnight it all came down to a choice between a major pain in the ass I hadn't counted on or a psychotic child. I opted for the major pain in the ass.

"What's that smell?" is the first thing Antonia says.

I can't tell, at first. Then I place it: The sharp, fetid odor of a million freshly fertilized suburban lawns traveling heavily on the breeze. But something is rotten in paradise: FOR SALE signs are toppling over with age. We take a taxi through a pretty snappy neighborhood, where every house looks the same, every street looks the same, and every street *name* is the same, for God's sake, mile after mile of "Pyramid Place," "Pyramid Path," "Pyramid Parkway," "Pyramid Passage." Who came up with this hypnotic, nightmarish sameness? I half expect to see Franz Kafka and Rod Serling splitting a pitcher of ten-cent lemonade on the next fluorescent green lawn.

The ride is getting long, and the meter keeps climbing. If this is how much it costs to get around out here I might as well sink my savings in a used car; five more rides like this and it'd pay for itself.

The cat is raising a fuss. She has been trapped in the carrier for nearly four hours. Antonia tells her to "Shut up." Can't imagine where she got that expression from.

"I have three cats," says Antonia.

"*Three* cats?" I ask.

"Puchungo, and Puchungo's friend—" A stray who used to howl at our window when Puchungo was in heat "—and Rosa."

She still remembers Rosa, who died when Tonia was a little over a year old.

"Rosa ran away," she says. "She doesn't like me anymore."

That's it. I used to tell her Rosa "went away," but I can't continue the nice euphemisms if it makes her think the cat ran away because it doesn't like her anymore. "Tonia," I tell her, "Rosa will *always* like you. She didn't run away. She died. She's with Snowball One—she's in cat heaven."

"She's in cat heaven?"

"Yes—"

Sorry, but I'm not about to enter into the whole do-animals-have-souls issue. It is of no comfort to a child to tell her that her cat is being eaten by worms two feet underground. And where is the soul of Antonia's sister? Poor little thing never stood a chance. Am I supposed to meet her in heaven—a three-month miscarried fetus whom I never knew? I rub my tired eyes, and hug Antonia to me. Do you believe that I still get them? The nightmarish infant mortality fears? Not as often as when she was a newborn but I still get them. Once you've lost something that innocent . . .

There better be a heaven. Or else . . . My thoughts conjure up the grim vision of the last surviving humans standing in the bloodred sun, lording it over a dead planet.

And speaking of dead planets, we're entering Fairhaven town limits: an industrial wasteland bleaker than any Gothic windswept heath. Transplanted shrubs are not quite enough to hide the razor-wire-capped steel-mesh fence that rigidly defines the perimeter of an adhesive factory. Four distant smokestacks belch a sulfurous smog so thick even the wind-borne traces sting my eyes and sear my lungs. And a linen handkerchief isn't much good against the Devil's own smelting works. My great-grandparents would have fled in terror from the smell alone. But the dingy line of prefab row houses across the street indicates that today's inhabitants don't have the sense my ancestors had. Or maybe the option to flee.

How about that word, "smokestack"? Quite a quaint throwback to an earlier era, ¿no es así? I'm amazed they're still called that. If they had just been invented, they'd probably be called "residual distribution enhancers" or something. You can charge higher rent across the street from one of those.

The stench shifts from a sulfurous, sweet, acidy sting to a thin, warmish wind with the same sweet aftertaste. Bleaah. Imagine my pleasure when the taxi driver pulls up across the road from a fenced-in wasteland of bulldozers and backhoes, dirt piles and stacks of fifty-five-gallon drums and sheets of broken glass and announces, "Forty-four Pleasant Valley Road. That'll be thirty-four dollars."

"Thirty-four dollars? Where are we—Khazakhstan?" I ask. He fails to appreciate that. If this is what the L.I. prices are like, I might as well head for home. As if I had one. Fortunately, I always keep some of that green-gray paper on hand just to pacify the na-tives in case they get unruly. Blighters worship the stuff, you know.

Nobody's there to meet me. The front door's locked. I recheck the address and look around for landmarks, but the taxi driver has already turned around and sped off. Should have told him to wait.

Having no other choice, I shoulder our bags and schlep around back, where a couple of chickens are tied up. They don't look happy to see me, either.

The screen door's locked, too. Inside a woman is chopping vegetables with a ten-inch carving knife. I knock. She starts and turns like she's been jumped from behind before (that *is* why I knocked) and stops the door with her foot. She doesn't put the knife down.

"What do you want?" she says. Oh yeah, we're off to a great start.

"Colomba?" Nothing. "I'm Filomena. This is Antonia."

"Raúl no tell you don't bring stuff? We got no room here."

"It's job interview clothes," I tell her in Spanish, hoping my intention to get employed right away will soften her up to me a bit. Not a chance.

She unhooks the screen and turns back to her cooking. I guess this means we can come in, so I prop the door open and haul two bulging suitcases and the cat carrier into the narrow hallway just past the kitchen. I hear the TV and go look: Two young men fully capable of helping me with my bags are slouching on a twenty-year-old couch, watching MTV through their feet on a formica particle-board table. On screen a nerdy voyeur gazes through venetian blinds at a soft-porn star doing sexual aerobics on an empty bed while mainstream rock thrashes on the soundtrack and rapid editing gives the illusion of action.

These must be the two boys, Elvis—yes, I said Elvis—and Velasco, who is called "Billy." Elvis is twenty, tall and very thin, with a thin, thin ponytail in the back, crew cut in the middle, and a half-bottle of moussed post-punk pompadour in front. Billy is seventeen, I think, shorter and considerably heavier, shirttails out, hair uncombed, slouching deeper into the couch. And possibly a blanker look on his face, but that's really tough to call.

Elvis looks up, his attention momentarily caught between a sex kitten on video and a tired-out mother falling feet first into fossil-hood live in his living room. He decides to privilege proximity over fantasy and gets up to have a closer look. I can tell he's thinking, "Hey, not bad for a mom." Kids his age still think they can look you up and down and you won't notice it.

"Where can I put these?" I ask, pointing to our bags.

"Not in my room," says Billy, without looking at us.

"Rosita's room, *chica*," says Elvis, as if that means anything to me.

While we're taking the bags upstairs I complain about the high-priced cab ride and Elvis says, "That trip costs twelve-fifty, *chica*. You were ripped."

Yes, I was! Of course I should've caught that. What is happening to me? Oh yeah: I'm worried about dying before July Fourth weekend. It's just that it's making me lose all my street smarts. And I'm going to be needing them.

Antonia's bored by MTV, so she's playing with the broken Nintendo in front of an altar to Our Lady of Shock Absorbers opposite the TV. Any kid under four years old is guaranteed to find the most dangerous thing in the room in thirty seconds or less, and sure enough, there's a battery of plugs overloading a socket under all the altar drapery, and Antonia's all ready to poke at it. I pull her away.

"We could use something to drink," I say.

"Help yourself," says Elvis, pointing to the kitchen.

I rinse a glass from the sink, turn on the tap, fill it and take a big glug. *Wrong*: I'm not making the best impression right now, but my first concern is spitting everything out in the sink. The water tastes like *crap*. Or more precisely, like photo lab chemicals. The only cold thing they've got for me is no-alcohol beer. I gargle with it. That goes over big, too. At least it clears the taste of Dektol out of my mouth.

I ask where the nearest grocery store is so I can buy some juice for Antonia. You understand I keep trying to show I'm not here to freeload. Might as well be talking to a wall.

"It's two miles west on Route 25, in Carthage," shouts Elvis from the TV room.

"*Two* miles?" I say to Colomba. Silence. Sure, this is fun.

I've got nothing better to do than wait for the grains of my life to run out, so I decide to kill another portion of whatever short life I've got left standing around this sweet-smelling kitchen waiting for my proxy sister-in-law to speak directly to me. She gets three onions, ten carrots, a *refrito* of green pepper and tomato and every spice on the shelf into her stew, stirs it, tastes it, stirs it, tastes it, stirs it, tastes it, before she addresses me:

"Don't you have something for me?" Oh.

"Yeah, sure," I tell her, reaching for the money. "This is for one month's rent—" $350: almost what we were paying in New York for a whole apartment "—this is for the phone because I'll be making a lot of calls trying to find work and all, this is for the electricity, water, oxygen and whatever the hell else we might cost you. There," I say, piling the cash on the wet counter in front of her. "That's about every dollar I've got. Another couple of hundred and I'd have bought two tickets to Ecuador instead." I don't want her to think I *need* this.

Colomba counts it twice as if I've got a history of stiffing her or something then stuffs the soggy wad into her apron.

Right now I need food, drink, the want ads and the phone number of the nearest hospital. In that order. Maybe it's respect for the kid, but Colomba silently puts out two plates of rice and ladles some watery stew onto both of them. She doesn't call the boys so I guess it's for us. We eat in silence. The only newspaper in the house is last Saturday's, opened to the Lotto results, but that's the day they run a special classified section, so I'm in luck. Lucky me. Elvis finds a coverless phone book for me and tells me to try the teaching hospital attached to the University at Running River ten or fifteen miles north of here. Everything's slow as can be, but it's cheap, he says. Wonder what he's been there for.

I call up and ask for an appointment with a lung specialist. They tell me I have to make an appointment with a student intern first. So be it. They ask me how's next Thursday at 9 A.M. with Dr. Chu? I tell them I can't wait that long. They put me on hold for a few minutes then come back and tell me that's all there is. Now I've always tried to be an honest, work-within-the-system kind of person, but right now my fuse is getting a little short. I thank them and hang up. Then I call back, tell them I'm Dr. Buscarsela of Bronx Veterans Hospital's radiology unit, and ask them what time tomorrow I can consult with Dr. Chu. They put me down for 3 P.M. Sorry, God. But it's for a good cause. I swear.

There is a tremendous crash from across the street as a dump truck starts unloading broken sheets of heavy plate glass onto the ground inside the fence. They must have been on their lunch break. Terrific. Scared the crap out of me.

I take Antonia out back to play so I can sit in the sun, breathe in the air with the peculiar sweet aftertaste, listen to the sound of bull-dozers piling up heaps of scrap metal and glass, and read the classifieds. There's not a lot of stuff. There's an opening for a telemetrical engineer with five years' experience in computer-aided design for F-15 jets, and the county wants a Recycling Supervisor with ten years' experience and an MA in waste management, but otherwise it's a couple of columns of Waitress ($2.25/hr plus tips), Asst. Beautician (ditto), Asst. Landscaper (must have own tools and truck), Asst. Plumber (ditto), etc., etc., straight down to the bottom of the barrel. "Positions Sought," however, is a fat twenty-five pages, ten columns each in six-point type, of professionals and middle-management with an average of twelve years' experience willing to take 50 percent pay cuts, desperate to do anything to stay in the area. I understand there's some Trans-Himalayan mule packer jobs opening up along the Nepalese border, but the commute's a killer.

There are a few prospects: a part-time job teaching basic English to immigrants, and a couple of pink-collar jobs that all say they want "bright, intelligent, innovative, fast learners." I consider myself all those things. Like the time I busted out of an Ecuadorian jail by throwing fresh-squeezed lime juice into a cop's eyes, pushing him through a window and shooting out the courtyard lights with his gun while four of my comrades scrambled down the back stairs under a barrage of machine-gun fire. That was pretty innovative. I pick up the phone and lie my way into three interviews. Fuck honesty.

Look what it's gotten me.

Colomba and Billy still haven't spoken directly to me in two days, so I decide to take Antonia with me on the interviews rather than leave her here with them. Rosita comes bounding down the stairs with all the bubbliness of a nineteen-year-old high school grad who can type sixty-five words per minute and buy a sports car with it. If her dress were two inches longer it'd be a mini-skirt. She squeals with delight at the sight of Antonia, and cootchy-coos her while Tonia admires her six-inch-high petrified hairdo.

I ask her, "Don't you know there's a mousse shortage?"

She shakes her cotton-candy conk and laughs at my joke, then she springs like a coiffed gazelle into a yellow convertible and *Vrrooooms!* off to work. I realize now I could have used the ride.

Rosita uses hot wax (no thanks), so I've got to shave my legs and underarms with a razor rough enough to plane a door. I hate job interviews.

Elvis's friends come by to carpool, and I charm them into driving me to the bus stop. Billy doesn't move from the couch.

I never knew the term "Bus Stop" was so open to interpretation. It takes me an hour and a half to determine that no buses are stopping here this millennium. I guess we're all supposed to drive. Having given myself nearly two hours' head start, I've now got fifteen minutes to make it to an interview in a town I've never heard of. I get to a deli phone and call a cab. Twenty minutes later a cab comes for me, takes us on a long ride and drops us at the door to absolutely nowhere. It takes me several minutes to realize that the place I'm looking for is a warehouse a thousand feet from the road. Going to have to check the classifieds for used cars.

Sweaty and stressed-out—and it's only 10:15—I arrive and I find out I needn't have rushed: The place has set up about twenty-eight interviews for "10 A.M. sharp," and the wait begins. They get to me just before noon. I tell them I've taught Survival English before, and they stop me in mid-speech to tell me that they are *not* interested in having me teach the immigrant workers filling the place anything besides what they need to know to follow simple commands. Like "fetch," "roll over" and "play dead"?

The next two jobs—the ones that wanted "bright, intelligent, innovative, fast learners"?—are boring, repetitive and mindless. Now that's false advertising. The last one wants a urine sample. I piss in the cup and shove the wallet-sized copy of the Bill of Rights I carry down into the specimen jar. Should be in a museum: "Piss Fourth Amendment."

I just don't have time for this crap anymore, but without the income I can't get to where I need to be in order to skewer Morse's head on a stake. It's just taking so *long*.

We hitch a ride to the hospital. It's eight miles out of the guy's way but I talk him into it. Sometimes the truth works, too.

Dr. Chu is kind enough to see me, but it still takes sixty dollars to confirm that I need to see the lung specialist who isn't available until next Tuesday. Damn. But I do get some help. The accounts payable clerk is one of those exceedingly rare lifers, permanently adhered to her institutional chair, who has *not* become a bloodless paper handler. She tells me the hospital has an income-based financial assistance program, but I have to apply for Medicaid first and be rejected. Makes sense. I ask her where the County Office of Social Services is, she tells me Coram.

Where the hell is Coram? Only about fifteen miles southeast of Running River, but twenty dollars each way by cab or three hours by bus. Screw this. Turns out we're walking distance from the train station. Running River's a pretty nice-looking North Shore village. It's good to know there are still some trees left on Long Island. Two hours later Antonia and I are chugging through the Sunnyside train yards and into the tunnel under the East River to Penn Station. We spend the night at my friend Charrito's and the next day I take all my stuff out of storage, sell half of it to the guy running the place and haul the rest downtown to sell it for whatever I can get. It takes all day for my music, my clothes, my couch, my comforts to fetch $350 in American money. And I take it.

Friday morning we're back on Long Island and I'm answering ads for used cars. The first two are pieces of crap, but the third has just been tuned to sell, and I bully the guy down from $500 to $225 in three minutes he'll probably never want to go through again (the ad said $750), but I'm already a week closer to death and not one minute closer to nailing Morse. The heap has a single sun-faded fuzzy die, minus its partner, dangling from the rearview mirror. I reach up reflexively to yank it off, then decide to leave it. They tell me God does not play dice. And He has the house advantage.

We drive to Coram so I can waste the afternoon at Social Services. Two claims processors are trying to screen seventy hot, frustrated people who spill out of the room and into the hall. Another fraction of my life is gone forever by the time they get to me. They ask me for "Evidence of Identity," which turns out not to be as easy as I thought. I learn that the card I've been carrying for more than a decade is *not* my Social Security card but the "receipt," and that they need to see the actual card—which means I lost it maybe twelve years ago and I have to apply for a new one, which will take three to four weeks at least. This is time I don't have. It takes another couple of hours to find out we're not even close to being eligible for Medicaid because we've got too many assets. I was honest and said I was living with family and that I had just bought a car. I won't make that mistake again.

Saturday morning we drive to a bank so I can apply for a short-term loan to cover medical costs. They're digging into my credit record when I realize that this is one of those S&Ls that my taxes are now bailing out. So I've got a better credit record than they do and they're checking *me* out! None of this makes me feel any better. I still don't know what I'm going to do about paying the doctor bills. I suppose I could probably run them up, die, and have them bill my estate. But then I remember they really do that. So Antonia will be four years old and $30,000 in debt.

I don't think so.

So what do I do?

I think. I know how Morse does business: He's slick, tough and greedy, but his cockiness sometimes makes him a bit sloppy. I nearly nailed him for tax evasion two years ago. If I can prove he's still at it, the IRS will pay me 10 percent of the first $75,000 recovered, capping the reward at $100,000, which would provide nicely for Antonia, at least until she's eighteen. There must be a few weak links in his chain of power, I've just got to find one. Something he's done that'll cost him a *lot* of money if I can get him on it.

And if that doesn't work, *then* I'll kill him.

*   *   *

"Hospitable economic climate," huh? Not for me or anybody else I've met out here, it isn't. Chain stores I thought were national institutions are closing up, putting thousands out of work, others are "trimming" staff by 50 percent, and those who are left with jobs are being blackmailed into double overtime at no compensation because if they won't do it, there's a long line of people who will.

By Saturday night I can't take any more and I find myself slouching on the couch next to Billy with about the same dazed stupor overcoming my features. Billy's excuse is the six empty beer cans in a rough semicircle around his feet. Mine is just mental strain, physical tension and extreme mortal anxiety. There isn't enough beer in the world to fix that (although some have tried).

"Man, that Elijah Watson can steal a basketball from a moving train."

I look over. Billy spoke to me. I've had other things on my mind, but I've learned to go for an opening wherever I can find one. I could use someone in this house who answers me back.

"It's those long arms," I say. "And twenty years of practice on the toughest playgrounds in the city." Pause. Then: "What happened to your arm?" I've noticed he doesn't use his left arm. He tells me he's had almost no use of it since nearly two years ago while playing high school football he was tackled and landed on an upturned shard of broken beer bottle left on the field from the previous week's victory party. Ouch. That explains a lot, but not enough. His arm may be no good for football, but I've seen a lot of torn cartilage in my years and his doesn't look that serious—I mean, he can open beer cans and change the channel pretty well with it. No, this kid doesn't *want* to move. I sense he needs help, but more than I can spare for anybody else right now.

Or so I think.

Sunday morning we all finally submit to the pretense of going to church as a group, and the Old Testament reading is a command from Proverbs to "Speak up for those who cannot speak for themselves," and "not to stand idly by while your neighbor bleeds."

Though it doesn't say anything specific about your neighbor slowly wasting away from lung cancer, I figure that's the general idea. After church Billy refuses the car ride, says he'll walk back with Antonia and me. That's news to everybody. We stop at a bakery and Antonia blackmails me into getting her pistachio cookies. I hand the cashier a fifty-dollar bill. She checks it carefully and *snaps* the change as she counts it off.

"You've done this before, I see."

We're halfway through the bag when Billy takes us past the school and stands at the fence, staring at the football field.

"This is the last time I fought for anything," he tells me. "At least I knew what was up. The game had *rules*. There's no more rules to follow."

"Sure there are."

"Like what?"

"Like it says in the Bible: to fight for the little guy."

"The little guy ain't always right."

We stare for a few more minutes, then walk past this school where for twelve long years he learned he was useless for anything other than football—and now he can't even do that. I tell him mistakes in life should be like mistakes in the kitchen—throw them right out.

"Nobody keeps spoiled pea soup on the shelf. The smell alone would be unbearable."

He says: "What are you talking about?"

"I guess I am babbling, aren't I?"

"You sure are."

And not one inch closer to my goal. Whatever that is. No, I know what my goal is, all right, the question is, How do I get there from here?

I get the answer from Colomba. We get home, lunch is served, and she hands me yesterday's classifieds, with four job openings circled in red. Two of them are at Morse's computer factory.

3

What's the point of women joining the mainstream if the
stream is polluted?

—Bella Abzug

Well, this hero is spending the night before battle trying to get
her kid to eat her vegetables. I explain the importance of eating a
variety of other foods, and I get nods of understanding, but no cooperation.

"You've got to eat your veggies, Tonia," I say. "Popeye eats his
spinach, that's why he's so strong; Bugs Bunny eats carrots, that's
why he's so smart."

"But Bugs Bunny doesn't eat *other* food," she says.

Colomba laughs. I have to admit she's got me. "Three-and-a-
half years old and she's got me."

"Mommy, you're silly," says Antonia.

Oh, no. My kid has finally discovered that her mother's not rational. I've had her fooled for almost four years but no more.

Monday morning I call to confirm an appointment I haven't
made with Techtonics, Inc. Typical Morse operation: The frenzied
receptionist is too overworked to admit she's never heard of me
and squeezes me in for 11:30. Rules are for *gringos*.

I decide it's okay to leave Antonia with the family today. I
wouldn't want to take her to Morse's place anyway. I think you'll

back me on that one. I kiss and hug her good-bye, fire up the heap and head west. The words "East Carthage" are superimposed on my Hagstrom's with the same authority as the words "Carthage" and "Minoa," yet it is conspicuously absent from the reality I'm driving through. In less than a mile "Minoa" becomes "Carthage" without passing through this intermediate stage. Okay.... But I'm too busy dealing with a guy in a black 'Vette riding my butt at 65 mph the whole way. Fuckhead. Like he's in a bigger hurry than I am.

Morse Techtonics is a snappy new steel-and-reflective-glass building with enough bevels and angles and shrubs to make it look like an oversized high-tech greenhouse, pristine and green and gorgeous, but it smells as bad as in Minoa. I've got to find out what that smell is.

I'll admit I'm a bit nervous about running into the guy himself and blowing it all too soon, but I'm banking on my knowledge of Morse's character, and I figure the Personnel Office is probably pretty far from the Executive Suite. Besides, he's only seen me dressed for battle. I'm fighting a whole different way this time.

I win the first hand, and breathe a lot easier after I sign the Visitor's Log, pass under the handheld metal detector and am directed to a quiet suite of rooms down a long hall in the opposite direction from the front offices. Two other applicants are ahead of me, hot-waxed legs crossed, seams straight, flipping through supermarket magazines that promise Better Sex in Three Days, and How to Get Him to Commit, but absolutely *nothing* about How to Murder a Bloodsucking SOB. And they say they've got "Everything today's woman needs to know." For shame.

I check in with the receptionist, who says she needs "another" copy of my résumé (she won't admit she can't find it), so I hand her one from my genuine leatherette business case. Much of it is actually true.

My sister interviewees do not look at me. Okay, I don't particularly want to be seen, anyway. I'm taking the place in—large parking lot outside (more than a thousand cars), six loading docks, and a pretty large office staff, or so it seems. Nice water cooler, too. This receptionist is only screening calls for the Personnel Director.

A one-to-one boss-secretary ratio is getting pretty rare these days. But my immediate use for this info is if this place is big enough, maybe I can get lost in this system. I hope so.

The door opens and the first woman ahead of me is told to go in. She's a good ten years younger than me, blond, svelte, and looks like she gets plenty of dates but might need a few lessons in Getting Him to Commit. The other woman is even younger, looks like she'll be graduating high school in about three weeks. I shift in my chair and flip open the company newsletter. Shipments are steady, which is about as rosy as a report gets these days. And the execs have sacrificed a ten-foot walk to the building for a twenty-foot walk so the row flush against the plant can be designated for HANDICAPPED PARKING ONLY.

A loud burst of confident male laughter explodes on the other side of a flimsy partition, the door adjacent to the room where the interviews are being conducted opens, and out steps a man in a light-gray summer suit. He's young, in his early thirties, but already going soft around the belly and jowls, and his dirty blond hair is getting pretty thin, too. Must be the fumes. Even with three air-conditioners running, the place still smells of the stuff. The guy plants his briefcase on the receptionist's desk like he's Pizarro conquering *terra incognita* for the Spanish Crown and starts putting the moves on her. He's crude, obvious, but careful enough to tread that fine gray line between flirting and sexual harassment.

When he asks to see the "Winston file" and she has to bend way forward in that loose-fitting dress to open the W drawer, I lose interest and start checking out the back issues of the newsletter. A tiny paragraph on the inside back page of the February issue suggests that some new air-handling ducts for the molding room may be arriving before the workers keel over from the fumes. It does note that the first requests for new ducts were made six years ago.

"*Here's* a long-stemmed wineglass," I hear from over my shoulder. I look up and he's staring at me. He is *not* holding a wineglass.

"What did you say?"

He kind of clownishly backs off like he's fending off an imaginary Popeye blitzed on three cans of spinach. "No, no, no: He's hit, he's going, he's *down*," and he doubles over and falls to his knees in front of me.

Well. *That* was different.

"What's your name?" I ask him.

"Hey, that's my line."

"All right: Get lost."

"I like my line better."

"Words are not your exclusive property, Mr.—?"

He smiles. "Okay. Stella. James Stella. But you can call me—"

"Jim."

"*Right*. Or Jim-bo."

"I'll stick with 'Mr. Stella' for a few minutes, okay?"

"Okay," he says, dusting off his knees and sitting down next to me. " 'Til when?"

" 'Til you tell me what you do, Mr. Stella. Don't give me that look: I saw you looking at my résumé. You know everything about me and I know nothing about you. Now is that fair?"

"I'd hardly call your résumé 'everything' about you, Ms. Filomena Buscarsela of six-one-seven West Two Hundred and Fifteenth Street, New York City."

"It's everything you're gonna get for now, Mr. James Stella of Meyers, Craig, North, Robinson & White, Attorneys-at-Law."

He looks at me. I go on: "An upside-down business card at twelve paces. Not bad, huh? It's that Andean air. I've got eyes like a condor's."

"Hmmm. What else did you get from this condor?"

Oh yeah: *His* interest is piqued. I tell him: "Oh, strength, perseverance—and I can smell a skunk two miles off."

He's not fazed. "What do you smell now?"

I give him a long, languid look. "I don't know. And I'd like to find out."

Funny thing is, it's the goddamned truth.

I have the interview, which is for a data-entry clerk in the billing department, oh boy, and they tell me they'll let me know in about a week. James Stella is waiting for me. He asks me to lunch. I accept.

I throw on this huge pair of sunglasses as we step into the hallway. Ten feet from the exit the security guard jumps to open the door and I get a sudden heart flutter, and half grab Mr. Stella by one shoulder so I can stare at his chest:

"Is that your school tie?" I ask, just as Mr. Samuel Morse himself walks *right* past us on his way to the elevators. But he's in the middle of bullying some bootlicker into submission and doesn't notice me.

"Look Vinnie," I hear Morse say, "The Kim expansion's gonna open up thirteen hundred local jobs, so you better make sure the committee knows that—"

"But the unions are saying it's only going to be three or four hundred full-time jobs, and the Pine Barrens people are all over the press: they've got a *lot* of community support this time. This ain't the right way of doin' it."

"Don't tell *me* how to do business—"

"No, no, no, Mr. Morse, but the timing—" And the elevator closes. Goddamn . . .

Back to my other reality, James Stella has already said, "Uh, no, I got this off the rack at Macy's. Twenty-eight dollars, marked down from forty. Real silk."

"Oh. It's nice."

"Thanks."

He's not sure what to make of me, but that's currently working in my favor. We get into his European luxury sedan and he drives us to a place that's about six times fancier than I expected. Business is good.

"Don't tell me you eat here every day," I say.

"Only with very special clients." This guy's about as smooth as a loan shark on payday.

He does the whole bit. Orders a full bottle of wine even though I tell him it's too early in the day for me; he sweeps that aside as if I were a child insisting on a carrot when he's offering banana splits. I tell him my mother warned me about accepting candy from men like him.

"I bet your mother'd approve of a lawyer bringing in six figures."

"Is that including decimals?" He smiles at me. "Nah, Ma'd probably have gotten down the shotgun."

"Shotgun wedding, huh? You know, for you, it'd almost be worth it."

I laugh. It sounds forced to me, but I think I'm supposed to be quivering with anticipation, so I guess it fits. Hell, I might as well go the whole hog, here. Trick #17-B from the Old Book: I start imitating him. He takes a drink of wine, I take a drink; he adds salt, I add salt; he cuts his meat, I cut mine. Take it from me, it's subliminal, and it drives men *wild*. Guilt? Sure—but there's that "good cause" clause in the contract.

He does a fair job on the bottle of wine (I remain resolute and stick to water after one glass) then orders two espressos, without asking me, and the check while I leave a breadcrumb trail to my groin wide enough for a blind ox to follow.

"But not if you work for Morse," I say.

"Huh?" His credit card clatters drily in the tray.

"Workplace flings leave me flat."

"Oh, that." I've succeeded in constructing an elaborate network of unspoken complexities between his sex organ and mine, and he tramples recklessly through it like a half-rutting boar to reach his goal: "Morse Techtonics is just one of my clients."

"How many others do you have?"

"Hundreds. We're a big firm. I usually have a dozen or so at a time."

"So what are you doing for Morse?"

A smirk crosses his lips. He chuckles at my no-nonsense business talk.

"I'm trying to help make the zoning for the Kim site more profitable."

"Oh. That's not going to be too easy, with all those environmental problems they've got."

All traces of the smirk have vanished.

"What do you mean?"

"You know that smell?" I say.

"Do I ever. I've had my nose right over those vats."

"Really? Tell me about it."

"Why?"

He's getting cagey. It's time to act up a bit.

"I'm just very sensitive to office conditions," I say, leaning forward and putting my hand near his. "My last administrative position was in one of those 'sick buildings.' I got a headache every single day."

"Aww, you poor thing. Well, the air quality in their offices is pretty damn good. Way above EPA standards. That's the advantage of being in the same building as Mr. Morse: He knows what kind of poison he's got in those vats, and he ain't about to let any of it get near him."

"So what *is* making that smell?"

"Well, it's not one thing that's doing that. That's a couple of hundred chemicals, and two dozen are bona fide killers."

"Go on," I slide a finger over his hand as I reach for my water.

"Ninety percent of Morse Techtonic's profit is PVC computer casings and wiring. PVC: Polyvinyl chloride?"

"Yeah, I know about that stuff."

"Yeah?"

"Yeah."

"Those guys in the molding room are breathing in enough parts per million to flambé their livers over the next couple of years."

"What's the lethal dosage?"

"In the air? You'd have to breathe in a thousand ppm for a couple of weeks. Not very likely."

"How about ingesting it?"

"Oh sure, with a side of fries?"

"I mean by accident."

"By accident? You'd have to take a swim in the molding vat."

"So humor me."

"Well, let's say you weigh about a hundred twenty pounds—"

"Thanks."

"So we're talking roughly fifty kilos, which means fifty thousand milligrams of vinyl chloride, or about two ounces."

"Two fluid ounces?"

"Yeah. But it'd be pretty noticeable. You can't exactly hide the taste with oregano."

"But I mean if someone fell into the vat, they could easily swallow that much."

"Oh sure."

"And it'd be fatal?"

"Look: Taking a header off the Hoover Dam would be fatal, too, but you don't see people selling tickets to that, do you?"

I laugh again. His credit card, his jokes. My plan.

"What about Kim Tungsten?"

"What about them?"

"It's the same smell."

"Oh, that? Sure, they use a lot of PVC. Everybody uses PVC. But the Tungsten place is an old tool and glass factory. Some of the workers started there as kids forty, fifty years ago, doing the spit-and-polish routine with rags and elbow grease. Nowadays they use a lot of industrial degreasers, like trichloroethylene, Circosolv, Fleck-Flip, Triad—"

"And what are the health effects of that one?"

"Pretty much the same. Hey, nobody's going to get lethal exposure and not know about it. Like I said, you'd have to take a bath in the stuff. They used to decaffeinate coffee with it," he says, pointing to our cups.

"With toxic chemicals?"

"Hey: You can drown in a vat of water, too. Nobody goes around calling that a 'toxic chemical.' "

"And nobody dies from a fifty-gram dose of it, either."

"Say, you're a fast learner."

"That's what the want ad asked for."

Now he laughs. Actually, we're getting along pretty well, but this turn in the conversation reminds him it's time to sober up, get back to work. He orders a refill espresso.

"How about dinner?"

"Tonight?" I ask.

"Sure, why not."

"Not tonight. I haven't seen my kid all day and we need to see each other."

"Oh. Tomorrow?"

"Okay."

"Okay? You're saying okay to a—a date?"

"Sure."

And he goes *yes!* like a tennis player who's just aced a serve. I shake my head and chuckle. I guess this I'm-still-a-clumsy-college-kid act works on some of these local babes. Otherwise, why would he use it? He drives me back to Morse Techtonics. I pretend I'm looking for a pencil to write down his phone number. Before he can stop me I open his glove compartment. Tissues, small change and—condoms. I'm sure Meryl Streep could pull it off. As for me, I let out a shamefully acted giggle and give him a knowing look as I return them to their enclosure. "Maybe later" is the message I hope he's getting. At least he gets the "later" part, because a slight incline towards me gets checked in mid-lean.

"I'll come by for you around seven," he says, as I get out.

"Why don't we meet there instead?"

"Why? Something about you you don't want me to know?"

I bend forward to talk through the window and give him just the briefest glimpse of the upper curve of my breasts. "What do *you* think?"

Pretty flagrant, huh? I will definitely get time in the penalty box for that one.

He smiles and pulls away to park his car. I give him a few minutes to disappear from the lobby, then I head back into the building. I tell the security guard that I left my sunglasses in the Personnel Office. He passes the metal detector over me, front and back, then escorts me all the way there and waits. I pretend to be looking, but it's hopeless with a cop watching me. I'm only about ten feet from the personnel files, but they might as well be under armored glass along with some artifacts from King Tut's tomb and guarded by the mummy's curse. Fortunately, I know how to work a glass cutter.

I'm pretty good with curses, too.

Not today, though. I tell the guard I "Must have left them in the restaurant" and thank him for his help as he guides me straight back down the hall and opens the exit door for me. Doesn't even count as a try. Mr. Stella is one possible angle, but I need more. I walk back to my car and sit there looking at the loading docks, but they, too, are fenced-off and guarded. From this side, anyway. Every workplace sucks in some way, and every one has a pissed-off worker.

I need to find him.

I get to Colomba's house and Antonia catapults through the air, full of life and love for me alone. I, too, smother her with kisses. I've been spending all my time with her lately, so I can't help longing to be away for a spell, then I spend a few hours away and I feel like it's been days. I don't let her out of my sight for the rest of the evening. We go to pick up ice cream for the family dessert, then I read to her from the few books we brought with us. After we say our prayers and I'm tucking her in and kissing her on the forehead she tells me:

"I don't have any balloons."

I look around. "No, you don't."

"Where are the balloons?"

"What balloons?"

"The balloons from my birthday!" Like it should have been obvious.

"Your birthday's not coming for another three months. Maybe we'll celebrate it in Ecuador."

"With balloons?"

"I hope so."

"I only get one birthday," she says.

"What do you mean, only one birthday?"

"Rosita has two."

Of course. Rosita still has favors pinned to her message board from her last two birthday parties. I try to explain to Antonia that we each get one a year, and that she'll have lots and lots of birthdays, my sincerest hope, but she is not convinced.

I stroke her forehead until she sleeps. All our problems should be so ephemeral. Where are the balloons of yesterday's birthday parties? They fade from glory faster than cut flowers, limp, rubbery and lifeless within twenty-four hours. Then I think, hell, most men get that way within twenty-four *minutes*. But balloons aren't as much fun. Generally.

Sweet dreams, my child.

The hospital sure makes me feel young again. Elderly patients crammed elbow to elbow in the hallway watch me hungrily as I walk past them to check in. I haven't exactly thought of myself as being enviable, but I can see by the lost looks in their watery eyes that my youth is something desirable to them, and gone forever. But I doubt any of them would be willing to trade with me.

The clerk punches my name into the terminal, confirms my appointment and tells me to have a seat. Fifteen minutes later a nurse leads me to a spotless examination room with floor-to-ceiling windows flooding the place with light. It's certainly an improvement over the last place I was examined in. Her tag says DORA. Dora records my weight, blood pressure, temperature, then instructs me to strip into a hospital gown and wait. Vertical blinds make for privacy, so why do I feel so aware of all my scars as I unclothe my imperfect body—my thighs are holding up, but my post-pregnancy abdomen will never be completely flat again—and suddenly feel cold, barefoot and barely wrapped in a thin piece of cotton cloth? The forensics microphone hanging from the ceiling doesn't help any.

I've got a few minutes alone with nothing but my own ugly thoughts that I keep at bay by focusing on the room's blandness. I think the Zen Buddhists would call it emptying your mind, or something like that. Soon the doctor comes. He's maybe a couple of years younger than me and a bit taller, with dark curly hair and a long, roundish nose.

"Ms. Buscarsela?"

"Yes."

"I'm Dr. Wrennch. So what can I do for you today?"

"I want you to have a look at my lungs."

"Oh, I need a parental signature for that—unless you can prove you're over twenty-one."

"Thanks." He probably says that to all his terminally ill patients.

"Seriously, what's the problem?"

"Don't you have Dr. Chu's report?"

"Sure. I want to hear it from you."

I tell him more than I'd tell some friends. Five years as a beat cop for the NYPD. Stress, family tragedies, love life disasters, all greased with the abrasive salve of booze and pot in quantities known to cause abnormalities in lab animals, and no solution. Then control, not cold turkey, but managed, like a slow-burning fire. But too late. Not before a corporate murderer I was tracking tried to sear my insides out with a barrel of cyanide vapor.

"Is there any history of cancer in your family?" he asks.

"I don't now. Records are pretty spotty."

"What did your mother die of?"

"Witchcraft." That raises an eyebrow. "I was just a kid. All the villagers said she was bewitched by my father's mistress."

"Oh. Uh, and what about your father?"

"I don't know if he's dead or alive."

"Oh . . ."

"Not your typical patient, huh?"

"No, none of mine are typical. It says you had an X ray done two weeks ago at Bronx Community Hospital."

"Yes."

"We've tried to contact them, with no results. Now, we can either wait, or we can take another one, which I wouldn't recom—"

"Take another one. Please. I want a completely separate opinion."

"You're sure?"

"Yes."

"Okay, let me see how soon we can have the room."

He leaves me alone in the pit of my fears for a few naked minutes. He comes back and says we can go in a couple of minutes. Then he takes out a light purple stethoscope and starts warming it in his hands.

I say, "I thought all stethoscopes had to be regulation black."

"Please, this is conservative. I could've chosen magenta or orchid, but I thought lavender went better with my scrubs. Deep breath."

He raises the back of my gown and presses the stethoscope to my ribs, so I guess he means me. I oblige, staring blankly ahead. "Again. Uh-huh. Again." He moves it over a bit, then down, then he steps back and unplugs his ears. "There's certainly a lot of wheezing, but not more than any former heavy smoker."

He asks me about the blood. I tell him it's happened a few times since I've been out here, like when a truck passes me on the road or the wind shifts and I get a lungful of incinerator ash from Kim Tungsten.

"I need to listen in front."

Maybe I'm just kind of slow today, but it doesn't really register. So he gently pulls down the front of my gown and places the thing on my chest. "Breathe." I oblige. He's in so close I can smell his cologne. Something leathery. Not my favorite. He straightens up.

"Let's go for the X ray." He helps me off the examination table and leads me out into the hall. And suddenly I am very aware of a chill breeze blowing up my back, and I feel pretty silly holding my two hands behind me, one high, one low. I wonder if Judgment Day feels anything like this.

He stands me up behind the big screen and stays close to me, making adjustments. I read his ID badge three times.

"*Please* tell me your name is not Alan Wrennch," I say.

"Well, I'm better off than my brother, Monkey," he says. "Just kidding. My middle name is Stanislaus. I use Stan."

"Then it's okay if I call you Stan?"

"Sure. They shortened it when my grandparents came from Byelorussia in 1916."

"From what? Wrennchowski?" He's spelling my name out in lead letters to identify the image.

"Nobody remembers. Could have been Rabinowitz for all we know."

"That's 'A.' "

"I beg your pardon?"

"B-u-s-c-*a*-r-s-e-l-a."

"That's quite a name yourself."

"I think it's two names run together. My family comes from a small mountain village in Ecuador. I think a few too many first cousins got married, half the town had the same last name and there was no way to tell anybody apart."

"Hold still. *Deep* breath and hold it." I oblige. *Crrzzzap!* "Okay, you can step down."

"How is that possible?" I ask.

"What?" he says, pulling out the X-ray film and handing it through the door to a lab assistant. "Rush that back to me in Room E-Six."

"That nobody knows your real name."

"Oh, my grandmother was only four years old when they came and if she ever knew the old name she took that secret to her grave with her fifteen years ago."

"Oh, sorry—"

"She had operable cancer, too. But the damn Upper East Side doctor didn't bother to do what he should've until it was too late."

"You mean, you know that now."

"Yeah. 'Oops. Your grandma's dead and I could've prevented it—sorry. And oh by the way here's your bill for twenty-three hundred dollars.' "

"So that's when you decided to become a doctor?"

"Yes, actually."

"Hmm. You see those shadows?"

"Yes."

"Those are the scars from your exposure several years ago. The lesions don't seem to have advanced beyond their initial state. But there are some odd shadows here—and here—they look almost tubercular. But it *could* be cancerous. We'd better schedule a biopsy. Can you come back on Friday?"

"Can't you do it now?"

"Mrs. Petrizzi is eighty-two years old. I can't keep her waiting."

"After that?"

"Two more."

"After that?"

"It's going to be at least a three-hour wait."

"I'll wait."

I keep insanity at bay for another hour-and-a-half by going through the much-thumbed and smeared waiting room copies of today's papers. U.S. Marines are in Italy trying to plug up an erupting Mount Etna with seven-ton concrete blocks. And they say *we* believe in witchcraft. A New York City program to buy illegal weapons with no questions asked has brought in 1,246 guns in three weeks, a local library is being closed for lack of funds, and a sharp entrepreneur is cashing in on the "Kill the Imports" craze by charging one dollar a whack for anybody who wants to stop by his Chrysler dealership and swing a sledgehammer at a Honda Civic. He's made $122 so far. But the human interest item that just brightens my day is a brief on the KKK's public disavowal of any connection with a group that has claimed responsibility for two bombings that killed a federal judge and a lawyer in Arkansas. The Grand Wizard says he never heard of the group and that it has no connection with the Klan. "I think it is a group trying to make the Klan and the racist groups look bad in front of the public," he said. I'm not kidding.

I call Colomba to see if everything's all right, and ask to speak to Antonia. She's playing happily, and doesn't want to come to the phone. I guess that's okay.

Two hours later Dora gives me a shot of local anesthetic in my butt (for my *throat?*) followed by a squirt of dark brown goo that I'm supposed to keep on my tongue as long as possible. As it slowly seeps down, I lose some feeling in my gullet. Dr. Stanley Wrennch returns, wheeling in what I learn is a bronchoscope. He's planning to send this fiber-optic tube down my trachea to my lungs, hack a bit off and come out again. Dora rubs my shoulders a bit to relax me so I don't bite down on $30,000 worth of fiber optics, and Dr. Stan gets to work.

"Are you taking any medication?" he asks. Why do they always ask you questions when your mouth is full of medical equipment?

"Just birth control pills," I manage to answer. Don't know why, since I haven't had sex in three months. At least he doesn't ask me that.

Okay, here goes. This one-centimeter-wide tube goes sliding past my tongue, down my throat until I lose contact with it. Thank

God for anesthesia. I guess I'd be throwing up by now, normally. Some of my mucus gets on the ocular, and he has to activate a fine spray, which makes me cough furiously and fogs up the lens even more. When I've stopped coughing, he risks a little more spray to clear the tip, and the tickle almost makes me cough. I suppress it.

"That's it, Filomena," he says. "Hold it. Just a little bit more."

"You're doing good," says the nurse.

Isn't this what everybody kept saying to me when I was giving birth? They haven't changed their material in four years? Inexcusable.

Finally it's over. Dr. Stan retracts the bronchoscope, bottles the sample and peels off his rubber gloves.

"Okay, we'll have the results in a couple of days." He scribbles a few lines in my file, checks off half a dozen boxes on the billing log, and tells me to take it to the receptionist who'll schedule me for a follow-up.

"In the meantime?" I ask him.

I can see that he doesn't have an answer. He's newer than I thought.

"Thanks, Doc," I tell him. He nods and is gone out the door.

I take the papers up to the desk, get it all processed, then take the bill to a small office down the hall. By some miracle I have brought all the right papers proving who I am and that I have been rejected by Medicaid. The woman's fingers fly across a calculator keypad and she tells me I will definitely qualify for the hospital's financial assistance program. The Federal Government may be in debt until the year two million, but at least the state's keeping aboveboard. I mean, if an unemployed mother and child aren't eligible for Medicaid, then who is?

"Please," says the woman, "we've got a guy here with multiple sclerosis. He's thirty years old. Hasn't gotten out of bed since January, but because he's under sixty-five he doesn't qualify for Medicaid because under the current guidelines he's considered 'able to work.' Reagan raised the cutoff, Bush raised it some more, and Clinton's done nothing to change things. It was better under Reagan."

Better under Reagan.

"You need your parking validated?" she asks, tearing a blue-green stamp out of a booklet.

"Sure."

"Here, I'll staple it."

"Oh, I was going to lick it."

"Girl, let me tell you something: Don't you ever lick *anything* in this building."

I drive south. Did you know you can't qualify for a driver's license on Long Island without taking a three-hour class in mind reading? Because that's the only way to predict what some of these crazies are going to do next. "Signal? I don't need to signal—*I* know where I'm going!"

Trapped at an eternally red light, I think about the alien living inside my chest. And how it got there. Leaving no obvious bruises on me. The folks who put the Bible together knew a thing or two about people. We've all heard about the commandments against inflicting physical harm, you know, "If a man shall smite his neighbor's eye," and all that, but it also commands against inflicting *psychological* harm. What, after all, are the *tangible* results of lying, dishonoring, coveting, and screwing around? Those crimes produce *emotional* suffering, which the Bible seems to take quite seriously (four out of ten commandments, at last count). Extortion laws criminalize the perceived threat of physical harm, but there is generally no legal recourse for the crippling mental anguish caused by, say, being given a disease that takes ten or twenty years to kill you. If Morse had just shot me in the back of the head a few years ago he'd be in jail. But cancer? Anything could have caused that.

I get home, make dinner for Antonia. I don't eat anything myself because I've got to get ready for my "date" with Jim Stella. Not that I could keep anything down after that bronchoscopy. I take her upstairs to read, and rearrange the framed photos in what has become my altar to Antonia. I take her hands in mine and pray, God, please, don't let my shrine become a memorial.

It's interesting. Unexpected. To feel your priorities shift from self-preservation to species preservation. I'm much more concerned that the kid should carry on than I am about myself at this point. Is that instinct? Parental hormones? Or am I just going nuts? I've got to stay focused here. I can't let anger blind me this time, but I can't let myself go soft either. What should I do? What do I say to you? Lord—why am I dying?

I come downstairs ready to go out. I wasn't kidding before. There really are shock absorbers on the main altar. Brand new Monroes, absorbing cosmic energy before use. Who am I to doubt?

It takes twenty minutes to drive to the spot where the restaurant is supposed to be, and another twenty minutes to find it. These Long Island commercial stretches are just mile after endless mile of McDonald's, gas station, Friendly's, gas station, record store, gas station, Burger King, gas station, Kentucky Fried Chicken, gas station, all indistinguishable from each other. I pass a law firm, a bowling alley and a real estate office three times before I realize that the real estate office is the restaurant.

Jim Stella pushes his second martini away and stops working the sweet young thing two bar stools over when I come in.

"Have trouble finding the place?" he asks. "You should have let me pick you up."

"I got stuck in the middle of a stampede. You ever seen a herd of bull Cadillacs in rut? It isn't very pretty."

"Ha ha *ha!*" He laughs, forcing it to justify a friendly slap on the shoulder that lets his arm linger around me for a moment. "Let's take a table. Say, that's some sexy outfit." He lets out a kind of snort.

"You just come out of hibernation?"

"It's just nice to be with a real woman for a change."

"You've been dating transsexuals?"

He laughs again. Must be I've got something *he* wants.

"No, no, but most of these babes, you know, show them a good car stereo and their eyes pop out."

"Yeah—what else pops out?"

Snicker.

"Sounds like you've been dating teenagers," I observe.

"Some."

"And you prefer a good challenge." And he's in for one.

He smiles a satyric smile, half sits, checks himself and comes around to pull out my chair for me. "There, you see? Not too many women appreciate gestures like that."

"Let me derail this runaway trolley car of a conversation before it hurts somebody, okay?" I say.

"Okay, so what direction do you want it to go in?"

"Tell me about yourself."

That takes up most of dinner. I stick to my absolute limit of one glass of wine. Jim Stella does not appear to have a limit. I learn more about the features on his car than I thought I'd ever know and I have to remind him that I'm a bit more mature than most of the women he has evidently been dating, and that I'm not impressed with the fact that he has a car with a fifth gear. So he switches to the *other* topic his mildly inebriated cerebellum can handle.

It seems that most guys have a "standard size" prick, but he claims to have a "legal size" prick that thrills and delights all the women he screws. I think he says "women" to show how liberated he is. Does this really work on these local gals? Somehow I doubt it, but his confident manner implies it's been working *just fine.* What do I know? Maybe I'm getting too old for this crap. I'm beginning to feel strangely like this whole evening is a fiasco. The cutie he was working at the bar when I came in is bouncing on the bar stool, talking to some guy and looking for a piece of paper, which she can't find, so she gives the guy her phone number on a dollar bill. This is all falling apart. Get me out of here.

"Why'd you become a cop?" he asks. That's a bolt out of the blue.

I don't bother asking where he got it from. He probably knows some more things about me, too, given a lawyer's resources and hyperactive testosterone.

"Because they wouldn't let me become a priest," I answer.

"Who wouldn't?"

"Who? My parents, my aunts, my uncles, my cousins, my confessors, my school teachers, my Popes, my presidents, my saints, movie stars, millionaires, beggars, men, women—other than that everybody else supported me."

"Somehow I just can't picture you carrying handcuffs and a nightstick."

"You and a million others." He probably can't picture me blowing Morse's brains out, either.

"Tell me about it," he says.

I stare at him for a second.

"I mean about how tough it was to get pimps and perverts to take you seriously as a cop."

Oh.

Don't lose it, girl. I think for a minute, have a sip of wine, and chase it with some Long Island water. "One time this big, burly truck driver was gassing the whole block—there's a city ordinance against idling, and the EPA says that prolonged exposure to diesel emissions increases the risk of lung cancer by about forty percent. So I told him to shut off his rig. 'Make me,' he says. I repeat my statement. He repeats his. I write a ticket. He tears it up. Now, he's a huge guy, enjoying it, looking for a fight. I should really call for backup—the rule book says so—but the guy's whole point is that I can't take him. I tell him, 'You make me take you and you're going to get hurt.' 'Yeah?' Now, the rules back me both ways here, and I generally prefer not to hurt people. But this guy urgently needs to get hurt. I tell him to get out of the truck. He blows a kiss at me. I say, 'What'sa matter? Afraid of me?' I give him plenty of room. I want this to be fair. Then—*slam!* I only hit his elbow, but it's right on the funny bone, and in about three seconds I've got him cuffed, knees on the asphalt, face against the truck. I tell him: 'You should have shut it off when I told you.' Bastard was nonunion anyway."

"Wow!" he says, nodding vigorously. "You know, the guy could've reported you."

"Yeah. A truck driver's gonna go public saying a 5'6" *latina* beat him up." I finish my wine in one swig. Damn cop reflex. I've got to watch that.

"I just love virile women."

And how about viral women? No, let me change that: "And what do you love about them?"

"I'd love to discover about twenty-five of your thirty erogenous zones. Single-handedly, and in great detail."

He's kind of a charmer, I guess. So why do I keep composing put-downs in my head?

"What's the matter with the other five?"

"Haven't you heard? The Decade of Greed is over."

"I need to get a job first," I say. "I hate economic inequality."

"Want me to put a good word in for you at Morse?"

"*No!* I mean, that'd be too obvious."

"So what do you want?"

"Well, I was figuring if I could find out some more about the people who already work there, maybe I'd have a better chance."

He nods. "Well, I've got some personnel files at my office—"

"Great. Can I come by and look at them?"

"Nah, it wouldn't help you."

"Why not?"

"All I've got at the office is the list of sickos."

"What do you mean, 'the sickos'?"

"The Disabilities. The Worker's Comps. Making friends with *them* isn't gonna get you anywhere."

"Well, I'd still like to see what you've got."

"You would, would you?" He leans closer.

"Yes."

"How about tomorrow, around lunchtime?"

"Sure."

I let him follow me home. He comes in for a few minutes. Billy's on the couch watching *El Show de Porcel* at ear-splitting volume. How 'bout those G-strings, huh? Jim's only comment is "This place would be nice if you decorated it." I walk him back to his car. I let him kiss me, but that's it. He starts his car up, then rolls down the power window:

"See you tomorrow."

"See you."

"I can hardly wait," he says. Then: "Oh, you know, you could try the business liaison office at the State University. Morse is using about half their incubator space. It's all public documents over there, so they *gotta* let you see 'em."

Hmm. "Thanks." Then it's off to bed. I've got to hunt for a sick, angry worker, find a helpmate at the State University, get a second interview at Morse's plant, call the EPA to initiate an investigation into the local toxicity, raise my child, save the environment, and not die of lung cancer. That's a lot to do.

I think I'd better let it wait 'til tomorrow.

4

Vivie: And are you really and truly not one wee bit
doubtful—or—or ashamed?
   Mrs. Warren: Well, of course, dearie, it's only good
manners to be ashamed of it: it's expected from a woman.
Women have to pretend to feel a great deal that they don't
feel.
                —BERNARD SHAW, *Mrs. Warren's Profession*

Wednesday morning I phone Gina Lucchese at the U.S. Environmental Protection Agency. Gina is one of the three Feds in the world you can trust. (Or is it four? I keep forgetting.) Because she *could* be making a ton of money doing the same work for the other side. Turns out she's in Puerto Rico for the week busting heads over some toxic leachate in the water supply. They had to throw in Puerto Rico because she got stuck with cleaning up all the toxic waste in New York and New Jersey, which is a bit like having to clean up the tiger cages at the Bronx Zoo—with the tigers still in them.

They think I'm just another hysterical mother whose drinking water tastes like brake fluid but they promise to put me on "the list." I ask to speak with the supervisor, who listens patiently for details, then announces, "Drinking water is local jurisdiction, call your County Board of Health."

Okay, so I call up the County Board of Health. Sixteen minutes on hold listening to the bulldozers rearrange the jagged metal landscape outside my window before some guy gets on and says, "Yeah?"

"I'm a homeowner right across the street from the Kim Tungsten Steel and Glass factory on Pleasant Valley Road. There's this terrible smell coming from the plant."

"You just move in?"

"Well, yeah."

"I figured. Newcomers're always callin' up the first week. But you'll notice it don't bother none of the regular people. See, the diesel-powered generators give off some carbon monoxide exhaust, but it's no worse than you just runnin' your car, ma'am."

"Thanks. Carbon monoxide fumes can kill you."

"Huh?"

"Even from just running your car. Anyway, the tap water's so volatile you could use it for jet fuel."

I can almost hear him shaking his head. "Now listen, miss—"

"No, you listen: This is a complaint about the water across from the Tungsten plant. It's your job to investigate that complaint, right?"

Pause.

"What's your name and exact location?"

I use Colomba's name, then take down his name and title. He promises to get right on it sometime before the next ice age.

Elvis moved out today, and I took his room. Colomba was pissed, but Elvis has wanted his own place for a while and I just gave him the excuse. With the warm weather coming, he's been getting a lot of work doing landscaping and lawn maintenance for independent contractors, but I don't know how he's going to get through the winter.

I figure I can safely take Antonia onto the State University campus. Besides, I'll need her afterwards to protect me from Jim Stella. I put on some serious business clothes and head out to the car.

I give the die a spin for luck. I'm getting used to the drive up now—except for when we almost get run off the road by a shirtless suntanned teen with a crew cut driving a jeep with a cruise computer that's better educated than he is. Parking on campus turns out to be almost as difficult as finding a spot in midtown Manhattan on St. Patrick's Day, and when I get out and look around, half-expecting to see a college green surrounded by ivy-covered Victorian brownstones, I notice that half the buildings look like they were designed by the same guy who built Hitler's stadium in Nuremberg. I take Antonia up to the first big building I see that doesn't look like it was primarily designed to withstand an air raid. It's the Vaughan Carter Memorial Library. I ask at the reference desk for the Business Liaison Office, and they tell me to turn around, go straight back out the door, past the Benjamin Carter Social and Behavioral Sciences Building and the brand-new Lillian Carter wing of the Indoor Sports Complex to the Administration Building.

"Just the plain old Administration Building? No Carters?" No answer.

Only about half the ceiling lights are on, and the "Down" escalators aren't working. Add a volcano out back and it'd be the State University of Ecuador. I find a nice, helpful guy, a graduate assistant in the Academic Vice President's Office. He's kind of cute, and I can see that he likes Latin women (he lets Antonia play with his computer), but I can also see the photos of his wife and two kids on the desk. He tells me the person I need to see is Phil Gates down in the Business Office. He shows me the way, leading us down the stairs to a bunkerlike suite of offices in the basement with only two windows—both in the boss's private office—and he's gone from my life.

The secretary's got about four phone lines buzzing, so I lean into an office and ask who I should be speaking to. The woman jumps as if a mongoose has been dropped down the back of her dress and blurts out, "What about?" as if Perry Mason's just caught her with a blood-soaked meat cleaver in her hands.

"About the technology incubator."

"You'll have to speak to Franklin Schmidt." And she turns back to her terminal fast enough to dislodge even the most determined mongoose.

"Frank," says the short, muscular guy in the next office. "Call me Frank. Everybody does."

He's got hairy arms and a raspy five o'clock shadow, and it isn't even lunchtime yet. He looks like he's been out of college maybe two years, where he majored in racquetball, and has connections of some kind because he's starting at the bottom as Assistant to the

Vice President. I tell him the company I work for is looking to try out some new production techniques, and we need affordable space and access to minds that are willing to experiment. I've worked enough with computers over the years to fake a pretty good line. But the presence of Antonia is putting him off. He's still enough of a kid to regard it as highly abnormal to have one yourself. It drops my credibility from an A– to a B+.

But I get in to see the boss. I can see that Frank Schmidt got all the hair in this duo, because Phil Gates is a pudgy, balding, middle-aged guy, and he is *totally* unhelpful. He takes one look at the kid and just *knows* I can't be a professional. I ask to see information about the companies that are already using the incubator space and he says, "Why?"

"It's public information, isn't it?"

"Rival companies aren't covered by the statute."

The fuck they aren't.

I tell him my supervisor will be contacting him, and prepare to go. But Antonia insists on a drink of water. So I'm wrestling with the cooler when Phil Gates leans out of his office and yells, "Kate! I wanted those cover proofs ten minutes ago!"

A woman skitters out of her office clutching a dozen glossy images and hands them over to Gates. He flips through them, tosses ten in the garbage, hands back two: "These are all right. Do the others over."

When he's gone, Antonia looks through the garbage and announces, "I like them." As I'm pulling her away from the garbage in front of Gates's office, the proof-woman treads lightly up behind me and whispers, "It's not a child-friendly office: I think the boss eats them for breakfast."

I catch myself for a moment, and look at her: She's—well—stunning, a few inches taller than me, thin, with a creamy Pre-Raphaelite complexion, thick jet-black hair and eyebrows and a wide, flat nose that must have come from some passing salesman or wandering Semite two or three generations back because the rest of her is purebred Italian American. The nameplate on her door says KATHERINA MINOLA.

"Is that you?" I ask.

"You know, I often ask myself that," she says, smiling, and she backsteps into her office like a kimono-clad geisha.

I follow her in and Antonia goes, "Oh my God!" at all the colors and shapes jutting from the walls and surfaces like Technicolor stalactites in an underground cavern.

"You wanna see this?" says Katherina, holding out a purple plastic tube. "Here. Look."

"What do you say?" I perform my parental duty.

"Thank you," Antonia performs hers.

"This end," says Katherina, reversing the tube for Antonia to look through, then she brings her swivel lamp down and shines it right at her.

"This is cool!" says Antonia.

"She got that from me," I explain.

"I figured."

Antonia is going nuts over this thing.

"You have to rotate it," says Katherina, demonstrating. Antonia gasps. Just the way I would have.

"Can I see it?"

"Sure."

"Give Mommy a turn, Antonia." I look in. What I see is a subtle explosion of color, nongeometric, just a jumble of shapes, but the blending of colors is a slight foretaste of heaven. "Wow. What is it?"

"It's a kaleidoscope. Only instead of mirrors and colored plastic I cut up paper-thin diffraction gratings and translucent polarized plastic and float them in a semiviscous polymer—it's the polarized light that does it: The pattern *never* repeats. Kind of like genetics," she says, patting Antonia's head. "Completely nonoscillatory and aperiodic."

"You lost me there," I confess.

"Oh, just designer talk."

"Is that what you do?"

"What I do is make all the flack these guys produce look good. And wouldn't you know—"

She must have the feel of this office down to an instinct, because at that precise instant Frank Schmidt pokes his head in the door and asks to see the page proofs for the new brochure that has to go to press by 3 P.M. Katherina angles the twenty-four-inch color monitor on her Unisystems 2000 towards him and gives him a whirlwind walking tour of the graphic layout she has created for whatever drivel they have churned out in the next office. All I can say is it looks beautiful, and this woman's talents are wasted in this place. Schmidt looks satisfied, but gives me the eye long enough for the fluorescent light to start playing tricks with me—his shirt is just so white, his skin, the walls behind him so white—that I just lose all sense of depth perception trying to focus on him.

"I've got to get back to work," says Katherina. That gets rid of Schmidt. Her volume drops a bit: "Now what are you looking for?"

"I'd like to see some information about what Morse Techtonics is doing with the incubator space."

"I don't see a problem with that. Why?"

I've got three stories prepared, but somehow I don't feel like lying to this woman.

"Private reasons."

She eyes me.

"I'm not after his secret formula for Coca-Cola."

Just then the shape of Phil Gates blocks the doorway and he says, "I don't see how it can be helping you get your work done when somebody's in here with you."

"I was just admiring the new logo. That's just what this university needs," I say. "We'll be going now."

Gates glares at me, then walks away, satisfied.

I turn back to Katherina, lower my voice even further: "It could be a good way to get back at your boss."

"And why would I want to do that?"

Because he's an asshole, that's why. But I say, "He doesn't want to give me any information about Morse's private use of the incubator site. Why not?"

Silence.

I continue: "Because I might find out something that'll screw him up a little."

She leans back in her chair. Takes me in. "Meet me in the print shop."

"I'd walk through fire for it."

Fire would be an improvement. Some sadistic lunatic decided to put the print shop in the windowless basement of the Administration Building. There's a half dozen thinners, cleaners and maybe two dozen inks fouling the air, and no ventilation. But the place is crowded and noisy as only a print shop can be, so we can talk. Katherina has reduced a poster-sized flow chart to a single 8½-by-11-inch sheet, so it's almost unreadable, but it's enough to give me a glimpse of Morse's leveraged empire. There are three tiers of overlapping company names with enough branch connections to wire a mainframe computer.

"Can I keep this?"

"Sure, just don't tell anyone where you got it from."

"Can we meet later and talk? The chemicals are really getting to me."

"Sure." We arrange to meet after work. I got less than a ten-minute dose of chemical fumes, but it's enough to start me coughing up blood, and my lungs burn for the next two-and-a-half hours.

For lunch we go to Jim Stella's office. The whole gamut of emotions washed across his face: Damn, she brought the kid—no sex today—oh, crap, now I gotta pretend to love kids—boy, isn't she cute?—just like her Momma!

He tells me my outfit would be really nice if I had it dry cleaned by professionals, and he actually gives me the business card of the place he uses.

"Best on the island," he assures me. Apparently it has never occurred to Mr. Stella that all this *takes money*.

I give Antonia her paper and crayons to draw with, and work on Mr. Stella a bit until he lets me look at his list of disability claimants who still work at Morse Techtonics. I see at least five names with addresses that I recognize as being within a mile or two of Colomba's, but I think that highlighting them in red would be a bit obvious. Hmm, I really don't like using my kid for a cover, but I don't have much choice at the moment.

Antonia's done a wonderful abstract drawing, already incorporating some of Katherina Minola's design influences. I draw Jim Stella's attention to it.

"What's that?" he asks.

Antonia says, "I don't know."

And he says, "You don't know what it is?"

"No."

"It *has* to be something."

"No it doesn't," I interrupt. "I'm not so hot to start making my kid put everything into a 'meaningful' and 'structured' context so soon."

"Well, they've got to learn the way of the world," he says.

"The world doesn't set such a great example itself, okay?"

"Okay, okay." His intercom buzzes. "Yeah?"

A voice squawks: "LaFehr on line two."

"Oh, *not* LaFehr on line two *again*." Jim Stella stands up, shaking his head, and goes back to his desk to take the call.

I put Antonia on my lap, with a legal pad for an easel, and start explaining some of the dialectical principles behind the early twentieth-century collapse of standard linear perspective, using Cubist and pre-Colombian motifs. Meanwhile, on a separate sheet partly covered by the drawing, I'm writing down the names and addresses of the six nearest disability claimants with a bright red crayon.

Now we're waiting outside on the Academic Mall for Katherina Minola to free herself from the Administration Building and rescue us from Investigative Dead End Number Three.

Here she comes, skipping down the stairs, full of vitality.

"You know, your talents are wasted on those geeks," I say.

"Yeah, well, what can you do? When I graduated they should have said, 'Here's your degree in design *and* your first unemployment check. Get used to it.'"

"Four years of art school and they've got you laying bricks."

"Don't knock bricks. My father laid them every day of his life so I could get that diploma. At least I've got a steady job. I had a fabric importer *break down and cry* on me after telling me business is so bad he might have to close. And this guy is based in the Hamptons."

"I want to go to the Hamptons," says Antonia.

"Later, honey."

"I want to go to the Hamptons!"

"Toni, it's a long way away."

"I thought of something else after we spoke," Katherina says. "Did you know that Morse Techtonics has put in a bid for the old Shore Oaks estate?"

"What's the old Shore Oaks estate?"

"I want to go to the Hamptons!"

"Seventeen acres of private woods and beachfront property. Do you want to go to the beach?" she asks Antonia.

"Let's go to the beach!"

"Okay, okay," I say.

"We'll take my car," says Katherina. "You need a university sticker to get in."

On our way to the parking lot, Katherina explains, "Old man Carter's place. Remember the Susquehanna Hat Company? Well, that was him. Made his millions back in the Roaring Twenties and bought up *all* of the land around here. Sold it to developers in the fifties and sixties with the stipulation that they build in the 'colonial' style of his mansion. All of this land we're standing on was donated to make the State University. About twenty years back the family donated their estate in Old Town. Too bad the place burned down."

"When was that?"

"Six or seven years ago. Damn shame. They used to have concerts there, and rooms for visiting faculty. But the upkeep cost too much. The SUNY system doesn't have much of a budget for the maintenance of mansions."

"What caused the fire?"

"You ready for this? Irony Department: A defective smoke alarm."

"Really?"

"Yup."

"So now what's this about Morse wanting to buy it?"

"Well, I normally don't pay too much attention to the Foundation's propaganda. But when somebody makes an offer of ten million dollars you sort of take notice. Besides, Morse owns half the town. You can't go for an ice cream cone without Morse getting his cut. Everybody loves the guy. I mean, when half the employers on the island are folding, his checks are still good."

"So what does he want to do with the site?"

"Well, the acreage is absolutely fabulous, there's just no house. I hear he's planning to build another."

"Is he going to find a buyer?"

"That's the market around here, sister. Two-hundred-thousand-dollar cardboard houses in Strathmore have been on the market for five years, but brand-new two-million-dollar homes on the beach are selling as fast as they can build 'em."

This is all very useful information. "How much are they paying you? Tell 'em I said to give you a raise."

"Thanks."

We're driving under a canopy of sunstruck leaves illuminated to a translucent green. The road narrows a bit, and the easy-to-read street signs start to disappear. I ask about that.

Katherina says, "The folks in Old Town want to keep the place as private as possible."

We come to a big iron gate topped by a gilded arc that says SHORE OAKS. The iron has gone rusty and has been painted over many times. Katherina makes a left and we start down the potholed and crumbling road.

"This place would be beautiful if we had the money to put into it," says Katherina. "I guess that's why the trustees are so willing to let Morse take it off their hands."

The driveway to this place is about half a mile long. Just before the seacliff drops down to the water, Katherina parks the car. We get out and walk.

"This used to be a millionaire's estate, woman," says Katherina. "Now look at it."

I look. I see. We have ruins left over from the Spanish conquest of the 1530s that look better than this. What is it about the faded glory of American money that makes a place fall this low after only ten years of neglect? To call the brick walkway overgrown would be generous. Two-inch pine tree hopefuls are shooting up five or six to a brick in some places. The surface is bubbled from so many advancing roots it looks like a still photo of boiling lava. *Onions*—green onions, scattered about the unkempt and corrupted grounds—are sprouting all over the unmowed, unmowable lawn.

And yet there is fertility, of an uncontrolled sort. In the dry fountain, the cracked brick is lush with thick, wet leaves, bright as any green in the Ecuadorian tropics, and a coven of tall white flowers, bell-shaped and drooping with wetness. Nature is reclaiming Mr. Carter's $10 million estate, and is converting it back to nature.

Day-Glo green moss invades from the borders and shoves between the broken parallels of reddish brick, crowding into any space not already occupied by some tougher organic formation. The question is no longer one of a battle between order and chaos, but rather which particular chaos will triumph.

We get to the flat stretch of blackened embers that used to be the house. The brick walkway from what used to be the second floor down to the gardens stills stands, and one can only wonder at the ghost of its lost magnificence. There's a circular red-brick lily pond, and after that the stairs lead to a couple of acres of well-tended lawn that drops sharply to a few hundred yards of North Shore beachfront property.

"Nice place," I point out. "Antonia, don't touch that, it's *fuchi.*"

"It's what?" asks Katherina.

"*Fuchi.* It means 'dirty' in Quichua."

"Sorry, but what's Quichua?"

"The dominant native language of the Ecuadorian highlands."

"You're teaching your kid *Quichua?*"

"No, not really. But a lot of Quichua words are used in Andean Spanish. I bet your family uses a lot of Italian American words that the good people of Wyoming have never heard of."

I bend down to dust off her hands and find the brittle, waxy remains of burnt pages among the ashes. "This was the library?"

"There was a library. Pool table and everything. Damn shame. About the only thing they salvaged was the grandfather clock."

"And where's that?"

"Oh, in a storage closet on South Campus. Nobody's got the money to rebuild a sixty-year-old clock."

I look at the fragments. I do not recognize the text. It's so badly burned you can't even tell what kind of paper it once was. It seems almost to have been glazed, as if the heat had turned it into ceramic or something.

One piece says: "*iety,* rules emerge"

Another says: "particular for ———— the competiti———— identi"

Others: "include one ———— participants"

"it must be"

"*ety,* rules emerge ———— of contract ———— erely"

And it goes on like that. Katherina opens an eye at me when I fold the fragments into a sheet of notebook paper and slip them into my purse.

"Is there something you're not telling me?" she says.

"Plenty, I suppose." I give her a bit of a fill-in, but not too much. I've got reasons for investigating this Morse character. And since I figure anything he's involved with has to be part nasty in some way, it's only a matter of time before I dig up *something.*

"Okay, just don't let the Board of Trustees know," says Katherina. "Morse is also offering one-and-a-half million to have a new wing of the library named after him. Lot of jobs connected with that project."

"Yeah, but what good is a paying job if it costs you your soul? Matthew sixteen."

"Say what?"

"Oh, nothing. Just my Catholic upbringing."

"Oh, *that* Matthew! Great evangelist, but he wasn't much fun on a date, was he?"

"No. Now how do I find out more about this place's past?"

"Check the town files."

"I haven't found the town officials terribly cooperative."

"Then try the reference librarians. They're always pulling old design motifs out of the vaults for me. They've got blueprints and elevations of the whole place."

We meander through a rock garden that Antonia thinks is just the greatest, although we have to sidestep some half-scorched beer cans and other such signs of campfires and partying.

I tell Antonia, "There goes a dragonfly!"

And she gasps: "*Uhh!* A *dragon?*" She's looking at the lily pond, the most likely spot for a dragon to be, I suppose.

"No, a dragon*fly*—See?" But it's too fast for her. Besides, she doesn't know what she's looking for. I ask Katherina about her boss, Phil Gates. She says he's one of those highly paid, minimally competent administrators who tries hard not to distinguish himself in any way except bullying subordinates, confirming an old theory of mine that bosses are all assholes in one way or another.

"How'd he get to be a freaking VP?" I ask. "By eating the competition?"

"By cloning himself. That butt kisser Frank Schmidt is really only about three months old, you know. I never thought I'd be working for someone who doesn't remember what life was like before *The Power Rangers* went into syndication."

We lean against a railing and look out at the sea.

"Man, who ever thought it would turn out like this?" she says. "When I was a kid we all figured that American Airlines would have commercial space flight by now. So what happened?"

"Ford came out with the Pinto."

She looks at me as if to say, "Come on, I was being serious."

"A car made of aluminum foil that explodes when it's rear-ended?"

She considers this.

"Planned obsolescence," she says, nodding.

"And when they realized that people preferred foreign cars that lasted a good ten or fifteen years, the way American-made cars *used to,* they tried to appeal to your patriotism to get you to buy American."

"Unfortunately, there's no law against screwing up the economy."

"I don't know, it got Louis the Sixteenth killed."

"That's what we need: The guillotine for white-collar crime."

"Why not? It would be a reliable deterrent."

"That reminds me," she says, "some of the rich Old Town kids actually go to the State University, and their parents actually endow."

"So?"

"So they might know a few things about the old Carter estate that might not be in the town records."

"Hmm. I—"

We're turning back towards the house and I guess I betray a start when I see a man standing there. Suit, tie, demeanor like he's lord of the realm and he's caught two peasants poaching rabbits on his property. It's Phil Gates.

"Aw, nuts," says Katherina.

Gates is standing on the ashes of the old mansion, looking down at us. But Ms. Minola is good. Damn good. She hasn't kept that job all these years by letting her boss know what she really thinks of him. She goes, "Hi, Phil!" like it's the pleasantest surprise on earth to run into your boss when you thought you were alone (and talking about him), waving vigorously and running up the old brick steps to have a chat with him about how wonderful the change is going to be as soon as the Zoning Board clears Morse's building permit so the deal can be sent to Albany for approval.

Oh, she's good all right. It's that kind of acting that doesn't look like acting, because there is a kernel of truth in it. Ms. Minola, after all, needs to eat, too. She is singing for her supper, and the boss is buying. If he called the sun the moon she'd probably agree with him and say how bright and goodly it shines. But I can see that he doesn't like my being here, and I wouldn't want Katherina to suffer for it. Mr. Gates looks like the kind of guy who would carry a vendetta into the next millennium, smiling the whole time.

Gates is not as good. He tries to fake a grinning interest in Antonia, who pulls away from him, as if he didn't just give me the dirtiest of looks for bringing her into his office just a few hours ago. What does he think, I don't remember that? Or maybe he's just so used to his staff's selective memory that he's forgotten that ordinary citizens don't have to put up with that crap. The mind of a boss is a mysterious, dark place that lies deeper than my plumb line cares to sound.

He keeps up appearances by giving me a rundown on all the fabulous things that are going to be done with this site. Since it's all going to be in private hands and sold for upwards of $30 million dollars, ask me why I should give a fuck.

I'm wondering how I can chase down this lead—that is, if it is a lead at all—when we get home, and Colomba says to me, "You got a call back from that last place. They want to see you tomorrow."

Later that evening I decide to call Jim Stella to ask him out on another date.

He goes, "Filomena? Shh—" I can hear a woman giggling in the background.

"Oh. I'll call you back tomorrow."

"Jeez, I didn't mean—"

"It's okay," I say. "Don't worry about it."

He calls me back about an hour later and starts in: "Listen. I'm really sorry about that—uh—"

"I said don't worry about it."

"Yeah, but—I mean, I hope I didn't mess anything up."

"Hey, we're not married."

"See, that's what I like about you, kid. You've been around the block. Nothing fazes you. I still want to make it up to you, though."

"Okay. Go ahead."

He chuckles.

"You really want to get something on this Morse guy, huh?"

I have to say that my heart almost stops. What's happening to me? I used to face down *los rurales,* mounted police armed with hunting rifles, without flinching: Hell, it *thrilled* me.

"Well, let me tell you something, Ms. Filomena Buscarsela, I am not what I seem."

"Yeah?"

"Sure, I'm working for Morse Techtonics, trying to make the zoning for the Kim site more profitable—"

"But?"

"But—I'm also gathering files for a major environmental lawsuit *against* Morse Techtonics."

Well, I hear that and go semi-nuts.

"You are? Tell me about it!"

"Ah-ah-ah, not over the phone."

"Okay. When and where?"

"Over dinner?"

"Sure."

"Great! My—oh, uh, I have to set up some meetings tomorrow. Then I'll know my schedule better. I'll call you, okay?"

"Sounds good. Uh, Jim?"

"Yeah?"

"Don't keep me waiting too long. . . ."

I pull out the bits of scorched paper from the ruins of the old Shore Oaks library and spread them out on the kitchen table. The text looks like standard business report language, duplicated, even. But the fragments are just too small to mean anything. So far.

Antonia's outgrown *Barney,* but I manage to find *Sesame Street* for her on channel 21. Billy stays put. If it's on TV, he'll watch it. "Gee, that Gina's kind of cute, ya know?" he says of the blonde actress doing a scene with Oscar the Grouch. I've got to leave Antonia with Colomba today, but I don't feel so bad about it this time. Now that we're getting along, we talk mostly in Spanish. It's warmer. Colomba insists that I not rely on the *agua sucia* (dirty water) that Americans call coffee and, fortified with two cups of Spanish coffee, my upper lip sweating from caffeine and nerves, I fire up the heap, spin the die for luck and take her into battle once again.

My second interview is with the Billing Office. With my identity blunted by KGB-issue sunglasses and my frizzy *mestiza* hair lashed into submission with damp leather thongs, I sign in, pass the metal detector and stalk the halls of Morse Techtonics with a security guard. When I ask to stop at the ladies' room, he knocks on the door, opens it a crack and announces, "Uncleared personnel coming in!"

Even the wastebaskets have one-way tops and padlocks. Shit. All the phones have at least five lines and *very* different phone numbers. I am starting to tingle, electric with the possibility of breaking this enterprise, or die trying (a distinct possibility). I count three radios quietly tuned to WBIW. "Lite" rock. Must be the official office Muzak. Desks are piled high with invoices I'd give an appendage to sneak out of here, but that's beginning to appear not too likely. One of the secretaries takes a coffee break, and before she leaves, she pops the Mylar ribbon out of her typewriter and locks it in her top drawer. Shit again.

Well, there's no lock on the water cooler. I think.

A middle manager named Joseph Kurst shakes my hand and leads me into a cubicle to discuss the job. I give a performance worthy of a Redgrave or a Plummer (or at least a Curly or a Shemp), trying to get the information I need from them while convincingly answering the nonstop barrage of hard-nosed questions. When you include the fact that we're *both* lying perhaps you can appreciate the mental juggling I'm doing.

I do keep seeing invoices for hundreds of "customized" Unisystems computers going for $28,000 each to Ergot Importers in Athens, Greece. Athens? Greece? After I've given them enough reasons to think I'm worth considering for the job and asking a few questions about the health plan, I learn they have a lateness policy (Show up after 9 A.M. more than twice for *any reason at all* and you're fired), and some pretty tight security, but that otherwise, everyone's just one big happy family. Do I have any questions?

Boy do I have questions. "What kind of computers do you sell for twenty-eight K?"

"Oh, we customize those. It's a very specific niche. We can't possibly compete with IBM, Dell and Apple in the PC market, but we've done remarkably well with the floor models and mainframes."

I see a weakness, but I can't do anything with it now. Steady, girl, steady . . . Morse is up to *something,* but I can't act without more knowledge or I'll risk losing it all. Hmm.

I ask for a tour of the shop floor. It's a bit unusual, but he sees no reason to keep me from it. Apparently, I've already seen the inner sanctum of secrecy, so there's no harm in letting me see the production line.

We walk down the wrought-iron stairs and skeedaddle between two adjacent rows of assembly stations. My nostril hairs prick up, excited by a sudden increase in chemical odors.

I ask, "Where are the twenty-eight K models?"

"Oh, we don't do the customizing here."

"Who does it?"

"A subcontractor."

"Maybe I've heard of them."

"Oh, I don't imagine so—"

"I've worked with hundreds of computer companies over the years."

He won't tell me.

"It's really very small. You wouldn't have heard of them."

And I guess I'm not going to hear of them from this horsefly. But I have to pretend I'm not pushing.

"Would you like to see the molding room?"

"Yes."

I wonder what inspiration Dante used for the Seventh Circle of Hell. A fourteenth-century meat market? A plague-infested mass grave? A sewer? A sulfur mine? Heaven only knows what images his renascent mind would have cooked up if he had followed Mr. Kurst deeper into the frightful acrid stench growing thicker and thicker around me. I gag. My head swims. Yeeacch! *This* is the source of the smell. I have to pull out my handkerchief, but it's useless. I'm trying to memorize the faces, hoping to match them to my crayon list as soon as I get out of here, but it's pretty hard to focus when you're choking back blood clots.

I still taste the stuff in my soup at lunchtime.

Pale. Afraid.

Rows and rows of eerie gray houses, walkway after walkway leading to dusty gray doorsteps and everywhere the oppressive sameness. Like when I first stepped off the train, only this is the flip side.

The days are getting longer, so I've still got an hour to catch them at home by the pale blue of fading daylight.

The first guy tells me in a hoarse growl to get the hell away. The second lets me in, his wife fetches tea, but when I ask about the skin rashes he says they're nothing and How 'bout those Mets? A constant cough keeps the third one from speaking to me. Number four: I don't get past the WELCOME mat.

The fifth guy lives across the street from a corner of the Tungsten site that's been neglected so long a bunch of neighborhood kids slip easily through a permanent trench under the steel mesh fence and play war games on stacks of rusty fifty-five-gallon drums. He can't hear so well, and keeps popping Mylanta for his ulcer the whole time I'm there. He tells me everything about his job—I now know in detail how many impact-resistant PVC casings for the 3600MBX computer Morse Techtonics expects a single worker to pull steaming hot from the molding vat and haul on his shoulder over to the trimming belt every hour (would you believe seventy-five?) and just how hard it is to keep that pace up (pretty damn hard).

But when I start in about his condition, he says, "Whaddaya mean my condition?" and when I explain that I mean his symptoms he tells me to get the hell out of his house.

The sixth guy won't even open the door.

Call me slow, but it's not 'til I'm driving back to Colomba's that it hits me: Every one of these workers saw me this morning down on the shop floor talking with a front office executive. Of course they won't talk to me—they all think I'm working for Morse!

Damn this cancer-clogged brain-pan! What a waste of time!

Blocked *again*. This is getting tough. And I don't have the time for this kind of tough. When I get back to the house there's a letter waiting for me. It's a card from Jim Stella with a condom inside it offering its use "Anytime." Boy, does he have a lot to learn.

I flop down on the couch and stare at the TV screen for half an hour with the cat on my lap. Billy's watching *Viva Zapata!* which ought to be great, but it's a disappointment. Why? They've got

white guys from Brooklyn playing Mexicans with horsehair mous-
taches glued over their lips. I know it was made in the 1950s, but
I mean, it *was* produced in *southern California* and filmed in
Texas—it's not like there weren't any *Mexicanos* around! Anthony
Quinn's just spilled taco filling on the Mexican Constitution when
Colomba comes in and asks me in Spanish how it went. I tell her
lousy, and when I show her the crayon list with all six names
checked off she says, "How about Reggie Einhorn?"

And I ask, "Who?"

"Reggie Einhorn. He lives three houses down."

"And he works for Morse Techtonics?"

"Fifteen years."

"I'll go see him right now."

"Uh, Filomena—"

"Yes?"

"A doctor called."

"Dr. Wrennch?"

"Yes."

"What did he say?"

"He got your biopsy results."

"And?"

"He wants to see you first thing tomorrow."

"Thanks. Anything else?"

"*Cuñada*—" First time she's called me that.

"Yes?"

"It didn't sound good."

5

Oh so young so goddamn young.   —PATTI SMITH

I watch her sleep.

I watch her, thinking about before I left Solano, in the high *sierra,* how my uncle Agustín broke a freshly baked cross-shaped sugar cookie in two and made me eat half of it, then buried the rest out in the cornfield, saying, "Now you have to come back, to eat the other half. Half your soul will always be here." For years I made my cousins smuggle in a few ears of Solano corn in their flight bags, just so I could get a taste of that food grown in the earth that made me.

She wakes up when I'm putting on my business clothes. She knows what that means.

"Don't go again," she pleads, in an irresistible childish whimper.

"But I have to, Toni, I have to go to the doctor."

She starts crying. Not a serious cry, but it requires treatment. I hug hug hug her.

"It won't be much longer," I explain.

"Then we'll be together?"

"Yes." And suddenly I'm holding back tears. No. No. No. I've got to keep control. I can't lose it. Not yet. Not before I can get back into the Morse Techtonics Billing Office.

I give the die a spin and thereby survive the ride up to the University Hospital. For whatever good it does me. The doc tells me straight out—

"It's a malignant chest tumor, Ms. Buscarsela. I'm sorry."

"Sorry? What does that mean? Aren't you going to do anything?"

"Of course there are options. Most cancers are treatable, but not curable."

"And what about mine?"

"I can't be sure yet. I mean—I don't know. We can schedule some chemotherapy, but I think your case calls for more severe treatment."

"Which is what?"

"Radiation. You'll have to spend the next several weeks in the hospital—"

"No."

"What?"

"*No.*"

"I don't think you understand, we need to contain this tumor immediately. I'm recommending an implantation of radium needles in the flesh around the tumor to isolate and cauterize it for removal, *then* we'll see if chemotherapy will inhibit the spread."

"Radium needles?"

"Let me show you." He brought a catalog with him. He flips it open to a four-color photo of gold and platinum needles arranged in a symmetrical battery of missiles but before he can begin my eye falls on the corporate logo in the bottom right corner: Sprilling. A division of Morse Techtonics.

Well I see that and I guess I go a bit insane. I think I accuse him of something ridiculous like trying to kill me but I know I push the catalog away so hard it fans out noisily, flaps to the floor, and I am already out of the office and on the highway before I realize I'd better slow down below 70 mph if I want to see Antonia, like I promised.

Hours later, when I've finally cooled off, I realize that I must have made quite an impression on young Dr. Wrennch. I can just see him writing in his log: "Very peculiar patient today. Absolutely *re-fuses* treatment. Almost became violent at the suggestion of using radium needles. Must have the staff psychologist observe her the next time she comes."

"Why are we looking at the sunset?" asks Antonia.

"Because the sky is beautiful when it's sunset."

"After the sunset is the sky going to be ugly?"

I laugh, and when she asks what's funny I tell her, so she keeps repeating the phrase the whole walk back to the house. I put her to bed and go downstairs to sit at the kitchen table so I can do some serious staring into space. Without asking, Colomba prepares an *agua de remedio* for my nerves. I tell her nerves are not my problem, but she dismisses that with an authoritative wave of her hand. By the time I've put myself around two cups of the stuff she's got me telling her things I didn't even know were on my mind.

I've been so single-mindedly pursuing my one questionable goal of trying to destroy a leech named Morse that I haven't been planning for what's going to happen to Antonia after—

"—after I'm not around anymore."

"We all face it, *cuñada*," Colomba tells me in Spanish. "At one time or another. *Así es.*"

"Because I *know* that sometime in her young life someone's going to try to make her believe some lies and if I'm not there to intercept it—at first, I mean—later on, I'm sure she can judge for herself, but 'til then—"

"The Lord will protect her."

"Some person is going to hurt her and I've got to be there to say, 'It's all right, Antonia, it's all right. I'm here. . . .' "

And I find myself cradled in Colomba's arms, tears purging my eyes while I recite a litany of prayers for the protection of my child, bargaining with God to please, please just let Antonia live a long and full life.

And just let me boil Morse's ass in a vat of hot tar and smear him across the Long Island Expressway.

*   *   *

The next day when I've recovered some of the sensation that's supposed to distinguish the living from the dead I take Antonia with me back to the hospital where we catch Dr. Wrennch unexpectedly.

"Oh, uh—" He's at a loss for words.

So I say, "Sorry. It's kind of long story. It'd fill a couple of books. Can we talk?"

"Sure." He closes the medical journal he was reading.

I explain: "Facing death is rough enough without being told you're dead before your time."

"Yes. Go on."

"I guess you know I used to flirt with death rather openly."

"You mean the smoking?"

"Yeah. And other things. Cop work revealed to me the humbling fact that the inside of a dead human smells pretty much the same as the inside of a dead rat. But now that—now that I'm trying to be a responsible parent to this wonderful daughter of mine—"

"That's me," says Antonia.

"Yes, that's right, Tonia. Now that—I'm a mom—the prospect of—"

I can't seem to find my tongue. It was there this morning, too. I don't know why, but suddenly I find myself unable to go on. It's nervous energy. Yeah, nerves. Tension. I've got to stop. Suppress. Ignore.

But I can't.

"Nobody really knows why you die of cancer," he's saying.

I'm back. "So tell me about the chemotherapy."

"I urgently recommend the radiation treatment—"

"No."

"May I ask why?"

"It'll weaken me, won't it?"

"For a few weeks."

"I don't have a few weeks."

He moves his chair closer and puts his hand on my knee. "Let me be the judge of that."

I'd like to kick him through the window. Instead the perverse imp of free-floating emotion puts my hand on his. This human contact is good. And we are not ashamed.

I should take the chemotherapy via a catheter, but that would lay me up longer, so he's willing to try injections. Twenty to thirty treatments, twice a day for two weeks.

"What about exercise?" he asks.

"I've been running around like crazy—"

"Panic and aerobic cardiovascular exercise are two different things."

"Thanks. I know that."

"Do you jog?"

"I used to. Can't anymore. Shreds the hell out of my lungs."

"Have you tried bicycling?"

"Not really. You need a car just to get a gallon of milk in this town."

"Please think about it."

"It'll mean an investment in helmets, a baby seat—"

"The nice weather's here, just in time for Memorial Day."

"I imagine your business doubles during the holidays."

"Not mine—by the time they get to me they're beyond help."

I cringe. And me, who used to haul bodies to the morgue on a weekly basis. *Other* people's bodies. He shifts the topic. "Now July Fourth is another story. Every year we get kids with hands, fingers blown off, glass shrapnel in their eyes, third degree burns—"

"Let's talk about something else."

"Well frankly, Ms. Buscarsela, I think we should begin your chemotherapy immediately. What do you say to that?"

What do I say?

"Call me Filomena."

We finally get on the state financial aid program, so I only have to pay 35 percent of the standard outrageous fee. I'd like to go see this Reggie Einhorn that Colomba told me about, but he's at work. Since the hospital is only about half a mile from the center of campus, we go to the Carter Library.

And I'd better start disguising my motives better.

Now, I know it's a stereotype here, but you've got to believe me when I tell you that the first reference librarian I talk to is an asocial ninety-seven-pound beanpole with thick glasses and permanently hunched shoulders. And when Antonia grabs hold of his leg he asks me to "get her off" him like she's some slimy creature with eight tentacles and hundreds of suction cups. Screw him. The next librarian's a polite, efficient woman who smiles at Antonia and says that her name is Prunella Isles. Small and thin, with a British accent that's closer to Mick Jagger than Margaret Thatcher, she has obviously grown up among *people* and is actually able to converse with them.

I tell her I'm seeking information about the history of the village for a class assignment. She tells me about the Revolutionary heroes from the area, including one woman, Cynthia Crane, who used to signal rebel ships hiding in the coves by hanging a specified number of shirts on her laundry line, how the Battle of Running River was a significant part of the Redcoats' struggle of pacify Long Island, and a few other things I can't use. Of course it would help if I knew what the hell I'm looking for.

I tell her, "I'm particularly interested in the early twentieth century."

I get the whole Carter family story.

"I understand you have architectural drawings of the Carter home," I say.

"Which one? The Revolutionary cottage that collapsed in a hurricane in 1857? The three-storey Colonial that was torn down in 1928 when Vaughan Carter built the Shore Oaks mansion—"

"The Shore Oaks mansion."

"Ah, we have the *original* blueprints," she tells me, taking me up a flight of spiral stairs into the Special Collections. Before long she's unfolding them—brittle, crinkly, illegible and turning to dust in some places. But a very classy act once upon a time. She asks me, Aren't they beautiful?

"Do you have any more recent ones?"

I see the 1932 west wing expansion, the 1938 swimming pool plans—never built because World War II came along and they felt "it wouldn't be proper" to show such ostentatiousness when everyone was sacrificing so—

"That was big of them," I offer.

The 1947 cathedral window additions to the north and west wings, the 1955 reroofing.

"Nothing newer?"

"Well, there's the revised blueprints from 1983 when the university was considering some major remodeling, but they're of little historical interest."

"I might find them easier to read."

That seems to serve. She lays them out for me. It's quite a spread. Servants' quarters down below (converted to visiting faculty housing), all-weather archway with hanging lanterns over the wide, circular driveway, two kitchens, eight bedrooms on the third floor, recital hall–sized drawing room and the library on the second. They've even got the rare books case, the walk-in humidor, the pool table and the grandfather clock outlined in pale blue lines. There's no indication of smoke alarms.

"Where could I find more information about the wiring?"

"What class did you say this was for?"

"It's an Engineering course: addressing the fire risks in historic buildings. Those third floor bedrooms would be a real challenge."

"It sounds interesting. Who's the professor?"

"He's new."

"Oh. Well, I suppose the best place to check would be with the Village Fire Marshall." We go back downstairs and she looks it up: "Three twenty-three East Main Street."

She writes it down for me. "And where would I find a report on the fire itself?"

"Again: The Village Fire Marshall."

Say, I'm going to have to see this guy.

New topic: "Did any of the Carters go to SUNY Running River?"

"Oh no, it wasn't endowed until 1958—they were all in their forties!"

"There are no more Carters?"

"Not around here."

"So SUNY has no illustrious grads from Old Town?"

"On the contrary, there've been dozens."

"When was that?"

"Throughout the university's history."

"Including now?"

"Certainly."

"From the old families?"

"Well, a number of them have moved here rather more recently, but we do get a few from the old families."

"I suppose their names are all in a *Who's Who in the Universe* or something of that sort."

"Well, most of them have *some* family member in the national volume of *Who's Who,* not that we'd need it. Everyone knows the Hustons, the Brackens, the Cranes, the Bateses, the Hugheses, the Moores, the Ridgways—"

"No Bernsteins, huh?"

"The first Jewish family moved into Old Town in 1964."

Well: Now I know *that.*

"Thank you, you've been most helpful."

"If there's anything else I can do for you?"

Now that you mention it: "Might I see a copy of the university telephone book?"

No Brackens or Cranes currently enrolled. Six Hustons, all from other towns, useless to me, one Bates majoring in Radical Surgery—no thanks—a Moore in the Development Office and a Hughes in Comparative Literature, whatever that is these days.

Kelly Ann Hughes.

That's lyrical.

The twenty-year-old daughter of a prominent family might be the best way to get introduced to some of the town elite, who always have quicker access to privileged information. Coming from the other side of the tracks, I just might be able to strike up a friendship with some of the younger, more liberal children of the proud, old families, if this place is half the college town I think it is.

I find out from the overworked department secretary that Kelly
Ann Hughes is in class. Old Agriculture Building, Room 109. But
first I have to take Antonia to the bathroom.

The place we're looking for is one of those low, red brick buildings built when the Carters were still hoping to cultivate a nice ivy-
covered small town look that has since been dwarfed by
state-funded science department megaliths. Some of the rooms
still smell of cow manure. It lingers around us as we count off the
room numbers, searching for the right one. Turns out she's *teaching* the class in Room 109. She's standing among the students,
demonstrating something with one of their arms. Her back is to
me, I can't see what she's doing. The students laugh and Kelly
Hughes straightens, walks back to the blackboard. She's wearing
faded jeans and a short-sleeved polo shirt. She looks nineteen.

But she doesn't talk like nineteen: "So we could say that Virginia
Woolf sets up the binary opposition of male-female writing then
proceeds to deconstruct it and call for androgynous writing. But
are the binaries real? What about her own writing? What happens
when she has dinner at the women's college?"

Pause. "The food's lousy," says a student. Some laughs.

"Right. The food's lousy. And what effect does that have on her?"

They don't get that one, and Kelly Hughes has to tell them what
page to turn to to find out.

"The food is lousy because . . . ?"

Long pause.

She spoon-feeds it to them: "The food is lousy because the
women's college doesn't have . . . ?"

"Enough money?" ventures a brave soul.

"Exactly. But instead of giving you an economics lesson, Woolf
describes the stringy stewed prunes, the tasteless meat. What else?"

"Water instead of wine?"

"Right. So rather than taking an essay form—and citing nu-
meric data to demonstrate the differences between the endowments at the men's college and the women's college—she's
physicalizing her feminine dilemma, trying to get you to respond
emotionally to the sensations created first by her descriptions of
the sumptuous meal at the men's college, followed by the tasteless

meal at the women's college, so that you, the reader, *experience* the difference: Is that 'female' writing?"

Pause. Nothing. Kelly Hughes has to fish for this one. "She makes it a *narrative* instead of statistics. Is this the 'female' voice that she argues she must assume?"

Pause. Then, hesitantly: "Well, yeah: 'Cause men are supposed to be logical. When you write an essay, you're not supposed to let your emotions into it."

"Good: Is the very idea of 'narrative,' then, a female form?" That gets responses ranging from half-sleepy bewilderment to bolts of lightning visibly striking two or three of the women students. "Or is it just the use to which she puts the narrative techniques that makes her writing 'female'? In other words, are there female *forms* of narrative?"

She lets that one go unanswered, as the notebooks are already slamming shut, papers are rustling, and she already has to shout out next week's assignment over the noise of scraping chairs and meaningless chit-chat.

"We're starting *Taming of the Shrew* next week, people: read Heilman's introduction and act one!"

I wait for her to finish dealing with the crowd of students who *still* want to know what they're expected to do for the final paper, then I get her as she's packing up.

I say, "You should always reassure your students that any material accidentally learned in class *can* be forgotten by next weekend if they really put their minds to it."

She looks up at me. Light brown hair, green eyes. Killer combination.

"I sure wish I had had a teacher like you at the State University of Ecuador in Guayaquil. But we were always striking for better conditions, so I probably would have missed most of your classes anyway."

"Excuse me, but who are you?"

"Let me answer that question by posing another: You say that language is male-dominated."

"I said that the *authoritative use* of language is male-dominated."

"All right. Well I have proof. Let me give you an example."

"Go ahead," she says, waiting.

"Okay. Imagine you've got a twenty-gallon pot full of warm spaghetti and tomato sauce."

"Uh, yeah?"

"And you think there might be a peacock feather in the bottom."

"Okay . . ."

"And you slowly part the spaghetti with your fingers as you reach down, until you're up to your elbows in it . . ."

"Yes?"

"There's no word for that."

"What?"

"There's no word for that. No *single* word to describe how your fingers feel when they part the buttery strands of warm spaghetti."

She thinks. Then: "Squishy."

"No, don't you see how *violent* that is, how *masculine*? 'Squishy'? No, there's no single word for what I'm looking for."

She smiles, then lets it drop. "I've got to prepare tomorrow's lecture—"

"But you need a break, don't you? There's a nice cozy coffee shop under the bridge and I'm dying for some intelligent conversation."

We slide onto some wooden benches at the campus coffee shop, where Antonia can run loose and play with other kids.

"My name's Filomena."

"Mine's Kelly. Kelly Hughes."

"Yes, I know."

She eyes me. "What is this about?"

Well, how would *you* begin?

"Okay, I'll level with you," I say, flipping my wallet open to a photo of Antonia. Whoops. Wrong side. I flip it over and repeat the gesture, flashing my old badge.

Kelly smiles nervously. "You're a cop?"

"Relax, ma'am. I left my rule book behind years ago."

"Then why do you still carry that badge? Isn't that illegal?"

"Legalities have not been working for me lately."

"Oh. Well, I've got a meeting with the Graduate Studies Committee—" She's gathering her things.

"Then why did you order coffee? No, wait. This is not starting out the way I'd like. Let me tell you something. Then you can go if you want. It'll only take a minute."

She hesitates. I've got too many dangling threads already. I don't want another loose one.

"I'm trying to solve a crime." *That* gets nowhere. Okay: "I'm also trying to protect Long Island from a company that's poisoning the environment with toxic waste."

"Then why are you talking to me?"

Because I have no freaking proof. Dammit.

"The man who owns this company—well, he hurt me. I know what he's doing is illegal, but I'm not a cop anymore, so it's not going to be easy to build a case against him."

She asks, "Then what is your method?"

Right. My method.

"Let me tell you something: I've been an American citizen for more than ten years, but I still get a lot of doors slammed in my face for being a dark-skinned *latina*. But it was a lot worse in my aunt's day. One time they wouldn't even let her into a movie theater. Said she was bringing in her own food. Was she mad? You bet your ass. What could she do? I'll tell you: She spent the night gathering moths from all the porch lights in the neighborhood, then she got someone to go back for her, smuggle in a jar of moths and set them loose in the darkened theater. They all went for the projector lamp and ruined the show." I look into her eyes, giving her a moment for the description of my method to sink in. "I want to release moths in his theater."

Slowly, she nods. I tell her, "It's a very fucked-up situation, and I can't fix it. But I've got to try to do some good, whatever I can."

"Sounds a bit like teaching at SUNY."

"And you probably pictured yourself reading Emily Dickinson and Alice Walker aloud to wide-eyed, rapt youths under the spreading elms of a northeastern university."

"Something like that."

"Another idealist goes down in flames. Well, Virginia Woolf isn't too far off."

"If they read it."

"But how much of that is their fault? I mean, all the math I was taught in school was *wrong*. Twelve times two does *not* equal six times four."

"Uh—"

"Then why are two twelve-packs of beer cheaper than four six-packs?"

"I guess I never thought of math that way. I mean, we're all used to indeterminacy of meaning in literature, but—"

"But you're always taught that numbers speak for themselves, immune to subjective interpretation. Bullshit. You Americans aren't trained to haggle. Most of the time you get everything handed to you with a price tag on it that's not negotiable. And you pay. But not us: the unenlightened masses of the underdeveloped nations of the world. No, we've got to bargain for a frigging pound tomatoes every day in the open market. They ask for twice what it's worth, and you've got to bring 'em down or else you're a darn fool. Now here they train you from the moment you go to school never to question prices. Check out all those math problems they give you: 'If you have twelve apples at fifteen cents apiece and eight oranges at four-and-a-half cents apiece and a half-pound of grapes at three dollars and thirty-nine cents a pound and you only have two dollars and twenty-five cents, how much more do you need? Choose from answers a, b, c or d' Right? They *never* say: 'e: How much do you need to *bargain* the guy down?' Whoever heard of such prices? Three thirty-nine a pound for grapes! It tests the same math skills, doesn't it?"

"I have to admit that it does." Kelly considers this new perspective. "We *are* creatures of duty. . . . I never looked at math that way."

"What do you look at?"

She lets out a cynical, quiet "Ha!" reaches into her book bag, pulls out a book. It falls open to a page with a bookmark in it.

I read from the passage she has highlighted: "Let us return to get a 'glimpse' of the disseminal structure, i.e., the no-possible-return of the letter, the other scene of its remnance [*restance*]. We have already recognized the effects of the indivisible framing, from frame to frame, *from within which* psychoanalytic interpretations (semantico-biographical or triado-formalist) drew their triangles. . . ."

I ask, perplexed: "Your parents approve of this?"

"As a matter of fact, they don't."

This may be a break. I haven't had many. And I realize that I'm rubbing my throbbing forehead. With clammy hands. Too much coffee, maybe.

Kelly says, "I bet you've got some strange stories."

"I don't have the stomach for them right now."

"Just one. Over easy."

"Over easy?" My tongue feels thick, gelatinous, alien. I swallow. "Okay. Ethics question: fine points of the law. I once busted a guy for selling pot. But he kept smiling at me, so I knew something was wrong. I look close: the stuff didn't look or smell right. Wouldn't fool anybody for a minute, so the guy must have been working a variation on the basic envelope switch. I ask: 'What is this garbage?' He says: 'We put oak leaves in a blender, man. It's legal, bitch.' Now you tell me what I should do."

"Bust his ass for calling you a bitch."

"That's good. What I mean is, I can't bust him for pot, 'cause he isn't holding any, and I can't bust him for selling phony merchandise just because the *real* thing is illegal. . . . *Oh God.*"

Now I'm really getting sick. Like seasick. I ask for some cold water and lean back, then lie down on the bench.

"You want some Rolaids?" Kelly asks.

"Sure. Thanks."

She reaches into her bag and pulls out what would be a year's supply for most people. "A lot of people have this reaction to literary theory," she explains, feeding me two of them.

"Thanks."

"Derrida and Rolaids. It's quite a combo."

I explain that it must be the chemotherapy. It takes a long time when you have to stop every third word and suppress the urge to retch. Antonia wants to climb on me and Kelly, thank God, kindly takes her off me and shows her around the room, holding her up to the window to look out while I recover.

When I'm well enough to sit up I order a cup of chamomile tea. Antonia comes back and asks me if I'm okay. I tell her I'm better. Better enough to take a stab. I ask Kelly, "Do you know Samuel Morse?"

"We both use the same cable TV company, if that's what you mean."

"No, really."

"Everybody knows Sammy Morse. Why?"

Suddenly I'm very nearly sick again, but it passes.

"Kelly, I'm afraid of losing my grip and going under before I get a chance to finish this. I'm feeling around in the dark, trying to find all the angles the Feds have missed, or ignored, without a friend to help, and I need one. I don't suppose you know what that's like."

Pause.

"What can I do?" she says.

"Introduce me to some trustees . . ."

6

The story of the hunt is always told differently by the lion.
— AFRICAN PROVERB

Fil, it's your boyfriend," says Billy, dangling the phone from one hand, both eyes on the TV.

"He's not my boyfriend," I mumble, irritated. Okay, so I'm not so original before I've had my coffee, okay? "Hello?"

It's Jim Stella. "Dinner tonight?"

"Who's buying?"

"Wha—? Who—?"

"Dinner tonight sounds fine."

"Great: Whaddaya want? Chinese? Mexican? There's a new Indian place on Route 347."

"You know, I really feel like plain old American food for a change." I can barely keep down a slice of bread and a glass of water.

"Terrific—I know just the place. Vincentio's. Best veal *parmigiana* on the island."

"Um, really, I've been having too much rich food and wine lately."

"Oh I get it. Gotta watch the figure, huh?"

"Right. So—American?"

"Sure, you can just get a plate of spaghetti if you want."

"It's a date."

Did I miss something?

The Memorial Day holiday is Monday, but today is the actual day, and all the local schools are rehearsing their bands down on Main Street. I figure Reggie Einhorn might just be old-fashioned enough to have taken today off. I figure right.

He lives in a house most folks probably don't picture when they think of Long Island. It's a company shack that'd be more at home in Ludlow, Colorado, in the early springtime of 1914 than here. Sheets of fake linoleum bricks nailed to the frame are eaten away and peeling back, revealing the rotting 2 × 4 beneath. The interior hasn't been dusted or swept since Mrs. Vera Einhorn keeled over from kidney failure three years ago.

Colomba told him I'd be coming over. He thinks I'm trying to get a job with Morse. I figure if I can get him to talk about his job in detail, it might give me a clue as to how they *really* handle the toxics at Morse's facility (another possible weak link). But getting men to talk can be pretty hard. And none of the workers are talking to me right now. I need to get to know this guy first. He'll talk when he's ready.

He's already up and shaving when I show up on his sagging doorstep with a bag of groceries.

"I don't have any trouble getting around," he growls, but he puts the milk away in his fridge. "What's this?"

"Tea. Mind if I make some?"

"Go ahead." And he goes back to finish shaving. He's a big guy, almost six feet if he stood up straight, but his back is curled with a permanent stoop from years on the shop floor. Most of the muscle has gotten sinewy and saggy, but he was a tailgunner in the Pacific from 1943 to 1945, so I bet he could once do Russian leaps and touch his toes. He's still got a fair crop of hair, almost pure white, which makes his red face look redder. He keeps trying to scratch an itch inside his ear.

I check the fridge. Mustard and half a hot dog. Typical. "Don't you have any bottled water?"

"At two bucks a gallon? Not on your life, girlie."

I reluctantly bring some tap water to a boil, find the teapot (obviously Mrs. Einhorn's purchase), swish some hot water in it to warm it up, open the box and steep the leafy blend for five minutes.

"Vera was always making tea," he says. "Me, I'm a coffee drinker. But she'd always be up early, makin' herself a cup of tea. Didn't help much."

"What do you mean?"

He sits down with a mug in front of him.

"She was always tired. And clumsy. Walking around like a boxer who'd taken one too many kidney punches. If it wasn't one side it was the other. Then her blood pressure went through the roof . . ."

Reggie stares at his mug of tea for a long time. Then he tries a sip, makes a bitter face and says: "Bleah! What is this?"

"It's tea."

He gets up, spits it in the sink and dumps out the mug. He reaches up, groaning with the effort, opens a cabinet and pulls out one of those fluorescent cardboard cylinders filled with quick-dissolve crystals of sugar, coloring and somewhere way down the list of polysyllabic chemicals, freeze-dried tea. He heaps three spoons of powder into his mug, then adds hot water. His movements are restricted, painful.

"Now *this* is tea," he says. "Try it."

It's a sugary confection that bears no resemblance whatsoever to a plant once grown in China. The aftertaste makes my nausea rise. "Well, it covers up the taste of the mimeograph machine fluid. Is that what they do down at the factory? Add saccharine?"

"Hey: Mr. Morse is concerned about us, young lady. He warned us not to drink the tap water in the washroom."

"That's the solution? Water coolers?"

"I know it ain't a popular idea among you kids, but some of us are actually loyal to our company. We work hard for them, and they provide for us. If there were more people like Mr. Morse, this country'd be in a lot better shape, young lady." He keeps calling me that. Pretty soon he'll be asking me if my mother knows I'm here. "No cheap talk, no speculation. He just goes in and gets the job done."

"Like the way his lab technicians came up with the first practical liquid crystal display nearly twenty years ago and he squelched it because it would've made his then-current line obsolete, and now the Japanese are leading the LCD field?"

"He gambled, he lost. That's business. He also started this adhesive plant here with his last hundred grand and *now* look at it. Every car in America's got Morse adhesives holding all the rubber and vinyl in place. You use diaper pins on your kid? No—you got disposables with adhesive tape. Convenient, huh? You can thank Morse Techtonics for that."

"Right. Just think what they can do for your lungs."

"Listen, if it weren't for people like him we'd've fallen to the Japs years ago. Is that what you want?"

"Okay, okay, forget it. I promised to take Antonia to the parade."

"Wait. I'll go with you."

Just what I need.

We watch the Cub Scouts, the Boy Scouts (three troops), Brownies and Girl Scouts (two each), three elementary schools, the junior high and the high school bands, then the volunteer firemen. Which reminds me—

"And there's that bastard Vitelli," says Einhorn.

"Who?"

"Mike Vitelli: Head of the town zoning board. Morse is offering to develop ten thousand acres near the South Fork. Do you know how many jobs that would provide? *Honest* jobs? And that bastard Vitelli is blocking it."

"Why?"

"The Pine Barrens lobby. They're all afraid that two-acre zoning'll ruin the groundwater or some tree-hugging bullcrap like that. So what are they gonna do? Five-, ten-acre zoning at a million bucks a throw? And where are the working people supposed to live, huh? But these politicians don't give a crap about us. No, they just show up on parade day and then—"

He stops dead. I duck down and spin around as if some stalker's about the strike. But I don't see anything unusual. As I'm straightening up, Einhorn takes his cap off and holds it over his heart.

"What are you—?" I ask.

"Shhh!"

It's the flag.

He grips the cap tighter over his chest as the colors go by. There's a dark, reddish splotch above his right temple that was covered by the cap. After the honor guard passes he puts his cap back on and says, "You know, this is the way it's supposed to be. We should remember Memorial Day for what it is, not just a day to go to the beach."

"Fine, then ask your boss to give people more vacation time."

He laughs at me.

"Whaddaya want?" I say. "We're strapped! We get *ten* paid vacation days a year. That's the seventeenth lowest in the industrial world!"

He stops and turns to me: "America is Number One. Do you hear that, young lady? Number *One.*"

"Okay, okay."

"Damn straight. I'll see you later. I gotta go buy a buddy a beer."

I spend my lunchtime being shot full of tumor-inhibiting chemicals, then try to go learn something about how Shore Oaks burned down from the Town Fire Marshall. Well, the fire report must have gone with Amelia Earhart on that last flight, because *I* can't find it. *Nada. Desaparecido.* You Americans may not have roving death squads, but you sure know how to make information disappear.

My trip to the Town Office of Records is rewarded with access to a box full of papers that I can't do anything with. That is, I'd be able to do something with them if I weren't shivering with cold sweat and dashing off to the women's room every ten minutes for a full session of the dry heaves.

The chemotherapy also seems to have made me a bit dyslexic. Word orders seem reversed, even the spelling of individual words is jumbled in my feverish brain. After twenty minutes of trying to read the same three paragraphs and all I'm getting is:

· "Ew mstu sd nlki, yjrtr ytjyjdf yo nr drkg rbufwnt"

I figure it's time to quit.

Damn.

I lose an hour of precious lifetime lying in the backseat with my legs curled up until it passes. Then I drive home.

I need to get back on Morse's site.

Jim Stella takes me for a drive, the long way, past some of the primo old-money North Shore property.

"Look at the *size* of those houses!" he says. "Nothing like that in Ecuador, huh?"

"Sure, there are plenty, they'd just never make the mistake of letting us get this close."

"What do you mean?"

"In Ecuador, the superwealthy live within fortified enclosures patrolled by armed guards."

"Oh."

"Look at that: They've even got stables for their horses."

"Great, let's go for a roll in the hay."

"Oh, is this where I ask you about your taste in horse racing?"

"Huh?"

"You know, 'Speaking of horses, I like to play them myself. But a lot depends on who's in the saddle.'"

"What?"

"Never mind. Let's go eat."

"So *'porque'* means both 'why' *and* 'because'?"

"Yes."

"Stupid language."

I start to tell him it's two different terms, *"por qué"* and *"porque,"* but he's not listening, he's looking around.

"Boy, the clientele sure are slipping around here, ever since that takeover was done in by Congress," says Jim.

"I don't see anybody going through my jacket pockets, if that's what you mean. What takeover was that?"

"Can't you stop talking shop for one minute?"

"Just making conversation."

"Well converse about something else."

"Like the obscene, criminally gotten wealth we just drove by?"

"There you go again, Filomena, talking like a Third World guerrilla warrior. Don't you know Communism's dead?"

The sudden sound of breaking glass startles him. Then he stares at me. I look down and see that the water goblet has fallen from my hand and shattered on the floor. The waiter dispatches a busboy to clean it up. I listen to the sharp fragments being swept together as Jim's empty stare probes deep into my eyes. Seeing nothing.

Nothing.

But.

Glass.

"Filomena? Are you all right?

"Let's just order."

I fulfill my minimum daily nutritional requirements, but it costs me two-and-a-half hours of listening to why the Mets suck but the Yankees suck even worse, why there couldn't possibly be a third political party, how the state should either abolish or else triple local property tax, and why condoms should be made thinner because one time he asked out a new secretary, let the cash and the drinks flow, and, while driving back from the city, just as they were entering the Queens-Midtown Tunnel, she bent down and started giving him head right there on the front seat (a very dangerous thing to do).

After this he invites me back to his car.

He doesn't notice that I'm holding back pale waves of nausea.

"Have you ever made it to Tchaikovsky's *Festival Overture*?" he asks me, inserting it in the car's CD player.

I listen. "It's nice," I say, "Very characteristic of him: Throbbing with barely suppressed phallic desire."

He grins. "Isn't that the idea?"

Suppression? Not around here.

To those of you who ask, Are there really guys like this? Yes, there really are guys like this. I tell him, "I think women approach the idea of sex differently from men."

"Oh, you wanna hear something else?"

"Yeah."

"What do you wanna hear?"

"I want to hear you say yes to something."

"Ooh, I'm all a-quiver. What? What?"

"Get me some invoices from Morse's Billing Office."

"Whoa, whoa!" he says, braking for an unanticipated stop sign. He punches the STOP button on the CD player. He looks at me. I smile at him. "You're kidding, right? That's it," he begins chuckling. "Boy, you really are something else, Buscarsela. You really keep me guessing. But no more."

He lunges over and presses his lips against mine, hand behind my head pulling me towards him, hard. I stiffen, but let him do it. For now. When he stops, all I say is, "The road's clear."

He throws the car in gear and pulls out. "What are you, obsessed with this fucking Morse guy or something? What's with you?"

"I'm just trying to help you."

"You help me? Oh, that's a good one. Get serious, will you?"

"You're suing him, aren't you? For environmental damages?"

"Yeah."

"So I can help you dig up some dirt on Morse Techtonics."

"We're not interested in Morse Techtonics."

"You're not?"

"No."

"Then—what are you interested in?"

"Ever hear of a company called Prosystems?"

"I wasn't born knowing the name, no."

"You wouldn't be. It was just a letterhead company. Morse dissolved it twelve years ago when it was cited for forty-three Federal toxic waste hauling violations. That's when he formed Union Carting. When that racked up too many violations he formed Morse Techtonics. Anyway, when Kim Tungsten Steel and Glass bought the old Prosystems site they didn't know the place was knee-deep in toxic waste. Gonna cost about twelve, thirteen million dollars to clean up, and Kim wants Morse to pay his share."

What a dodo I've been: "Let me get this straight: You're suing Morse *on behalf of Kim Tungsten*?"

"Yeah. Sure."

"The company that's polluted East Carthage's drinking water?"

"Hey: Morse has *at least* half the responsibility for that. Maybe more." I think I'm about to explode. He looks at me for a second, goes back to driving. "Morse isn't the worst offender, you know. The Fairhaven National Lab leaked radioactive tritium into the water supply, for Christ's sake. We've even found traces of plutonium."

"In East Carthage?"

"Yeah."

"*Where I live?*"

"Oh—uh—"

"Stop the car. I'm getting out."

"What the fuck? Oh, come on! If this is more of your fucking bullshit—"

I bring my foot down hard, shoving it between his feet and jamming on the brake, then throw on the parking brake just a bit too soon, sending us both forward with a severe lurch. The engine coughs out of gear and dies.

"What the fuck are you doing?" he tries to stop me from unbuckling my seat belt.

Damn these new automatic shoulder straps! I kick the door open and the thing retracts. I yank my wrist loose from his grasp, snap the belt and step out.

"Okay, okay," he says. "Now get back in."

"No. Good-bye."

"Oh, stop this fuckin' bullshit! Why the fuck are you doing this? Why? You know, plenty of women are just waiting to take a ride with me."

"Then go pick one up."

"Okay, okay. It's okay. Go: I've left my mark on you."

"Oh, fuck you."

"No. Fuck *you.*"

An accelerated roar. The exhaust comes billowing out, mixing with my nausea from dinner and putting it over the top. After a few contorted minutes a good samaritan stops, headlights blinding the poor woman bent over the guardrail retching her guts out.

She takes me a couple of miles out of her way to a train station where I can get a cab home that uses up nearly one-third of all the cash I've got left in the world. Principles are painful.

*   *   *

The next chemotherapy session leaves me rolling around in brain-dizzying agony on a hospital cot for an hour-and-a-half. This is a foretaste of death, being sucked down by the dark, plutonian forces beneath this poor little island that was once as lush as the jungle.

I wipe some of the sweaty clumps of cold sick from my face with a clammy towel and I ask to speak to the doctor. They tell me he's out to lunch. Good for him. One of the more painful hours of my life goes by—and that's saying something—then Dr. Wrennch comes in and says, "What seems to be the trouble, Ms. Buscarsela?"

"The trouble is I'm seasick on dry land twenty-four hours a day."

"I can prescribe THC for the nausea."

"That's one of the things that did this to me," I explain.

"No, no, this would be in pill form."

"You know," I say, trying to smile but it hurts too much, clenched teeth holding back vomit, "five years ago I would have leapt at the chance. Okay, *two* years ago. But not now." Another wave engulfs me, and I fall back and let it wash over me. It's a bit easier when you don't resist it. He's trying to tell me something and I'm not listening. When I can swallow again without gagging, I interrupt whatever the hell it is he's saying: "I want to stop the chemotherapy."

"Stop? You just started two days ago."

"I said I want to stop."

"Why?"

What is it with men always asking me why?

"It's slowing me down."

"You need it to live."

"Just three more weeks."

"Why on earth should we postpone your treatment three weeks?"

"Okay, two weeks."

"I mean, I suppose we can, but what would that possibly accomplish?"

I look at him. I'm thinking. "You idiot," but all I say is, "Justice."

7

Now still another generation is being erased by a civil war
    and Rome's own power is bringing her to ruin,
she who was never destroyed by her enemies . . .
we shall destroy her, an ungodly generation, a curse in our blood,
    and once more animals alone shall dwell here.
                                        —HORACE, *Epode XVI*

You're out of your mind!" he says.

"Yes. I am."

"Why?"

"Why am I out of my mind? I don't know, *you're* the doctor."

"I mean why postpone treatment?"

"Because I've *got* to do this. I've just got to."

"Do *what*? Ruin your health? What could possibly be worth that?"

"I told you: Seeing justice done."

"That's what we've got cops for, and courts, and—"

"Listen, I've had enough of you interpreting the world for me: This happens to be something I know a little more about, okay? I told you the facts, not the feelings."

"And what are the feelings?"

"I'm doing this for others, not just for me."

"Will you stop being cryptic and just tell your doctor what's wrong?"

"What's wrong? Good question. What *is* 'wrong'? I seem to be having trouble with that one lately."

"Miss Buscarsela—"

"Listen, Doc: I ran away from an abusive home when I was fourteen. I would have joined the church but they were way too old-fashioned back then, always happy to be giving bread to the poor but never attacking the root of the problem. So I joined a group. Well—kind of a gang." I've got his attention now. "Militant activists. They gave me a home. And I rode with them. We were revolutionaries, with noble ideals of fighting the rich and helping the poor. Some were real heroes to me. . . . But a lot of them turned out to be gun-crazy bullies who blew our chances of connecting with the peasants, so when I came here I joined the cops because—well, because I thought being a cop would be the next best way to help people in this country, but it wasn't, because the cops turned out to be just *another* gang of gun-crazy bullies. 'We've got cops and courts.' Jesus! I'm a crime solver, okay? And this one's pretty close to home."

I do get talky around him, don't I?

"And what is this wrong you're risking your health to right?"

"Tell me: Do you think it's ethical to kill a sonofabitch who is responsible for dozens, maybe hundreds of deaths?"

"No: Absolutely not."

"Okay, how many does it take? A thousand? Two thousand? Ten thousand? How many relatives you got left in Poland, Dr. Wrenn-chowski?"

"None."

"Used to be a big family, right?"

"Like all families—"

"Do you think Israel was justified in kidnapping Eichmann?"

"Yes."

"So there's some point where it's *not* okay to let a murderer walk, even if the 'cops and courts' won't touch him. And where is that point? Five deaths or fifty? Does it have to be five hundred thousand before you'll consider him a murderer?"

"Eichmann was brought *to trial*—"

"Okay, so I'll bring him to trial."

"Why?"

"In order for my life to have meaning."

"All life has meaning."

"Then in order for my *death* to have meaning!"

"It's not worth sacrificing your life just to take another stab at him."

"Then what is my life worth?"

No answer.

I go on: "What if I stop being your patient for two weeks? But I still want to see you."

"I don't understand—"

"So I can come see you not as a patient but as a friend."

"Um, yeah. Sure. But what are you trying to prove?"

"We're not doctor and patient now, we're friends. You're Stan and I'm Filomena."

"Okay, Filomena."

"Okay, Stan: I think one of the most important things you can do in life is raise a kid to be a skeptical, independent thinker, who's ready to fight to make the world a better place."

"Then do *that* instead—"

"Don't you see? That *is* what I'm doing. But it has to be *by example*. Not just words. Just two more weeks."

"I don't know . . ."

"Okay: Ten days." Our eyes meet. Feels like the first time, though it's not. I smile at him. He concedes.

"Okay. Ten days . . ."

I hope I've got that long.

I call the county again. Twenty minutes later the guy comes on and tells me the Tungsten site's got a clean bill of health.

"What?" That's me talking. "You could develop photos in the drinking water!"

"Must be residual leachate, ma'am, the site's clean as a whistle."

Well, *that's* bullshit. It's time to call the EPA again.

Gina's back. Hoorah. "Gina? Fil. Call out your dogs. There's two places: One's called Kim Tungsten Steel and Glass in East Carthage, the other's Morse Techtonics in plain old Carthage. Did I mention I'm on Long Island?"

"You might have said it faster than the speed of sound, 'cause I didn't hear it. Slow down, girl. What's going on?"

"Two companies out here are poisoning the air, the ground-water—"

"And what makes these companies different from all others?"

"Because both sites were run by a selfish bastard who'd kill your mother if he thought it'd make him some extra pocket money."

"*My* mom? She'd gut him and stuff him like a cannoli. Get real, Fil. You got a site for me? How do you know they're Superfund?"

"I don't."

"Then there's nothing I can do. You have to call the county first—"

"I called the county, Gina. They're getting a bigger dividend than the stockholders."

"That's quite a charge. Can you make it stick?"

"No. That's why I need you."

"Well—" I can hear her flipping through pages. Must be her map of Region 1, Long Island Section. Yep: "East Carthage—oh, the old Prosystems site?"

"You know about that?"

"Hey: We're the government. We know everything."

I cough excessively.

"You're also right near Fairhaven National Lab. That's been Su-perfund since 1989."

"Y—" I stop myself from saying "You know about that?" again.

"That site's reasonably under control. We've had to slap them around a bit for improper handling of asbestos, not fixing broken emissions monitoring units, stuff like that, but that's an air qual-ity issue. None of their radioactive compounds have turned up in the residential drinking water, although maybe that's because the County Water Authority switched sixteen hundred homes from private wells to public water at the first sign of trouble. Nothing like nuclear waste in the drinking water to get people hopping."

And lower the property values so that only the *latinos* will move in next to the living dead. Colomba says when she bought the place, the real estate agents told her that FNL was a drug company. Nobody mentioned the Relativistic Heavy Ion Collider.

"Yeah, it's a little unsettling to say the least," I say. "Kind of like finding out one of your neighbors has a vengeful, emotionally disturbed teenage son with ready access to high-powered rifles."

"Plutonium's pretty heavy, though. It would tend to sink rapidly and bond with the sediment, so it's fairly unlikely that it would get into the drinking water." I'm beginning to think about just how I could get it into someone's drinking water, when Gina says, "There's a much bigger risk on Long Island from breast cancer."

Oh, no. Something *else* to worry about. "What's that about?"

"Well, we're just starting to study it. But Nassau and Suffolk counties rank among the highest incidence of breast cancer in New York State, which already ranks high in the national average. We think the most likely chemical agents are organochlorine pesticides like chlordane, toxaphene, DDT—"

"DDT was banned years ago."

"Yes. Suffolk was the first county in the U.S. to do it, back around 1970. But the stuff's persistent. Any woman who's been living in the same house for fifteen years is at risk."

That means Colomba. And probably Rosita, too.

"Chlordane was banned in 1988, but it can stay in the soil for twenty years. Traces have been found in the Arctic food web, and in almost every human being on the planet, but it's particularly high in people who work with pesticides, like exterminators and lawn-care workers."

And that means Elvis. Strike three. "What else have you got? Come on, don't hold out on me."

"It's still being manufactured for export."

"Where to?"

"Where do you think? Poor countries with flimsy environmental regulations."

And that means Ecuador.

All of Latin America.

"Ay, ¡mierda!" And a chemical change comes over me, submersing me in a cauldron of wrath, which I pour out for several minutes, constructing elaborate curses about what I'd like to do to the SOBs who allow a known poison to be shipped abroad, in a mixture of English, Spanish and Quichua, before I resolve to get

down to Ecuador somehow and help them outlaw this shit before it's too late.

I also resolve to insist that Colomba and Rosita start going for regular mammograms, and to tell Elvis to make sure he uses rubber gloves and a breathing mask the next time he has to spray some shrubs. But Gina tells me it's not that easy. No one uses chlordane anymore, so he wouldn't be in danger of breathing it in. The greatest risk would be physical contact from digging in chlordane-contaminated soil. He does a lot of digging. And the only way to determine if a house he's working on was treated with chlordane would be to find out from each and every homeowner if they or their exterminating service have records from before 1988 indicating what chemical pesticide they used for termite treatment. Right.

I listen to Gina tap her pencil and hum, as she studies the situation.

"Tell you what I can do, Fil, I can check with the state Resource Conservation and Recovery people to see if there are any existing violations—"

"That's too slow. You've got to move in *now.*"

"Just like on TV, Filomena. 'I need *evidence,* Detective Buscarsela, *evidence.*' "

"You *do* sound a bit like my lieutenant."

"Fuck you, girl." We laugh.

"You want evidence?" I say. "I'll get you evidence."

"Okay, but be careful."

"I will."

" 'Cause the phone might be tapped." It's a joke.

So why aren't I laughing?

It's one of those cloudy days that's threatening a thundershower sometime, you just don't know when. I'm moping about the house, at my wit's end. I've been blocked five different ways before, but with the machine to fall back on. Cops may not be too brilliant all the time, but they generally know what they're doing, they get paid to do it, and if there's evidence out there, they'll find it. I'm on my own here. I feel like calling up Van Snyder for backup, but I know it'll be the same story: "I need *evidence,* Detective Buscarsela, *evidence.*"

So now what? I think about the workers. They've lived there so long they're used to it. They may look okay to each other, but to me they all look gray and bloodless. Of course, hazardous workplaces are nothing new. Nineteenth-century clowns were dropping like flies from the whiteface makeup before they found out that the chemical they were using to make it was deadly. Now *there's* a situation some surrealist ought to explore.

I've dealt a lot with the flip side of legality, but this one's got me caught between the two. Guess I'm showing my age there: I suppose CD-bred kids don't know what a "flip side" is. Well, maybe they do. Am I sounding old-fashioned? Oh, no. Is it old-fashioned for me to get angry when I hear that Elvis's girlfriend cooks his meals and cleans his apartment for him? (Does she cut his meat, too?) Is it old-fashioned of me to want to pull the plug when I go in to see Billy, and he's watching a porno movie on Pay-Per-View?

I accost him: "Why are you watching this garbage?"

"I dunno. Porno's really gone downhill."

"It has? How is *that* possible?"

"I mean, it's always the same: the guy and the girl meet, strip and fuck. Bo-o-oring! They even use the same actors. At least this one's got some new faces. Cute Asian babe. And there was this gorgeous black woman on before with—uh—"

"Any *latinas?*"

"Sometimes. See that one there? She's from Iran. Man, they'd stone her to death back home if they ever caught her!"

Hmm. So that's what our struggle for equality has given us: Multicultural pussy. It is a sad commentary on our condition when *pornography* represents our society at its most "egalitarian."

"See?" he says.

"My, he's large."

Billy laughs. "Yeah, his cock takes up half the screen."

I look at Billy. "You're getting a hard-on watching *a cock?*"

He shifts uncomfortably. "No, I'm not. I'm watching this Iranian babe give him head."

"You're watching both."

"I am not!"

"Look at it! It's right there on the screen!"

Pause. He zaps the channel. To a commercial: "And the taste? *Great!*"

"Yeah, that's what I'm looking for in an antacid: great taste. Come on, Billy, let's get out of here."

"And do what?"

"I don't know. Go for a walk. Antonia! You want to go for a walk?"

"I want to go for a walk!" she comes running in from the kitchen.

Tree-lined streets and lengthening afternoon shadows. It's pleasant enough, until the wind shifts.

"Pew! What's *that* smell?" I ask. I mean, in addition to the usual smells that we've all gotten used to.

"Every year they spray the trees," says Billy. "Right after Memorial Day."

"So it's insecticide. Great. More poison." Going to have to ask Gina about what they use in place of chlordane, too.

"Come on, Aunt Filomena. You know how much it'd take to kill a person?"

"No. Do you?'

He doesn't.

"We didn't go to see *tía* Yolita," says Antonia.

"She's in Ecuador, Antonia. I showed you on the map. It's very far away. We're going to see her soon. I promise."

"She's in Ecuador?"

"Yes, in South America. Remember, I showed you—?"

"*Freeze!* You're dead!"

"Jesus—!" I'm all instinct, pushing Antonia back and lunging forward into the bushes, grabbing a throat, thorns, squeezing—a knifelike slice cold across my cheeks begins dripping, then a second blast squirts it in my eyes. It's a water pistol. A fucking water pistol. Filled with ice water.

"Jesus shit bricks!" I explode, but I'm just letting off steam now. My forearms are scratched and bleeding superficially. The kid rolls out of the bushes, laughing. Thank God I didn't hurt him, but if it had been for real I'd probably be dead. He's about twelve years old, but big, with a voice like a man's. *That's* what did it to me. I wipe my face with my T-shirt and he shoots cold water all over my abdomen.

"Goddamn, that's enough!" I shout, grabbing him. "Don't you have kids your own age to play with?"

"My mom won't let me go when they're in there," he pleads, like that's supposed to make it okay.

"In where?"

He points. The fence.

Of course.

"What's your name?" I ask.

"Tomás. Tommy."

"Okay, Tommy, why doesn't your mother want you to go in there?"

"*She* thinks it's dangerous." He makes a face that says—*mothers*—as if I'm supposed to sympathize with him.

"Is it?"

"Nah."

"Why not? What's in there?"

"Just a bunch of barrels and shit."

"What do you mean 'and shit'?"

He makes another face: "I know, I'm not supposed to say bad words—"

"No, you're not—now what do you mean, 'and shit'?"

"You know, stuff."

"No, I don't now. What kind of stuff?"

"Just stuff."

"Just stuff. Solid stuff? Liquid stuff? Gas?"

"Oh, *that*." Like it was obvious. "Liquid."

"Liquid?"

"Maybe."

"What do you mean, maybe?"

"I mean I guess it's liquid. It's all thick and gooey."

"What color?"

"*Black*." Like *everybody* knows that.

"Black. Like motor oil?"

"Yeah, I guess."

"Billy, you got film in your camera?"

"I don't think so."

"Here's five bucks. Run to the store and get some. Go!"

He runs like an out-of-shape athlete who's over the hill at 17, but he runs. Haven't seen him move this much since I've been here.

"And there's five for you, too, if you'll do me a big favor."

"My mom told me not to take money from strangers."

"Your mom told you right. But now that you've soaked me twice we're *not* strangers."

"You're not?"

"No. I'll make it ten dollars."

"What's the favor?"

Fifteen minutes later Billy's back with his Instamatic and a roll of film and I'm explaining to Tommy that I want him to sneak in and take pictures of anything unusual. Since he doesn't know what constitutes "unusual" at an abandoned waste dump I tell him anything *messy*—like barrels that seem to be leaking oil.

He says, "There's one spot with this mess of big black metal things, like, ya know, like part of the Bat Cave."

"Good. I want pictures of that. And anything with labels on it. Make sure you get close enough so the labels are legible."

"Are what?"

"So you can read them."

"I know what I'm doing," he says, like I've insulted the U.S. Marine Corps or something, and he's gone, slipped under the hole in the fence like a dusty ferret after—whatever the hell ferrets eat.

There's a nasty surprise waiting for us when we get home.

"I think you need a lawyer," says Colomba, meeting us at the door. Her voice is trembling.

"What are you talking about?" I say, then two big guys in county-issued plainclothes get out of their easy chairs and confront me. One's kind of yellow-skinned like he's not getting enough sunlight, the other's a bit more robust, with a drooping red moustache and a nose you could open a beer bottle with. He speaks first:

"Miss Filomena Buscarsela?"

"Yes?"

"You have the right to remain silent. Anything you say can and will be used against you in a court of law—"

I almost panic: "Whoa, whoa, whoa, what the heck do you think you're doing?"

"We're reading you your rights, like in *Miranda versus Arizona*."

"Yeah? Well, 'No person shall be deprived of liberty without due process of law,' like in the Fifth Amendment of the Constitution. You've heard of it?"

"You're under arrest, Miss Buscarsela—"

"On what charge?" It can't be. I'm almost getting worried.

"We got a report of child abuse. We're placing you under arrest and putting your child under protective custody. Is this her? Is this Antonia Buscarsela—" he says, bending down like he thinks he's going to give her a kiss or something.

Now I get mad: "You got a *report* and you're here to arrest me on unsubstantiated charges? Get the hell out of here! Address all further communications to my lawyer. I'll send you his address. *Now get out of my house!*"

Droopy moustache straightens up, looks at me smugly like he's got every cop in the county on his side.

"Look, we know it ain't your house, lady."

"Then get out of my *sight.*"

"We checked the records: There is no record of you living here."

"Well I'm living here now."

"You got any proof of that?"

"Yeah, I'm standing here."

Colomba says, "She's staying with us."

"Yeah, but—"

"I said I-AM-LIVING-HERE-NOW."

Yellow-face turns to his partner, his features clearly asking the question, What do we do now? Droopy moustache looks right at me and says, "We'll have a hearing in a couple of weeks. Who knows? Maybe a couple of days, even."

"*Get out. Now.* Before I get your badge numbers." They go.

"Fuckhead."

Good thing I didn't panic, huh?

*　　*　　*

"Hello, Gina? I've got some evidence for you."

"Fine, come on in."

"No: You come out here."

"Fil, you heard about decaf? It'll take *days* to arrange that. I thought you said you were in a rush."

"I *am*, it's that—Gina, I'm broke. I spent my last twelve dollars on one-hour developing for these pictures."

Pause.

"You don't suppose you could lend me a couple of hundred bucks to live on while you're at it, do you?"

"Christ, you have got it bad, haven't you? What are you on to out there?"

"You trust me?"

"What kind of question is that? Course I do."

"How soon can you get out here?"

I hear papers rustling. "Well, I suppose I could tell the Navy to go to hell. God knows they've done it to me a few times. The meeting's in two days, and I've got to get through about fifteen hundred pages of turgid bureaucratese before then."

"So read it on the train."

"It's not *English*, Fil—"

"It'll take ten minutes to look at the pictures. And don't forget that portable water sampler."

More rustling. "Okay—How about tomorrow afternoon?"

"Beautiful. And thanks, Gina."

"Yeah. They should issue me a bugle."

I hang up and breathe the first easy breath I've had today.

Antonia walks in. She's all dressed up, and I mean purse, hat, shoes, sunglasses, everything. She announces: "I'm going to Ecuador."

I laugh like I haven't laughed in weeks and hug my precious daughter to me like this hug has to last forever. Thank God, I've got my child. Thank God.

Hell yes.

The phone rings. It's for me. Kelly Hughes.

She asks: "Want to go to a party?"

8

El mundo habrá acabado de joderse el día en que los hombres viajen en primera clase y la literatura en el vagón de carga.
(The world will be completely fucked up the day men travel first class and literature goes as freight.)

—GARCIA MÁRQUEZ

I warn Colomba of her rights. I want her to understand that we are probably in for some major hassling, but that she is not to relinquish custody of Antonia to *anybody*. Somebody has called in a complaint to Child Protection Services, and that's as easy as picking up the telephone. I explain that there's supposed to be an investigation, questioning of neighbors and witnesses, an official examination of the kid, *then* a charge and a hearing, not this bullcrap they cooked up 'cause they didn't know they were dealing with an ex-cop. Somebody's getting sloppy.

Did I say "bullcrap"? Jesus, that's Einhorn's phrase. Something about that guy. I'm going to have to give him another try. He knows something, and he hasn't seen the last of me.

I've been wearing the same black dance dress every evening out because that's about all I have left. Well, this crowd hasn't seen me in it. I hope. I shower with Antonia, who stands right under me, making it hard to move, and I let the shampoo and conditioner flow down from me to her—a fine form of recycling. Then I dry her off, comb her hair and explain that I'm going out but I'll be back later, and that *tía* Colomba is going to stay with her until I get back. She's not thrilled but she accepts it. Like her mom. But when I ask for multiple kisses good-bye she pushes me away, saying, "Go." Sharper than a serpent's tooth.

I give Colomba the numbers where she can reach me, then I drive up to Kelly's house so we can go together in her car. I wouldn't want to pull into a swanky party in the heap. I meet her parents, who are nice enough to me. The place isn't a mansion, but it's big enough to hide a grand piano in the living room that I don't spot until we're ready to leave. The floor is so clean a good-sized roach would die of starvation, and I don't know how they maintain a plush, white shag rug in the same antiseptic state. Witchcraft? My kid would have it looking like the siege of Stalingrad in less than a week. Did I say a roach? A *microbe* would die of starvation in there.

Kelly's not quite ready, so I go with her up to her room to chat while she finishes primping. The place is so spic-and-span every noise reverberating off the pristine tiles spirals around your ears, amplified like in a library whispering gallery. Downstairs—three rooms away—Mrs. Hughes coughs.

"God, how did you ever sneak your boyfriends in here?" I ask.

Kelly smiles at my reflection in the vanity mirror. "I didn't have to. I always snuck out."

"Hmm: I'm going to remember that in about twelve years."

"Oh that's right! I'm talking to a parent! Oh, no! I've betrayed my generation!"

"Easy, woman, we're not *that* far apart."

"Far enough: Don't you have relatives who were already grandmothers by your age?"

"Yeah—my mother."

"So you see . . ." She concentrates on putting on her eyeliner, which is just as well.

"Is Phil Gates going to be there?" I ask.

"Who?"

"Vice President of University Relations. And a total creep."

"I shouldn't imagine so. No. It's a small affair. Strictly upper crust." She's only half kidding.

"Good."

"Why? Who's he to you?"

"Just someone I don't want to run into."

She's already putting on her character, so I don't bother her with my policewoman's just-the-facts questions for a while.

"How far is this place?" I ask.

"Little over a mile," she says, brushing on the shadow. My God, she's made up. I guess I didn't notice she wasn't wearing makeup when we first met because so few of the younger women I've been dealing with lately wear any at all.

Oh no, I said it: "Younger women."

She puts on some blush, powders it, dusts it. It's a remarkable transformation. "So when are you going to tell me the rest of this big mystery?"

"When I know it myself."

She ties her hair back with a gold ribbon and pumps a little hair fixer into it. "Just don't make the mistake of trying to fit everything snugly into a preconceived hypothesis and committing what Nietzsche calls 'metalepsis,' when you reverse an effect into a cause, especially when you're thinking causally."

Like thinking that cough syrup causes coughing. My God, Antonia's committed "metalepsis"! Wait 'til I tell her.

"Of course, Sherlock Holmes was a master of the art of deductive reasoning, and Conan Doyle and Nietzsche were contemporaries," she says. "I'm sure that would be useful to you as a detective."

"I didn't study any Nietzsche in college."

"What *did* you study in college?"

"Well, let's just say I've learned a lot that isn't on my transcript."

She eyes me in the mirror like she sees something there she hasn't seen before.

"Could you snap this on for me?"

She holds a string of pearls behind her neck for me to clasp. Remarkable.

"Thanks." And she reaches for her watch.

"Wait a minute, can I see that?"

"Sure."

I give it a look. "Jesus, this is the real thing. Where the hell do you wear a 24-karat-gold watch?"

"From your house to the car, to the dance, to your house."

"During which time you don't have the *slightest* need to know what time it is."

"Right."

"Let me ask you something, since you're an expert on philosophical reasoning: If beauty is truth, as Keats said, and the truth hurts, as we all know, then does it not follow that beauty hurts?"

Kelly smiles at me. "It sure does."

And we're off. Would you believe I'm actually excited? I mean, I realize I've lived surrounded, nay, *immersed* in WASP culture for nearly fifteen years—hell, my whole life if you count *yanqui* influence on the Southern Cone—yet I've never really penetrated it. I feel like a pioneering anthropologist with my trusty native interpreter who knows the rugged hills, the strange, clipped language and the local customs and who is going to help prevent me from being eaten alive. I even brought some of that funny green paper they worship, just in case.

Kelly's car is nicer than anything I've ever driven, though I'm sure it's considered modest by her community's standards. I mean it's domestic, few features, but it's new.

"So how would you define WASPness?" I ask.

"Part of being a WASP is not having to define it," she says, gunning the motor and sending up a spray of gravel behind us.

"So how do you deal with traditional anti-intellectualism? Your parents don't approve of your career choice, right?"

"They don't even think of it as a career, Filomena. Reading books? What kind of a career is that?"

"Uh-huh . . ."

"And whenever I take on some of the tough guys, like Althusser, Foucault, Lyotard, you know—"

"Oh yeah, sure—"

"All these male professors act like, 'Isn't that cute? She's trying to read the hard stuff.' Like, excuse me, but I don't happen to believe that my vagina interferes with my reading comprehension."

"Although it does sometimes get the pages all bloody."

She laughs, taking a curve she's grown up with because I didn't even see it coming.

"They really told you that?" I ask. "That a woman can't think complex thoughts like a man?"

"Not directly, in those words, but yes. Yes, all the tenured former sixties 'radicals' have turned into macho shit professors who I'd like to sue for motherfucking sexual harassment."

"Why don't you leave them to me? Ecuadorian women have a very special way of dealing with troublesome men."

"So I've heard: *snip snip*. My parents still regret not sending me to a Christian college."

"Really? Why?"

"Because I was a good little girl before I went off to the evil State University, learned all that horrid 'logical' reasoning that fed my intellectual pride, and lost my faith completely."

"My God, Kelly, you're the embodiment of the last thousand years of European history in one person!"

"You see? That's a hell of a burden to have to carry around with you. It's tough being a WASP, even when you don't have to struggle to define it."

And we laugh about it until she makes a sharp right onto a private road with no streetlights to guide her.

"How do you read the signs?" I ask.

"There are no signs."

Right. I forgot.

This "house" could pass for a plantation. A half dozen Doric columns spaced every twenty feet or so support the overhanging roof and the second-floor balcony above a porch you could play rugby on and still have room for a modest shuffleboard game. All at the central axis of a six-acre entranceway and perfectly symmetrical garden. The only thing that's missing are a few dozen slaves. Maybe it's their day off. There's even valet parking, but he's white. Times have changed. The guy has just finished parking a solid white 1950s-era Bentley that puts all the sleek-but-indistinguishable modern luxury cars to *shame*. I wonder whose car that is.

"Good evening, Miss Hughes," he croons.

"*Ms.* Hughes, Mickey."

"Yes ma'am."

"Oh yeah, there's a victory for feminism," I tell her on our way up the stairs.

"Leave your preconceptions at the door, Detective Buscarsela, it's showtime."

"Don't call me that in front of—"

The front door opens and Kelly explodes with delight, "How have you been, Mrs. Crane?" She and the hostess kiss each other on the cheek, rapid, passionless, perfunctory kisses, and she slides effortlessly into the role of good, traditional daughter of the WASP community.

Mrs. Crane eventually gets around to asking after me, and Kelly says, "And this is Filomena."

"Well, I hope I can live up to *that* introduction."

We all share a titter, and I scan the horizon for cocktails. Having spotted them I make my way over, avoiding all obstacles 'til I'm cradling a drink in my hand and don't look quite so much like I don't belong there. And I'm thinking, Aristophanes wrote a play, *Wasps,* but I haven't read that one. Going to have to look it up in the university library when I get a chance.

Right. In my spare time.

After I learn ancient Greek.

Safely camouflaged behind a glass of thirty-year-old sherry that was probably harvested by one of my distant cousins, and *damn* good, I begin surveying the room. Hidden stereo speakers gush soft, spineless music that would send any serious composer screaming into the night. Kelly finishes her opening scene, comes over and drags me over to a loose circle of younger people near the blackened fireplace. Some of Kelly's friends. Anne's an unemployed MBA currently staying at home while her husband works, Brett's a corporate lawyer, and Jordan's a successful physician. I do *not* want to think about doctors tonight, but the Lord won't let me forget. No, He wants me to stay reminded. I notice Brett the corporate lawyer is also drinking sherry, so with nothing else to say I ask him how he likes it.

"I've had better," he says.

"I haven't."

"Well, you must come by then and I'll show you how to get wonderfully smashed comparing vintage sherries."

"Maybe in a couple of weeks."

"Shall we make an appointment? Where can I call you?"

"You can't." He looks at me. "I'll call you." He smiles hesitantly.

After a few minutes of this, Kelly introduces me to an older bunch of people, among them Donald Seaver, who turns out to be *the* Seaver of the "Seaver's" national hardware store chain. It's hard to believe there are still families behind some of these names, that they haven't all been swallowed up by The Very Big Corporation of America, Inc. During this conversation I learn that America was made great by the great rewards held out to the great men who founded and run the great corporations. Isn't that great?

Seaver, in addition, "appreciates fine literature," and he half kids, half patronizes Kelly, asking her opinion on various canonized nineteenth-century male writers, and dismissing her opinion when she gives it, then he asks me, "And what do you do?"

"Resource conservation and recovery for an independent arbitrageur."

"Really? Sounds fascinating."

"It means I sift through other people's garbage."

"Oh."

That stops the conversation for a moment, then everyone laughs, and I explain that I'm a consultant working for companies that are trying to increase profits in these lean, mean times by cutting back on waste and reusing old materials, while Kelly slides back into her role.

"Would you like another gin and tonic, Mr. Seaver?"

"Thank you, Kelly," he says, handing her his glass. She skips off and leaves me alone. He watches her skirt swish as she goes, then turns to me. Second billing to another woman's butt. I'm honored.

I find out his idea of "appreciating fine literature" is collecting rare first editions. He invites me to come have a look at his collection.

"First editions?" I ask. "Of what?"

"Oh, Melville, Hawthorne, Dickens. The masters. The Melville is particularly valuable because his works were out of print for so many years."

"He must have had a lot of financial problems."

"I beg your pardon? Oh, I suppose."

"Those books should be in a museum," I say.

"But they are."

"A *public* museum. Or the rare books room of the university library."

He harrumphs a few times. I think it's a chuckle, but I'm not sure. I excuse myself and ask one of the women which way to the bathroom. The bathroom is not as opulent as the Loire valley original, but the Duc de Guise would still find a place to hang his doublet and hose. I finish sullying the pristine place with my Third World bacteria, wash up, then drink a glass full of water. Mmm. At least the water in Old Town is still drinkable.

Fortified with a fresh glass of fabulous sherry, I feel free to wander about the room without attracting attention. Nice try. With my equatorial coloring and jet-black hair I stick out like a scarred cane-cutter's machete in a polished silver service for twelve. Finally I get the high-sign from Kelly. She says she's located the trustees for me. They're out back, second floor balcony, overlooking the dark, moonlit waters of Long Island Sound.

"Well, what do you think?" she asks me, leading me upstairs.

"I could do without that music. Don't you have any Anthrax?"

"I'm not sure: Wasn't there a 'Rebecca Anthrax' on the Mayflower?"

I walk right into a conversation about how it's much easier to get your employees to work overtime these days without complaint, because in today's economy, the market will bear it. Oh, there's also a nice view.

Kelly goes up to a group of men, among them Mike Vitelli and—the guy I saw talking to Morse. Turns out he's a town councilman. Fortunately he doesn't recognize me, because he's obviously emptying Morse's drool buckets for him: the cuffs of his pants are dripping with it.

Kelly says hello to all of them, saying their names for my benefit. They are, left to right, Mike Vitelli, Head of the Fairhaven Town Zoning Board; Vince DiMaggio, Town Councilman; Art King and Derek Gordon, successful businessmen and members of the SUNY at Running River Foundation Board of Trustees. They both act like they've known Kelly since she was a little girl, which apparently they have. Art King turns to me: "And you are—?"

Kelly begins to say "F—"

"Carmelina," I say. Sorry. That's just how it comes out. Kelly plays along, bless her little WASP heart. Call it crazy, but I've begun to sense that Morse has a fix on my *every* move. He's probably got my name flagged on sixteen different databases, so I'd better start playing it cooler.

"What a lovely name," says Mr. Vitelli.

"It's short for María del Carmen." We talk about names, then about how jurors' names used to be pulled from the voting records but now they're pulled from the Department of Motor Vehicles driving records because more people drive than vote, hmm, and finally I flatter him by mentioning that his championing of the Pine Barrens groundwater protection program is sure making the news a lot. He launches into a premeasured package of platitudes about how the East End constitutes more than half of Long Island's undeveloped land, and that large-lot zoning is needed for groundwater protection.

"That's the trouble with these politicians," jokes Art King. "You handpick 'em, set 'em up in office, and the next thing you know the job goes to their head and they start *doing it.*"

There's laughs all around with that one.

Kelly says, "It's the 'Beckett' syndrome," but nobody notices.

"Thomas or Samuel?" I whisper.

"Both."

"That's a popular answer with you."

A caterer's helper brings up a tray of coffee and cake, and Kelly helps herself to a slice of cake and a big glass of milk. *Milk.* In an eyeblink she's a fifteen-year-old virgin. I mean, I like the taste of whole milk, too, straight from the udder of an Andean cow when I can get it, warm and foamy, but I haven't been able to have it by the glassful for years now. Strictly skim for my slowing metabolism.

Since we're all getting so chummy here, I feel it's safe to ask about Morse's offer to develop the Pine Barrens. Now, that's another subject. All four men begin talking at once, but the general idea is that Morse is a guy who gets what he wants. Gordon tells me that Morse once bought sixty acres of farmland back in 1984 for just over $1 million. Less than one year later he had pushed through town approval for rezoning for a 348-condominium complex, and sold the newly razed land for $14 million. Not a bad markup for an empty lot. And that was just sixty acres. Now we're talking about ten thousand.

"Of course, that was back in the eighties," says King.

"Yes, yes," they all agree, the era of the Big Deal has past for now. I can see the streaks of teary-eyed nostalgia beginning to form behind the wine-and-coffee coated corneas of the four upstanding citizens, so I ask, "Where does that leave the Pine Barrens project?"

"Well, it's still great for development," says DiMaggio. Both politicians agree here.

"Oh, we'll reach some compromise," says Vitelli, "where some of the Barrens is spared and some goes to development." Both pols agree again. I'm glad we're all agreeing so nicely.

Then they both invite me to come visit their offices any time. I ask why, and Vitelli comes up with something about how I'm obviously a concerned citizen who would probably be interested in seeing how public servants serve their constituents. So I grab that ball and run with it and mention that actually I've had a problem with a county agency—then I realize this is a big mistake even as I'm saying it. They both ask, What, what? My, my. I wish I had Kelly's talents. How do you smile and titter your way out of this one? I fall back on the old lie about trying to get some of the university's low-rent incubator space, and Vitelli explains, "That's the state, not the county," which defuses that problem for me, but idiot's luck only lasts so long. During the ensuing discussion I find out that the incubator space is home to high-pressure physics experiments, biotechnology projects, medical prosthesis, skin grafts and burn treatment, everything but Morse's section.

Trying to sound innocent, I just ask: "What's cooking there?"

"What's cooking indeed. He's being very secretive," says King. "Won't even tell *us*—"

Just then a valet reappears and says, "Miss Filomena Buscarsela? Telephone."

I look around at the other guests before I realize what I'm doing, and how stupid that looks. Fortunately the four men are all looking at the other guests as well, so they don't see me looking stupid. I think. When they turn back I've had time to think and I say, "My partner. We get each other's calls all the time."

And I walk away, thinking "Shit." Okay, what would *you* say? Poetry, no doubt.

The valet holds up a phone in a little alcove at the top of the stairs. I put it to my ear. "Hello?"

A voice I don't recognize says, "Why aren't you home watching your kid?" Click.

Oh shit. I try to call home and I get electronic garbage. Shit shit shit. I grab Kelly, make some excuse about the babysitter that kind of contradicts what I said before about my partner, but I've got to get Kelly to drive me to her place. Once there, I run inside, try to phone again. Nothing. Dead air. I make my apologies, thank her for everything, and rush home, speaking out loud to the Lord above asking him then and there to take me, take me, take me, don't take her.

I cover the impossibly lengthened miles of twisted back roads and stoplights-every-fifty-feet highway in maybe twelve or thirteen endless, unreal minutes where time and space have been compressed and exploded beyond meaning. No cops stop me, though they couldn't if they tried. I screech to a halt, raising a cloud of dust even in the darkness in front of Colomba's house. The lights are on, I can hear the TV. I rush inside. Everyone's there. Everyone's okay. Antonia's in bed. She's okay. Even the phone's okay.

For now.

9

Even in the greatest crises public money can always be found for a really stupid purpose.

—MANZONI, *I Promessi Sposi*

The next morning they're interviewing neighbors and poking their heads into Colomba's kitchen to "investigate" if the kid is being fed properly. Colomba gets rid of them quick for *that*. Yeah, I'm getting to like Colomba. (Too bad her brother's a shit.)

They're out of there, but not before they hand-deliver a letter to somebody named Flora Baskarseller, who is supposed to be me, I guess. It's from the County of Suffolk, Department of Social Services, and it goes like this:

> Dear <u>Ms. Baskarseller</u>,
> This is to inform you that you are the subject or other person named in a report of suspected child abuse or maltreatment received by the New York State Child Abuse and Maltreatment Register on <u>5/22</u> of this year. This report has been transmitted to your local child protective service for commencement of an investigation and evaluation of the report as required by the New York State Child Protective Services Act.
> The Law allows your local Child Protective Service 90 days

from the time of the receipt of the report to complete a full investigation of the allegations contained within the report as well as an evaluation of the care being provided to your child(ren). You will be notified in writing of the findings of the investigation. Where appropriate, services will be offered to assist you and your family.

Which is a polite way of saying, "We will take your kid and put her in a foster home." And it goes on like that for several paragraphs.

Rotten way to start the day.

That afternoon a stranger rolls into town on the 3:15 from the city. A hush falls over the plains as she kicks the dust off her heels and squints her eyes at the disease-plagued town. A black crow watching from a dead branch shatters the silence with a screech and flutters away, casting its dark shadow across the flat, dry wasteland behind the 7-Eleven.

She spits in the dust, then reaches for the handle of her government-issue water sampling kit.

"Gina!"

She turns. She squints. She sniffs. She sneezes.

"Your hay fever acting up again?"

"Yeah," she says. "What a way to reproduce: like, why couldn't there just *not* be pollen?"

"Well, sexual reproduction comes with some rather cumbersome of baggage of its own, too."

"Yeah, I guess."

"Get out your hankies, 'cause that burning in the air is only going to get worse."

I can't even wait to get her home. I throw her stuff in the car and show her the pictures while I'm driving her back. There's one of a stack of fifty-five-gallon drums leaking bright orange foam.

"Sorry you can't read the labels," I say. "The kid didn't get close enough."

"That's okay."

"What is that stuff?"

"It ain't cotton candy."

"I got the film," says Billy. He insisted on coming along.

I tell her to look at the series of black metal boxes. She flips through them. None are quality photos, but he took enough of them so you get a sense of what's happening there.

"I *ran* and got the film," says Billy, who hasn't stopped staring at Gina since she got off the train. She's not his pornstar fantasy—small frame and breasts to go with it—but she's a dark-haired, Italian American beauty and, most important, *she's real.*

After a while, Gina pronounces sentence: "Those are transformers."

"Then what's leaking out? Oil?"

"Yeah, oil: PCB-laden oil."

"PCBs? I keep hearing about those. What are they?"

"Polychlorinated biphenyls. The proposed MCL is point five ppb."

"The proposed what?"

"Sorry. The proposed Maximum Contaminant Level for the National Safe Drinking Water Standard is half a part per billion."

"Half a part per *billion*? That's pretty damn toxic. How much would it take to kill a man?"

"Well, dermal exposure and inhalation are the primary routes of occupational exposure to PCBs, not drinking water."

"So how much would it take to kill a man, say, if he got it on his fingers?"

"It's even more toxic in the vapor phase, but since it's not volatile, it wouldn't tend to get into the air."

"But how would it get into the air?"

"If it caught fire, for example."

"Like if it got on somebody's cigarettes?"

"No: That'd only be a trace. I mean like a big electrical transformer fire."

"Oh. Think it'll get on the Superfund list?"

"I don't know yet. There are more than twenty-nine thousand candidates for seven hundred and seventy slots, but if it's bad enough we'll take it."

"Now I've got to ask you, Gina, if it's so goddamn deadly, why would anyone want to use that stuff? What's it good for?"

"Electrical conductivity. It's chemically heavy, with a low viscosity—"

"And what are the health effects?"

"Well, that's not really my turf—"

"Ballpark."

"Ballpark?" And she recites a litany of symptoms, each one tolling like an iron bell in my brain: "Tightening of the throat, hoarseness when speaking, three-day migraines, skin rashes, constant coughs, burning and watery eyes, ulcers, inner ear problems, high blood-lead levels, breathing difficulties, pain in extremities, abdominal cramps, blood clots, even cases of complete immune system breakdown in children, so we're not talking about fifty years of accumulation here."

"Gina, I've seen workers with those symptoms."

"How many cases?"

"A couple of dozen."

"That means hundreds. Maybe thousands."

Gina sets her sampler case next to the sink, takes a glass of water straight from the tap, holds it close. Her nose wrinkles in disgust. She lets the water run for a few minutes.

"Why are you doing that?" asks Billy.

"To get a representative sample."

"Oh."

"We've all heard stories," says Gina, "of old-fashioned housewives, the early risers who got up every morning and made tea for themselves, then made breakfast for the family, and fifteen years later *she's* dead of lead poisoning but nobody else is: The lead builds up in these old pipes and the first few gallons to come out of them is usually full of it."

Billy asks, "What does lead do to you?"

"Hoo-boy," says Gina. "You got your brain and kidney damage, your gastrointestinal colic, anemia, slowed nerve conduction in peripheral nerves, interference with Vitamin D metabolism, high blood pressure—"

And I say out loud, "Oh my God: Mrs. Einhorn."

"What's that?"

"No, no, Gina. It's something else." Something we're too late to do anything about.

She unwraps her own sterilized beaker, fills it with tap water and shuts off the flow. "We'll see in a second," she says, centering the beaker on the dial-crammed board of the portable sampler. She submerges a pen-sized metal tube into the beaker, about five inches long on the end of a coiled black cord, and stirs it around for a few seconds, then watches it settle. She whistles.

"What? What?"

"Have to shift it up a couple of decimals," says Gina, adjusting a knob past the 100s and into the 1000s.

She completes the procedure in about fifteen seconds. Then: "Goddamn," she says softly. "Over ten thousand—"

"What?" I ask.

"Well, I don't know what's responsible for it. I'll have to send it to the lab. But the conductivity's practically off the scale."

"Meaning what?"

"Meaning that ain't water, sister. You better tell everyone to stop drinking it. Give me the phone. I'll get a public notice to the Town Supervisor immediately."

"If ten thousand's high, what's normal?"

"For drinking water? Two hundred fifty to three hundred's nice if you can get it."

"Is that good for us or bad for us?" asks Billy.

I tell him, "Both."

"Hello, Ron? Gina. Yeah. Well tell them it can wait. Listen, I'm authorizing a full-scale investigation of the Kim Tungsten Steel and Glass site at East Carthage. Can you fax the public health warnings to Fairhaven Township before five o'clock? Standard language. Great." She lowers the phone, speaks to us: "And tell those kids to stay the hell away from those barrels. The orange stuff's probably low-level radioactive. Ron? Right. Okay. Now?" To me: "Can you take me back to the station, Fil? I've got to make a train."

"Can I go?" begs Billy.

"Yeah, yeah . . ."

Now I'm going to find out what on earth Samuel Morse is doing with the university's incubator space. But the workday's over. Long lines of bloodless workers tramp listlessly up their front walks and sit down to tainted meals. The unbearable funebrious rhythm of it all makes my head pound with profound, abysmal melancholy. So I put Antonia to bed and veg out in front of the TV because I simply can't think anymore. The show's in color, with a lot of quick close-ups of isolated fragments of female flesh, but these qualities alone are not enough to hold the plot together for me.

I wonder if this is what Shakespeare had in mind when he wrote:

> When in the chronicle of wasted time
> I see descriptions of the fairest wights,
> And beauty making beautiful old rime
> In praise of ladies dead and lovely knights;
> —Something something something—
> Of hand, of foot, of lip, of eye, of brow . . .

Dammit, I used to know the whole thing by heart.

One too many kicks in the head.

And I keep getting phone calls from beer-bottle-opener nose and other anonymous voices pretending to be asking after Antonia's condition but really just trying to make me squirm. Oh, it is getting to me, but the feeling it's engendering is rage, not fear. But you can't say, "One more call and I'll slit you open like a carnival pig and make sausages out of your intestines" to a county detective. So I tell him he'd better start going through regular channels or he'll regret it, legally. He tells me he *is* going through channels.

Don't they realize I know the law? Maybe I'm giving them more credit than they deserve, thinking that Morse must be behind everything just because he knows my history and is smart enough to exploit that knowledge. He may not even know I'm out here yet. Maybe it's just some local dweebs who don't like what I'm doing. Strictly bush league. That would be nice.

Jim Stella also calls a few times, trying to get ahold of me. When I finally relent and take his call, he says, "Man, sex is just like telemarketing: a two percent response is as good as it gets."

That's only one in fifty. "More like one in a million," I say, and hang up.

Colomba tells me to stop answering the phone and go to bed. But I can't sleep. Every time I hear the phone my heart jumps. See, I used to get middle-of-the-night calls so often I got sick of them. Then one night there came a 3 A.M. phone call that I never answered. The next day my roommate's best friend had committed suicide. And I still wonder if that call was him asking for a last chance at help. I think about that.

Motherhood has also changed my sleep patterns. I went from sleeping through fire alarms to being able to detect a change in breathing patterns two doors away. And now I'm lying here, listening. Hearing sounds. Every time I start to drift into dreams a twig snaps somewhere in the county and I spring awake. It goes on like this through the faceless hours until I accept and give up.

Antonia's asleep. Otherwise I'm alone. I sit on the bed and whisper, "Bless me Father, for I have sinned."

I don't want to go to a priest with this, I choose to confess directly to God for sins I have committed with weapons and pain, for sometimes following the path of violence, and for having violent thoughts—and the desire to kill, because I cannot go before the Lord with such a sin.

God gives us good and bad, but the day I was told I had no life left I ripped all the pages from the calendar of my life, and the sleeping giants chained beneath my skin awoke, and broke free. I could never bind my demons as well as God does it.

A life is a flash of light that streaks across the sky, then burns out and fades forever.

But when I see ugly souls living in comfort on the bodies of their prey, I ask why. I ask the birds and the fish, they know what God wants. Why do the flesh-eaters live, and grow old, and powerful? What's the point of serving God when the killer's refrigerator is always full, his bar is always stocked, his skin is smooth, while his victims fill their empty stomachs with bitterness. Yet they both end up the same in death.

The meat packers go hungry, the fruit pickers go thirsty. The murderer hides his face, and kills in the dark. I must shine a light on that face, see what others cannot see, seek out what others cannot find, and yank the victims from the jaws of the wicked.

But the disease, the disease is powerful, it sticks to my skin like mire. Those who hate me did this: I want to laugh as I destroy them cruelly and savagely. God says it over and over, and I still don't follow. Yet He keeps back my soul from the pit, and has saved me from many a violent and sudden death. Can I clean the oceans alone? Close the hole in the ozone layer all by myself? Make apples ripen on the vine? Feed the children?

Their poisons have seeped into the sunken earth and dissolved the bonds holding the dark forces prisoner. They don't know what they've awakened. . . .

My penance? I've done enough penance for one life.

It's still dark when I take a shower, but it's starting to get light as I put on some jogging clothes and go for a walk.

There's an odd peace over the houses. Even the stacks have ceased their belching for a spell, and the crisp, clear light of dawn almost cleans the air. I walk all the way to the twenty-four-hour deli on Main Street, get what passes for bagels out here and donuts for the family, pick up the early edition of the newspaper and walk back. Alone, awake before the rest, I check once more on Antonia and then put up a pot of government-issue water for coffee.

The sun is beginning to shoot through the trees as I sit down to a warm cup of real coffee and try to find solace in how fucked up the rest of the world is. It doesn't work. The last President's son has just landed an exclusive oil contract in a country we went to war to liberate. Gee, I wonder if the President needs a daughter? I'm sick of working for a living.

The NYPD now thinks the traditional police lineup is more likely to produce false identifications than newer methods, and critics of the "genetic fingerprint" say that DNA analysis does not accurately pinpoint identity. *Now* they tell us. For all I know, I could turn out to be someone else.

Even Long Island is getting more violent. A teenager from Levittown was fatally stabbed in the parking lot of the Tri-County

Shopping Mall, and yesterday a varsity lacrosse player from Rocky
Point was shot to death on the beach a few miles east of here.
Guns? Knives? This was supposed to be suburbia.

And there's an interview with Morse in the business section. A
sample:

> *Q: Does it ever go smoothly with transitional management?*
> *Are they cooperative or do they resent taking orders from new-*
> *comers like yourself?*
> *A: Executives are human, too. When I take over I try to un-*
> *derstand that someone who has given twenty to thirty years of*
> *service to one company, and has worked his way up to the ex-*
> *ecutive management level, would probably shoot anybody who*
> *tried to take his job away from him. But most of that is ego, and*
> *money usually patches things up . . .*

Hmm . . .

Well, the world's a total mess and there's nothing I can do about
it, except clean up one little corner of it. Now for that Morse incubator site.

I turn the key and the car dies. Oh, crap! *Not now.* This is Long Island, you might as well cut off my legs. I fume and despair for a moment before I remember a suggestion my doctor made a while back
that seemed pretty crazy at first. I call a tow truck and get him to
drop me in town, where I shell out three-quarters of what Gina lent
me for a new bicycle, with tire pump, water bottle, biking shorts,
helmet with rearview mirror attachment and a baby seat and helmet. I figure it'll serve the dual purposes of working off some tension and perhaps making me a little harder to follow without being
really obvious—like a car crawling along behind me at 12 mph.

Feeling brittle as a sheet of glass from lack of sleep and fortified
with three cups of Spanish coffee, I bike all the way up to the hospital to see Dr. Wrennch. He's not in today, so I make an appointment for tomorrow, then I head for campus. Now you might think
bicycling on Long Island would be a healthy pleasure, but not
•when you're stuck biking uphill behind a car that hasn't been
tuned since *Uncle Tom's Cabin* was the number-one draw on the
vaudeville circuit. Even the main drag of the well-to-do town of

Running River has enough commercial traffic to mimic the air quality of the Brooklyn-Battery Tunnel at rush hour. I'm just catching my breath from the stoker when along comes a truck pulling yard landscaping equipment for all the fancy homes north of Route 25A that spews a thick cloud of carbon monoxide up my nose and into my lungs, then a truck with Jersey plates delivering fancy furniture does the same, followed soon after by a truck with pool-cleaning supples, one delivering heating oil and—¡chusa!—a cesspool cleaning service, *five* trucks savage my delicate respiratory system and what's supposed to be clean air in order to service the wealthy quicker. And I have to pull off to the shoulder, risking collapse, coughing up until blood comes.

Some college kids packed seven to a Camaro drive by and one shouts, "Nice helmet!" while another says, "There's something about a Spandex butt," before they're gone 'round a curve in a bubble of laughter.

I channel my rage into a loud "Grrrrrr!" And a guy stopped in a car stares at me. I look at him: "Whatsamatter, you never heard a woman growl before?" He looks straight ahead until the light changes, peels out with a screech.

I lock the bike to a pole in front of the Administration Building. Naturally I have to run into Frank Schmidt, who seems to have a permanent public relations smile frozen on his face. "Hey, Filomena, how's it going?" he asks. Well, he remembers my name. It's probably his primary job skill. But I'm here to see Katherina. She's in a staff meeting, and a mere forty-five minutes of my life ebb away forever before she's out.

"Coffee?" she asks.

"Sugar free or unleaded?"

She looks at me, raising one eyebrow.

"Just cold water," I say, using the cooler. I am not in shape for this kind of haul under ideal conditions, much less while breathing in enough carbon monoxide to rival a mid-Manhattan traffic jam, and I wander into Katherina's office on rubbery legs and collapse on one of her drafting tables. She pulls over a high cushioned stool for me.

"Try this," she says. "It's much more comfortable."

"So how've you been?"

"Oh, okay. Where's the kid?"

"She's at home with her aunt."

"She design any buildings yet?"

"As a matter of fact she was just playing with blocks and some of her cousin's old cars this morning, spreading them out on the floor, and she says to me, 'That's a city—but it's not a city,' like she wants me to know she's only pretending."

"Sounds like she already knows the difference between image and reality. Some of our top administrators don't even get that. I'd say she's a genius."

"Thanks. Maybe I should put her on the case."

"You know, I meant to tell you, I remembered something else: I've got a living witness to the Shore Oaks fire."

"You *do? Who?*"

"This plant," she says, pointing to a four-foot potted palm with a pinched stem and four withered brownish leaves.

"Thanks."

"I'm serious. This plant is one of the sole survivors of the fire. They pulled it out, and when the Foundation moved to the third floor, Pamela Moore left this down here with me. It was doing okay 'til Frank Schmidt tripped over it and I had to repot the whole thing. I suppose I should really take better care of it, after all, it is the last living witness to the fire."

"Let me ask you something, since you brought it up," I lower my voice. "Why would anyone want to burn down Shore Oaks? Insurance?"

"It's state property, Filomena, there's no insurance."

"Oh yes, of course. The state insures itself. How about to make the property valueless so it could be bought at low cost?"

"Now there's an interesting possibility."

"But I didn't come here to ask about that."

"You didn't?"

"No, I'm—" I look out her office door. I lean closer to her. "I'm interested in the incubator site. You know where I can get a floor plan?"

"I can't give you a detailed plan, but I can show you on the campus map."

"You can?"

She looks at me as if I've insulted her. She hits a key on her computer and calls forth the menu of all the publications she has worked on this year. It's a huge list. In a few minutes she has isolated the file, clicked it on screen, and forwarded to the map. She scrolls down and over to the South Campus buildings, highlights the area and doubles the size to fill the screen. It's just a loose conglomeration of black outlines, like what Antonia spills out of her box of building blocks.

"That's too small. Can you print it out and enlarge it on the Xerox machine?"

"Hey, I'm the one who designed this map, remember?" She copies the screen and opens a new file, pastes the image in, then she speeds the mouse around the screen, knocking off buildings like a squadron of bombers armed with laser-guided weapons over a hostile target. Highlight. Click. Erase. Highlight. Click. Erase. Until there's only one building left. Then she doubles the size again, and again until the outline fills the screen. She expands and draws in everything she can remember about the layout.

"I was only in the place once for the ribbon-cutting ceremony," she says. But I put my faith in her designer's eyes. She draws in the walls, the doors, even some of the partitions and wiring details. After a few minutes she prints it out on laser paper.

For God's sakes. A fucking typeset map. "Kate, I think I love you."

"Try not to let it show."

I smile. "Any idea what Morse is doing in there? Electrical conductivity? Microprocessing? What?"

"Don't know."

"What if it's chemical? I don't know how to handle chemicals."

"We do have an excellent chemistry department."

"Lots of grad students?"

"Lots of professors, too."

"I'll stick to the students. Where's the Chem Building?"

"Jesus, what do you want me to do? Draw you a map?"

I go to the bathroom to piss out those three cups of coffee, then I have to stand there wasting more of my precious lifetime because all they have in there are those ridiculous hot-air blowers that claim they "Dry hands more thoroughly and *keep washroom free of towel waste.*" Oh yeah, that's always been a big problem in my life.

The first chemistry grad student I talk to is nice but incompetent. The second one is too absorbed in his work to be of any use to anybody. The third is downright asocial. The fourth eyes me with suspicion. The fifth, sixth, seventh and eighth are not interested. The ninth is hostile. The tenth is not interested. The eleventh is hostile *and* not interested. The twelfth—

The twelfth is a Chinese American woman wearing a white lab-coat with a button on it that says, KISS ME, I'M POLISH. A sense of humor is a definite sign of humanity. She is bent over the valve on a four-foot vertical graduated pipette, trying to regulate to flow of a dark blue liquid into a 500 ml beaker of something clear. The lab makes me feel like I've been shrunk and stuffed inside a Wurlitzer organ: A network of foot-wide pipes runs up the wall and snakes alongside the air ducts on the ceiling to God knows where. Some of the pipes are clear glass. I remember one time Gina told me that means they contain liquids that would eat through normal metal pipes, which is not a pleasant thought.

"Got a moment?" I ask. Okay, so it's not brilliant. The caffeine's wearing off.

"Not really. I've got to verify the structural formulas for the four positionally isomeric carboxylic acids that have the molecular formula $C_5H_{10}O_2$ and identify any carbon atom that is a source of stereoisomerism, then I've got to identify the monosaccharides produced by acid hydrolysis of this compound." She slides a sheet of paper along the lab table towards me. The structure looks like this:

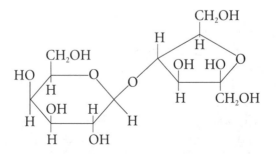

"Any ideas?" she asks me.

"Hell no."

"Actually, this is basic freshman chem stuff. I've just got to set up an answer key and correct two hundred and thirty exams of it by Friday *and* set up Professor Ling's NMR session by lunchtime." She moves swiftly and confidently among the flasks, glassware and hypersensitive digital balances, doing whatever the heck it is she's doing. "Fooled you, huh?"

"Sure did."

"No, this is strictly for beginners."

"You really know this stuff, don't you?"

"Either that or I'm fooling some real experts."

I like her. She's got irreverence, wit and nerve—i.e., just what I need. I introduce myself. We talk. Her name is Wai-Wai Choi. She also uses the Americanized "Vicky." I tell her I like Wai-Wai. Wai-Wai's dad was Chinese and her mom's American. She's *gorgeous.* She, too, looks about nineteen. Everyone looks nineteen. One thing about dealing with a university is everyone seems so goddamned young.

"By the way," she asks, "What the hell do you want?"

I look at her. Does she mean it? She's not even looking at me, drying and stacking test tubes at a pace that would have left Speedy Gonzales panting for breath. I figure that's just the way she talks.

So I go for the blunt approach. "I need some chemical advice."

"Go on."

"I used to be a cop."

"Really? I've always wanted to know, is it really possible to shoot at a moving car, pop the tires and make it explode in a white-hot ball of flame?"

I tell her your average car tire takes about two minutes to deflate after being pierced by a standard police .38 bullet.

"Not like on TV, huh?" she says.

I shake my head.

"Figures," she says. "Oh, I don't know how much longer I can take this relationship. I continue to worship my TV, but it just keeps lying to me, making up these ridiculous stories, spending all night in other people's living rooms, oh, I don't know why I put up with it. Someday I'm just going to throw it out into the street."

There's a moment of silence, then we both burst out laughing. I like this woman. I ask: "Will you help me?"

"Help you what?"

I'm about to speak, when the wall phone rings. She tells me to hold on a second and she goes and answers it. She switches into Chinese and I'm astounded. I guess I shouldn't be, being a cross-cultural hybrid myself. But she just seems so Americanized. Born here and everything. She's writing down a long message in Chinese. I glance at it. It looks like a piece of found art to me, infinitely more foreign than that chemistry stuff, and a humbling symbol of the limits of my abilities, of all that I will never know.

She tells me there's nothing I can't learn if I don't want to. So I tell her I want to learn what Samuel Morse is doing on the South Campus incubator site.

"Oh, *those* assholes," she says.

"You know them?"

"Sure. They come in here all the time, pulling talent for their little problems."

"You collaborate with them?"

"Yeah, the department's got a deal. We give them chemicals and brain cells, and they let us keep our kneecaps."

"Seriously, what do you mean?"

"I mean they always take over like they own the place. Damn obnoxious bunch, too. Gets on my nerves."

"What's so obnoxious about them?"

"They always want us to drop whatever we're doing and wait on them whenever it suits them, okay? I call that obnoxious. It's usually just piecework, which wouldn't be so bad, but they never tell us how the pieces fit together, and they don't want us to discuss the details of what they're doing with anybody—which is inappropriate at an institute of higher learning, if you ask me, and it's also pretty damn hard to do with a department full of chemists."

"Seems like Mr. Morse is working real hard to keep a secret."

"Sure is. Why? What do you want to do?"

"Find out what his secret is."

"No shit? How?"

"Tell me, if I brought back a sample of what he was working on, do you think you could analyze it?"

"You mean like Sherlock Holmes and his study on distinguishing thirty different kinds of tobacco from the ash?"

"It was a monograph on the ashes of one hundred and forty different varieties of pipe, cigar and cigarette tobacco."

Wai-Wai whistles. "He was some kick-ass chemist."

"So what do you think?"

"With absolutely nothing to go on, it could take weeks to get what you want. You'd have to lift some of his software, too."

"Who said anything about stealing?"

Wai-Wai eyes me like she's saying, Oh, *nobody*. So I tell her: "Okay, here's the deal. I've tried to find some information at the Morse Techtonics plant, but even the toilet paper is classified. But I figure the security at a State University site can't be what it is at Morse's corporate headquarters. And if I'm caught, it's only going to be by campus security. Them I can deal with—"

"But chemicals, analytic software—"

"Yeah. That's out of my league." I sigh. Blocked again.

'Til Wai-Wai says: "Sounds like I'll have to go with you."

10

Science without conscience is but the ruin of the soul.
—RABELAIS

I shoot over to Old Town beach. On the way a local cop for the village of Old Town stops me and asks me for ID. I ask, "Is biking considered suspicious activity in this neighborhood?"

His face hardens, but then I pop my wallet open to the badge. He smiles. "Off duty?"

"You got it." For the past several years.

Now we're brothers in blue, so it's okay with him if I want to bike to the beach, but I am left wondering what constitutes probable cause around here. (Driving without a cell phone?) I hang at the beach for a while looking at the couples, the parents with kids and the teenagers playing volleyball and whatever that ankle-ball game is called.

I lock the bike, take a long drink of water from the squeeze bottle and look around. I spotted one group when I biked in here, but I've been giving them some time to get used to my presence.

I casually unhook my helmet and amble over to a bunch of kids. They look about sixteen, seventeen. Not out of high school yet. Most have long, kinky hair, mass-produced Day-Glo tie-dyed T-shirts, skateboards, the works. And I can tell by the air that somebody's just pocketed a joint. I figure that'll work in my favor, if they don't get paranoid on me.

I go up to the guy whose car they're leaning on and extend my hand. "Hi. My name's Filomena. What's yours?"

"What's up?" he says. Not moving. My hand's out and he's not moving.

"What's up?" he repeats.

I drop my hand. "You kids from around here?"

No answer. Damn. This is not working.

And I realize I'm an old lady to these kids. Couldn't possibly be cool. They close in around me, protecting their friend. Glad they ain't bikers.

I tell them, "Look, I'm not trying to bust you." You idiots. "I'm just trying to find out if you know anyone who's ever gone up the beach and partied up at the Old Shore Oaks estate."

. . . *ting!* Was that the sound of a pin dropping in Poughkeepsie? Or just another thread snapping in the enigma I'm trying most unsuccessfully to unravel?

I have to give up. I wander along the beach trying a few more possibilities, but it all turns up the same—empty.

I unlock the bike and gear up. I've got a long way to bike and plenty of time to think about cops—especially county cops pushing their way in past my door and me faking them out once or twice but knowing that, if I don't come up with something better, eventually they would have all the power they wanted to use on me and I'd have none.

My only hope is that Suffolk County's too far out of it to have anybody who's that good, but after these past few days, I don't know. For all I know those kids work for Morse and they've got a videophone hookup under one of their skateboards and they're phoning in a report right now with a description of what I'm wearing and which way I'm headed, south along Running River Road towards Route 347.

That's how out there I'm getting. Gina was right. I've got to switch to decaf.

*   *   *

I bike home and Reggie Einhorn's there.

"Let's go fishing," he says.

"I don't have time for that."

"That's just when you need it the most."

"It's clouding over."

"Trust me."

Rosita wants Antonia to stay with her but I say no, I'm taking her with me this time. I change her clothes and throw on a little of the baby cologne that Colomba got for her.

Reggie Einhorn walks in and says, "Jeez, it smells like a French warehouse in here!"

"I don't think that's quite what you mean," I say.

"I know what I mean. Come on, let's move out."

We go over to his place so we can gather the fishing equipment. He's got a couple of decent casting rods and a deep-sea rod that he doesn't take with him. He's got a two-foot-long, three-tray tackle box that's pretty damn serious. And that's before I notice a Colt All-American Model 2000 double-action semiautomatic pistol down on the bottom.

I look it over. "Fifteen rounds?" I ask.

"Ain't it a beaut? Only eight pieces. Easy to break down. And you can take off the barrel bushing for easy concealment."

"We going to catch these fish or assassinate them?"

"You don't want some varmint stealing your fish, do you, young lady?"

"No, I guess not. Uh, Reggie?"

"Yeah?"

"What exactly is a varmint?"

"Oh, foxes, raccoons, possums, there's more than fish in them woods, you know."

"There's still woods left out here?"

"You bet your sweet p-toot."

I heft the gun. It's got a good, solid feel, almost like a police .38, with black composition grips. Interesting detail about the removable barrel bushing, but I wouldn't want to remove it. It's got a luminous dot on the sight for rapid alignment in darkness. Not a feature I'd choose to do without. Especially since it's getting dark and cloudy. Though why the hell you'd need it for hunting (on a fishing trip) I don't know.

"Thing got a rave in *Shotgun News*," he says, tossing me a copy of that venerable semimonthly publication.

I glance through it. I don't mind the ads listing vintage Czechoslovakian resistance carbines from 1943, but do we really need kits for converting the Chinese assault rifles to full automatic, or for every family to own their own flame thrower? *Flame throwers?* I guess that's for going after *really* big fish.

I put a light summer sweater on Antonia and have to drag some rain gear, just in case. Reggie swings the tackle box behind the seat of his pickup and groans.

"Oh, to be sixty-five again," he says, rubbing his sore arm.

"You want me to drive?"

"I can handle it," he barks.

"Okay, okay."

He starts the truck. "Where'd you learn so much about guns?" He asks.

"I thought everyone in the county knew I used to be a cop."

"Did you now?" And that gets him laughing. "A lady cop! Oh, that's good!" He laughs some more.

"You done?"

"Listen, young lady, my father and two of my uncles were city cops in the days of Jimmy Walker."

"I'm impressed. It must have been pretty tough to survive: That was a pretty corrupt administration."

"Sure, kid. And Patchogue's been corrupt since Dutch Schultz ran rum out of here in the twenties, but it wasn't like it is today. It was just old-fashioned patronage. My old man told me back then there was only *one* supplier of police uniforms for the whole city, and you had to buy from him if the bosses said so. At an inspection, they'd say, 'Einhorn: You need a new uniform,' and—" He snaps his fingers, then rolls them together in the sign for money.

"Yeah, well, some things never change."

"Yeah, except today you got the guns, the drugs, this mob, that mob. Even the Vietnamese got a mob. So what'd you do? Huh? You have tea parties with all the other lady cops?"

"I don't want to talk about it."

It starts raining.

The temperature has dropped twenty degrees since noon and the fog is coming in. We turn onto a gravel road and fifteen slow, bumpy minutes later we pull to a stop under a wet canopy of trees. The sky is dark and foggy, but Reggie says the fish are jumping. We walk down a path, wet leaves slapping at my face and thighs, and come to the edge of a pristine pond with ducks, geese and swans in it. Yes, swans. There's a plaque from 1938 dedicating the pond and environs to Vaughan Carter, who donated the land to the county on the condition that it not be developed.

In contrast to Shore Oaks, the memorial park is trimmed, well-kept, with an old stone bridge persisting through the decades in sharp reflection of the English style. Antonia's antsy from the car ride so I take a walk with her while Reggie sets up the fishing gear. There's some kind of pine tree I've never seen before whose incoming pinecones are utterly obscene flaming pink protuberances, and we come to a huge beech tree, black and shiny with rain, with a Code of Hammurabi–length list of lovers' names carved on its trunk, scarring it like a tattooed elephant.

We come to the bridge, where the pristine pond drains into a fetid, foul-smelling marsh and becomes a murky, narrow creek twisting and winding through high, windblown reeds to the Sound somewhere not visible from here. Not even enough of a flow to start the waterwheel by the dark empty old mill.

We rejoin Reggie, who has opened a cooler with soda and two Lite beers.

"What'll it be?" asks Reggie.

"Soda's garbage," says Antonia.

I have to laugh. "She got that from me."

"I want juice," she says.

"I'm sorry, I forgot to bring some. I didn't think of it."

She gets upset. Reggie offers her a sucking candy. They're bad for her teeth, of course, but it calms her down so I accept it.

Two cans of Lite beer. "I'm glad to see you're not one of those people who think hunting is an occasion for heavy drinking."

"People like that make me sick," he says, casting the rod. "Give the rest of us responsible gun-owners a bad name. Darn drunken deer hunters're always shootin' up some housewife who's hanging up the laundry in her backyard. Don't deserve the right to bear arms. Nosiree." He reels in. Nothing. He casts.

"Speaking of beer, who was that old buddy you had to go buy a beer?" Nothing. "On Memorial Day?"

He looks at me. "How'd you know about that?"

"You told me."

"Oh, I did, huh? Well, I guess I did."

"Yes, you did. What's his name?"

"Sol Weinstein."

"Where does he live?"

"Veterans Memorial Cemetery."

It's my turn to look and wait. He casts again, watches the lure bob and ripple away to stillness.

"You want to tell me about it?" I ask. "I'm a former soldier in blue myself."

Reggie tugs the line, reels it in slow, making it skirt and shimmy. Not a bite. He casts it again, lowers the rod and reaches for a beer. He cracks the top, takes a sip, takes another sip, takes a long gulp. It digests for a couple of minutes. Then:

"We were trying to lay down some ground cover in the middle of nowhere when we took a couple of forty-millimeter shells right in the belly. Smitty pointed the thing out to sea but we went down too fast. Our boys had maybe one-third of the island, the Japs had the other two-thirds. We just crash-landed right smack in the middle of it, cradled in the treetops for a couple of minutes. By miracle we all got out before she blew. We were strictly flyboys, didn't know diddly-squat about jungle fighting. We were dazed from the crash, didn't even have on our cartridge belts. Then we heard a bolt being thrown.

"Sol saw the gun and never hesitated. He lunged and grabbed the Jap and took three bullets in the gut while the rest of us un-holstered our pieces and got the guy. He saved me and two other guys. We turned the opposite way the Jap had come and met up with advancing Americans. They were just moving bodies at first. I tell you, when I finally saw the two-inch Stars and Stripes on that corporal's shoulder patch—"

He's choking back something in his throat, and is bothered that I can see it. He reels in the rod for another cast. "Why don't you cast your rod? I brought it along for nothing."

I oblige him and cast my rod. "And where are they now?"

"They're both dead. Bill in fifty-six in a steel mill accident and Sal in seventy-eight of silicosis."

"Silicosis?"

"That's the word, isn't it? You know, black lung."

"Oh. Sal?"

"Yeah. Salvatore. Lombardi. We kept in touch for a good long while. Twenty years running, we'd meet on Memorial Day to buy the guy who saved our lives a drink. I missed a few years, but I've been doing it every year since sixty-eight. It's the least I can do. We're getting old, and there ain't a gol-darned thing we can do about it."

"Yeah, that's the truth. And the word you're looking for is 'goddamned.'"

"Don't curse at me, young lady."

I chuckle. "Sorry." I shake my head. "You're one of those old-fashioned guys, aren't you, Reginald?"

"That's funny: The only guys who ever called me Reginald were my old Air Force buddies."

"How about that?"

"You know, in fun."

"Yeah. In fun . . ."

Reggie finally catches a fish. He whoops, hollers (it's a big one), then he unhooks it and tosses it back.

"What'd you do that for?" I ask.

"Are you kidding? You can't eat these things!"

"Why not?"

"They've got too much mercury in them. It's strictly catch-and-release fishing here."

"I don't believe this."

"Now what is it?"

"You spend the whole afternoon trying to catch a fish that

you've got to throw right back because the company you work for has poisoned the water?"

"Mommy, he's silly," says Antonia, who knows that you catch fish in order to eat them.

"Listen," says Einhorn. "Don't go blaming Morse again for our problems. There's much worse than him out here."

"Like who?"

"Like who?" He chuckles. "You couldn't've been much of a cop."

"Oh?"

"Let me tell you something about Minoa. One guy in the neighborhood tried to go into trash carting and the mob threatened him out of it. Now who do you think runs the toxic waste carting business?"

I guess my head goes "click" or something real audible like that because he goes, "Uh-huh? You see? Cop, huh? Remind me not to need *you* in an emergency—"

"Okay Reggie, just let it alone, will you?"

He chuckles. "You women's libbers just hate it when you're wrong and we're right."

"Yes. We do."

Antonia asks me, "What do you call someone who's deaf in their nose?"

"You mean someone who can't smell?"

"Yes."

"I don't know if there is a word for that."

"Why not?"

"Because there are things that don't have names yet. And I bet there are names that don't have things yet, too. Maybe Dr. Wrennch knows."

"I want to go see Dr. Wrennch."

"Not now, Toni. We're fishing."

"I want to go see Dr. Wrennch."

And you know? I do too.

Late that day the U.S. EPA shows up at the gates of Kim Tungsten, but they're not allowed in. I call Gina and she says the obstruction's legal, they'll have to get a search warrant, which means a couple of days' wait. Meanwhile, she'll send a letter to confirm that the EPA was denied access so that penalties will begin accruing at a rate of $25,000 per day.

Wai-Wai comes by and says she's ready. Colomba insists on feeding her, and Billy sits down next to her and says, "So you know all that chemistry stuff, huh?"

"Why? What's in the food?" she asks.

"So, like, you can synthesize anything you want, right?"

"*Billy*—"

"It's okay, Filomena. I get this all the time," says Wai-Wai. "Yeah, I can."

Billy's eyes widen.

"But I can't legally order most of the essential precursor chemicals without significant justification. I'd have to misrepresent my research objectives."

"Ethics don't get you bucks, dude," says Billy.

"But they do tend to keep you out of jail," I say.

"And it's dude-ette," says Wai-Wai.

"Come on, let's go."

"Can I go?" asks Billy. "Well, can I?"

Wai-Wai looks at him: "Another couple of years on the vine, *dude*."

"What? What's that supposed to mean?" he asks.

Antonia says, "Watch this."

I watch, and tell her, "Antonia, there's not a big future in being able to stick cereal to your forehead."

"Why not?" says Wai-Wai. "It's more than the Vice President can do."

"Come on. Let's go."

Wai-Wai parked the car a few blocks away like I told her to. We walk to her car, me checking our backs every two seconds. I'm pretty sure nobody's reporting us back to headquarters.

It's an interesting car ride. Wai-Wai asks me about being a parent, and if I'm interested in more children. I say that another would be nice, but it would have to be with the right guy.

"Watching your biological clock, huh?" she says.

"Uh-huh. And my biological TV, my biological radio, my biological blender and my biological desk lamp."

And how many people get to discuss earthly geology on their way to an illegal break-in? Wai-Wai tells me she's flown over the Andes (her father has some relatives in Peru), and that they look just like waves of the sea from high up. And why not? She tells me that it's the same forces at work, as if the earth's crust were not solid at all but a somewhat slower moving fluid.

"So the earth is liquid, always in flux," I observe.

"You got the makings of a scientist."

"Ha! Me?"

"Why not? We're all just searchers."

Darkness. Emptiness.

The void. The all-encompassing way.

God it's tough to get your bearings on campus. It would help if we weren't in the woods on a rainy night. Wai-Wai says she knows the way. It is tempting to hope this is true, because right now it's like a scene from a grade-C horror-slasher movie: "Ooh, we're lost." "Look, there's a house." Yes. Even the dialogue is trite. So I'll skip it and get to the good part.

It's a long, low flat building and all plate glass siding—no working windows—and three entrances. Main: Impossible, without alerting security. Side: Pain in the ass. Two steel doors and some serious deadbolt locks. Rear: A possibility. Because it doesn't lead into Morse's space, but to the other one sharing the building, the hospital's Burn Unit Research Center.

Guess what? They're all med students. They're all in there, lights on, working. *They let us in.* Jesus. That was easy. One of them knows Wai-Wai. They say "Hi" to each other and Wai-Wai introduces me and turns it into a twenty-minute social session. By far the best way of getting into the building. And great cover.

My map from Katherina shows a back door leading to a corridor shared by the building's occupants. Wai-Wai gets us shown to this isolated door, the entrance to a neutral, dusty storage space.

There should be a back door to the Morse space about fifteen feet down the hall on the left.

Wai-Wai asks, "Uh, can we get out this way?"

"Uh, sure," says the woman. "Just go right, then keep going 'til you get to the stairs. It's half a flight down."

"Thanks," says Wai-Wai. And we're out.

The woman says, "It's dark."

And Wai-Wai says, "That's okay, we brought a flashlight." She shines it in her eyes. "Bye."

And we're in.

"That's a novel approach," I say. "I would have lied."

"Eyes open, Filomena: They've been working on the same experiment for thirty-three hours straight with the help of *mucho* java. I could have walked out with the ultracentrifuge and they wouldn't have cared."

"*Damn* you're good. You know, I could really use a partner in this. Are there any more like you at home?"

"Not like me, sister."

Morse's door is *really* solid, but there's no light coming from the crack under it, so I'm happy. I'm beginning to like this. The ceiling's been dropped with that awful Celotex institutional interior ceiling tile.

"This is some really cheap shit," I say. "I bet we can go over the wall up there and get in."

"Good thing this is a state building. Lowest bidder gets the contract, which means some mighty cheap shit."

"And the contractors fix all the bids anyway—so you pay more and get less for the cheap shit."

"What is this: A contest to see how many times we can say 'cheap shit'? Let's see, one more—cheap shit—I win!" She preens. Then she says, "So who goes?"

"You know, I think I'm going to let you do it."

"Gee, thanks."

"I'm getting too frail for this garbage."

"Nonsense. You just need a few weeks back in the Andes. Tell you what, I'll go and I'll describe it for you so you can be there with me."

I make my hands into a stirrup, support it with my knee. Wai-

Wai climbs onto me and I straighten up, raising her about three feet. It's enough. She pushes up the ceiling tile and shoves it aside. I give her a few more inches, all I can manage. She makes a spring for it and grabs some piping and hauls herself up into the darkness like she was born doing this.

She reports back to me: "Gee, it's dark, it's cramped, it's—*filthy*. The real ceiling's only about a foot-and-a-half above me. I'm shining my flashlight around. I see a solid cement wall, Fil."

"What about over the door?"

I can hear her crawling over.

"Ouch!"

"Careful," I say.

"Damn conduit! They hang it like shit 'cause they know nobody'll see it. *No* sense of the aesthetic whatsoever."

"Wai-Wai?"

"Guess what, Fil?"

"I don't like guessing games."

"There used to be a window over the full-height door. Now there's just a piece of sheet metal. Got a screwdriver?"

Wai-Wai opens the ceiling panel right over the door and I have to jump three times before I pass her my specially modified Swiss Army knife.

"Nice work," says Wai-Wai. "Who did this?"

"A guy names Waxman. I did him a major legal favor one time. He owed me big, and offered to share some of the tricks of his troublesome trade."

"Nice trade. I mean, it's nice to get out of the lab once in a while but what kind of guys can I meet doing this? There's no future in it. Though *you* seem to keep doing it, Fil. Why?"

"Because the dental plan is so attractive."

"Hmm." The sheet metal falls loose and noisy. Wai-Wai slides past it and drops down inside. She tries the door.

She says, "It's locked." Big surprise.

"Describe the lock."

"It's a big box in the middle of the door with steel bars coming out of it in all four directions, three into the door frame, one into the floor."

"Through form-fitting steel guides? Square-shaped?"

"*Yes.*"

"I know this one."

"Say, you *did* go to night school, didn't you?"

"Let me think." Oh God, I've had so much else on my mind. Where is it? Where has it gone in this muddle of images? "Okay, okay—got my knife? Take the *third* spiral shaped screw in from the white cross—the thinnest one."

"Got it."

"Okay. How many holes in the box?"

"Just one."

"Uh-oh . . ."

"Sound unfamiliar?"

"Hmm. I think *it's* been modified, too. Okay: Hold the knife horizontal with the cross up and the screw facing the hole."

"I love it when you talk dirty."

"Now insert the tip of the spiral so it enters at nine o'clock— your left."

"Ooh."

"Do you feel resistance?"

"Some, I guess."

"Don't force it."

"*Never.*"

"Okay. That should be the guide thread. Try to keep a light pressure on it, and slowly turn it in counterclockwise. Is it going in?"

"Oh baby, you know it."

And I just burst out laughing.

"Just got to you, huh?" says Wai-Wai. And I can't believe I get a case of the F-ing *giggles,* for God's sake.

When I finally recover, I say, "Okay, let's get serious. And the simplest way to say this is: Is it in?"

"There's some more . . . There."

"You got it?"

"Yeah."

"Okay—pull it towards you."

Wai-Wai grunts. "I can't."

"Try."

Wai-Wai grunts again. "I can't."

"Okay, try turning it more."

"It won't go."

"Try harder."

Wai-Wai grunts. *Snap!* "Oh shit. It broke off!"

"Okay, okay. You know, maybe it would be easier if you just climbed back up in there and hauled me up."

"No, no, no, I'm going to get it. You stay right there."

"Yes, ma'am."

"So what do I do now?"

"Try the thickest one. Maybe you can guide it over the first one."

"No way José."

"Okay, the middle one."

"You know this is really hard to do while holding a flashlight?"

"So turn on a light. I'll give a hundred to one the windows are blocked off."

Pause.

"Goddamn, you're right Fil."

"Good, I'm glad. Now see if you can find some oil or other lubricant."

"Ooh."

"Stop it."

I hear her searching around. "Now you're talking *chemicals,* girlfriend," she says. "I don't need instructions for *that!*"

She finds some kind of viscous oil and guides the middle screw over the first one. She has to do a lot of teasing and jiggling, but the oil makes it go in pretty far before it jams.

"Now, unjam it," I tell her. "Turn it back the other way—just a bit."

"So *that* was our mistake."

"I think so."

"Okay."

"Ready?"

"You got it."

"Pull."

"*Ungh! Ungh!* Okay, I am plunking both feet on the door and pulling with both hands while—*rrrgh!*—pushing with my legs—*arrrgh!*"

It pops.

"*Now* turn it to the right," I say.

"Wait. My hands are all sweaty. I'm wiping them off." More sounds of exertion. *Clink!* It opens. Wai-Wai leans on the door frame, smiling. "They ought to have *that* one in the Kama Sutra."

What do we find? Enough Chemrel Max Coveralls to outfit a small army, three emergency full-body showers and four eye/facewash stations. Looks like these guys were prepared for handling some major toxics. There's a five-foot-high cabinet labeled ACID in huge red letters, which was awfully nice of them, and a few dozen plunger cans. Wai-Wai explains that these are designed specifically for use with highly flammable liquids. And if it weren't for her I probably would not have opened the huge yellow plastic drums to reveal the solid steel drums inside.

Wai-Wai gives them a rap. "Muffled," she says. "There's another layer of protection. This is some serious hazard containment."

"I want a sample of it."

"Why don't we just lift the red drum of BIOHAZARD WASTE?"

"Because I want this one."

"Oh. I'm going to have to put that phrase in my next grant application."

Wai-Wai locates the cabinet with the empties, takes out a small container-within-a-container, rinses it out in a deep lab sink and dries it, just to be sure, and proceeds to extract a couple of quarts of something black, gooey and repellent. Now she wants some software. I figure the most important stuff is in the drawer with the biggest lock. Will these goons never catch on to that? It takes some work, and a little obvious damage to the lock, but I get it open. She flips through the stacks of diskettes, grabs a few that seem to be copies no one will miss immediately. We close the drawer and relock it. I shut and lock the back door and we both go back out up through the ceiling, replacing the tiles after us.

"Not bad for two little maids from school," says Wai-Wai.

We stumble, wet and tired, through the woods and get Wai-Wai's car seats all dirty driving back to main campus and the Chem Building.

"At least I've got a key to this front door," she says.

Up in the lab, she siphons off a few milliliters of the black ooze and runs it through a few routine tests.

"Yep," she says. "Just as I thought: It's gunk."

"Can you get more specific?"

"Not without some parameters. That's why we brought this," she takes out the software. We go to an office adjoining the lab. She turns on the light and jumpstarts the computer. But it doesn't take long to find out the access to the software is pretty effectively blocked.

"I'm good at ripping these things apart physically, but that's it," I say, rapping the top of the computer.

"Okay, I can't do it. But I know who can. Let's meet back here tomorrow, okay?"

"Sure. What's another day? . . ."

The next day the EPA is at it again, banging on the gates of the glass factory, but they don't have the warrant yet and the place is still stalling. Gina says they're trying to slow the process down by requesting copies of every public document on record, which she's then required to provide. That's a Morse tactic, all right.

A salesman comes to the door and tries to sell us a water purifier. I ask, "Does it filter out trichloroethylene?"

And he goes, "Mbeuh-euh, I—"

"Never mind."

My car won't be ready 'til tomorrow. So I bike up to Wai-Wai's lab, and she grabs the software and walks me over to the campus computer center. There's a supply store, classrooms full of desks and display monitors and computers, and, way in the back, some offices. Wai-Wai takes me into the smallest one, with little slits for windows like the architects were expecting the place might have to be defended from Saxon longbowmen or something, looking out onto the it-came-from-another-planet windowless concrete monstrosity that Wai-Wai tells me is the Lecture Center.

Wai-Wai introduces me to her computer whiz friend Faith Wiegeneest. She's a white girl, of Dutch descent, like that isn't obvious with a name like Wiegeneest, and *finally* one who's nearer to my generation. In fact, she's a couple of years older and even a little bit more frazzled than me, which I was beginning to think wasn't possible.

"That's a pretty name," I say. "Does it mean anything?"

"Yes. 'Healer.' "

"Oh, no. First I meet someone named Alan Wrennch, now this: Your name isn't really 'Faith Healer,' is it?"

"I'm afraid so."

"Jeezus."

"What's yours?" I tell her my name. "Philomel's a kind of bird, isn't it? But what does Buscarsela mean?"

"It means 'hip deep in sheep shit.' "

Faith chuckles.

"Enough of this chit-chat," says Wai-Wai. "We've got something for you. Heal *this*, Faith."

Wai-Wai hands her the diskettes. Faith slips them in and punches up some stuff. She explains to us that she's trying to identify the operating code, but even that is blocked. However, she knows of only a handful of codes that can do that, so once again the excess of security on Morse's part has the opposite effect of pointing us towards a solution.

She says, "You know, sometimes people's pigheadedness amazes me. And sometimes it doesn't. Now, this really isn't the right terminal for this. Trying to bust a code on a Unisystems 1200 is like trying to perform an appendectomy with a backhoe. I mean, it can be done, but it's *messy*."

But I don't care. Fifteen minutes later we're printing out a list of chemicals fifteen pages long that Wai-Wai identifies as toxic organic volatiles, everything from alkylamine nitrates to xylidene triethylamine, and a corresponding list of configurations and words she does not recognize.

"They look like trade names, not chemical names," says Wai-Wai. "They could mean anything."

"But will this help you analyze the sample?" I ask.

"I'll let you know by tomorrow."

I bike home. Tired out from last night's activity and the round-trip biking, my wits really aren't about me as I dismount and walk towards the back of the house. As I round the shadowy corner something heavy and metal swings towards me. I get off the first hundredth of a second of a duck-and-roll reflex when it slams down on my head and knocks me to the ground; it probably would have killed me but he wasn't expecting this helmet (bloody fool doesn't know how to handle a wrench).

I roll to a stop flat on my back. The guy slices off my belt pouch and runs. I'm stunned, but I shake it out of my head and suddenly find myself on my feet and chasing the bastard. But after a block-and-a-half the pain starts oozing through the protective sheets of brain-made painkiller and fight-or-flight juices, and thick, hot blood is pounding like a dull metal clapper against my bell-shaped head while someone drives hot metal tent spikes into my chest and lungs. But the beast within me rages through the pain, ignoring it.

I chase him down and tackle the guy, but I've got a death grip on a shadow. My head all but abdicates into total blackness while the tent spikes turn to molten lead, burning holes in my chest. I crumple around prickly icicles of nothingness, and we both go down. I twinge uncontrollably and curl up, helpless as a flipped beetle. He kicks himself free, then keeps kicking what's left of my head and chest. Then he falls across me screaming:

"Aaooowwww!"

He must have burnt himself on the molten lead.

Claang!

The clapper in my head goes off, but he's the one screaming: "Aaah!"

Claaang!

Him again: "Aaaggh!"

Weight is lifted off me, and another *clang* drops it next to me.

I push myself away from mother earth's grave embrace one more time and roll over. My eyes still see. I look up. Reggie Einhorn is standing over the guy and clobbering him with a four-foot section of lead pipe. A few more swings and the guy stops moving.

The molten lead cools enough to condense, withdraw, re-form. I'm still breathing.

"Thanks," I say. "I think you saved my life—"

"What? With this flyswatter?"

"Ow!" Sharp stabbing pains in my neck and chest.

"Let me go call a doctor."

I give him Stan's number.

My assailant gets arrested. The cops tell me he has been arrested four other times in Suffolk county, twice for muggings. They want me to believe that it was just a mugging. But still. I wonder . . . Then why was he waiting *for me*?

II

I think love is terribly primitive.   —Helen Fisher

Antonia's very upset to see me in pain, but I talk to her and calm her down and tell her I'm going to go to the doctor and that he'll make me feel better.

"Can I go, too?" she asks.

I say, "No, I don't think you should."

"Please?"

"No."

"*Pleeeeese?*"

"Oh, okay."

Rosita's shocked but supportive, until Billy foolishly tells her my paranoia-inducing it-sure-seemed-like-he-was-waiting-for-me story and she gets completely spooked, so Colomba sends her off to Elvis's apartment for a few days until things calm down.

Reggie drives me up to the hospital in his pickup truck. It's too painful to sit the whole way and I have to curl up on the seat with my head resting against his leg. When we get there he helps me down to the sidewalk. The odd thing is *he's* shaking. This must have been more of an ordeal for him than I realized. He's not satisfied when I tell him thanks, I can handle it from here, but I manage to send him home.

Antonia says, "It's raining."

Is it? I'm not *that* far gone.

"No it's not."

"Yes it is." And she goes: "Shhhhhhhhh—"

"Oh." Pretend rain. "Well, let's go."

"No, we're going to get wet."

"Well use an umbrella."

"I don't have an umbrella."

"Well pretend you do."

"I don't want to get wet."

"If you're going to pretend it's raining you can use a pretend umbrella."

"Oh. Okay." And she walks with me towards the hospital entrance. "We're not getting wet."

"No, we're not."

"The umbrella's keeping us dry."

With Antonia leading I hobble down the newly buffed corridor that reeks of cleaning fluid vapors. A nice chaser to the carbon tet I've been breathing all month.

Stan looks up in horror. "Filomena? What happened?"

"Somebody hit me over the head with a wrench. Fortunately, they weren't expecting the bike helmet."

"Show me the spot." I do. It's very tender and sensitive to his hard, professional palpations. But no concussion.

"We're going to have to clean and bandage those abrasions. How about the rest of you? Does it hurt much?"

"Only when I move."

"Let me see you walk."

I hobble a few more feet. He lays me flat on my back and stands behind my head, placing both hands on either side of my neck, just under the chin. His fingers firmly probe and prod.

"The shock was distributed unevenly. Slight subluxation of the first cervical vertebra. Your upper body muscles are going to be very stiff and painful by tomorrow. Relax." He's cradling my head with two hands. "Deep breath. Let it out—" Before I realize

what he's doing he quickly twists my neck and moves the vertebra back into place with the sound of an enormous knuckle
cracking. Antonia laughs at the sound. "Oh, you like that?" he
says to her.

"Thanks. I already feel better."

"Good."

"Except for the searing pain in my lungs."

"Say ah."

"Aaaaaaaaaaaaaaaaaah."

"Yes, the passage is quite irritated. Have you been breathing in
a lot of—"

"Chemical fumes? Yes."

"Well, that's part of your problem. You're going to have to move
to a cleaner neighborhood."

"That's funny, that's why I left New York City."

"It can't be doing her any good, either," he waves at Antonia.

"Daddy," she says.

I can feel my face flushing involuntarily as I quickly explain that
she doesn't mean that, she calls every man with short, dark curly
hair "Daddy." Although Mommy is sure starting to feel like she'd
like to play Daddy with him. I don't tell him that.

He starts cleaning the scuff marks from my face, neck and
shoulders with antibacterial towelettes soaked with alcohol and
disinfectant. "I really think you should go back on chemotherapy.
Why are you resisting it?"

"Because sometimes it seems like the therapy is only prolong-
ing my suffering."

"Filomena, why do you have this attitude towards me? I'm trying to help."

"Yes, you're trying to help, but . . . I'm sorry. I just—well, I know
you're different. I feel you're different. But, you know, I had one of
the most beautiful moments of my life ruined by an asshole male
doctor, a condescending, chauvinist obstetrician from hell who
spread my legs and reached in as if he were pulling a hair clog out
of a drain or something."

"I'm sorry to hear that—"

"And when he bends down to perform the episiotomy, he tells

the support staff, 'Will you look at this? She's been hit up more times than a prostitute.' "

"God, I really—"

"Then when it's over and he's going to sew me back up he turns to me and says, 'What size does your boyfriend want?' That kind of sums up a lifelong dislike for male docs."

And yet I get such a jolt of adrenaline when I'm with him. Or maybe it's not adrenaline.

Nervous energy. Tension.

Attraction.

No.

Yes . . .

I crack and confess: "Whenever I'm with you, I feel like I'm holding myself back. As if I'm keeping myself from letting go with all I have in me. I feel myself holding back."

"From what?"

I can only imagine. Well, he hasn't run away yet. He's still here. I don't know what I'm going to do but it feels good to picture it. A warm surge is welling up inside me. Confession feels good. It's healthy, like how your eyes feel clean after you cry.

And I'm going to cry. I try to suppress it. But the warm surge mixes with a cold stream. He's about to form an explanation or an apology and I just burst out with, "Please, Stan you've got to help me: I can't die and leave her alone," meaning Antonia who's there and gets real upset herself. So Stan's stuck with two weeping women.

Eventually I recover. I tell Antonia everything's okay. I wipe her eyes, blow her nose, then do the same for myself.

Stan asks a teenage community service volunteer to take Antonia to the daycare area for a few minutes.

"I feel ridiculous. I shouldn't *need* to turn to a 'strong male' to save and protect me."

"Our needs aren't always rational, Filomena."

"Are you saying I'm not rational? Maybe it would be better if I weren't: After all, rationalizing got us thrown out of the Garden of Eden. Maybe then I wouldn't deserve this punishment."

"Oh not that again. We have *very* different viewpoints on that."

"What do you mean, 'Not that again'?"

"That pat Catholic-school answer to explain why innocent people suffer."

"Go on."

"Well, traditional Judaism is a lot more mysterious than your standard eighth-grade catechism. There is a great gap between ourselves and the Almighty, and no one claims to know the mind of God. And you can't tell a post-Holocaust Jew that physical suffering is a just punishment for sin."

The atmosphere in the room gets heavy and still.

"Yes, Stan. You're right. You can't."

I breathe for a while. Nice to know I can still do it. "But—" It's hard for my recently addled brain to form these complex thoughts into words. "But, tell me—"

"Yes?"

"Hitler planned to take over Europe, meet the Japanese halfway, somewhere around India, and then move on to Africa, the Americas, and Australia, too, I suppose."

"Yes?" His intonation skirts the edge of irritation, but he keeps it in check.

"The Holocaust cost Hitler the war in some ways, didn't it?"

No answer.

"He was being battered on two fronts, but he chose to pursue a suicidal devotion to seeing his Final Solution through to the very end. And so his plans to dominate the world went up in—in the same smoke that carried away the souls of the cremated."

Silence.

"I just mean that their deaths may have meant something in the sick, mysterious working of things: Just as you *could* say that Jesus died to save humanity, you *could* say that the Jews of Europe, and the other victims of the Holocaust, died to save the world from Fascist takeover."

Silence.

Then: "So you're saying—" Stan can barely say it: "The Holocaust—could have served some—some 'good' purpose—by saving the rest of the world?"

"It's just something to consider."

"Meaning—in your interpretation—that God so loved the

world that he sacrificed his only son, and then his beloved chosen people, to save it?"

Somewhere outside this room, time is flowing by. Not in here.

"You'd think he could come up with a new method," I say.

Stan stares at me, through me, then rubs his eyes. "God knows, I never thought of it like that."

"It's not the only answer," I say.

"But you're saying such suffering *could* be part of God's 'larger' plan."

"Something like that."

Some more time flows by. "So my question is, Why is God doing this to me?"

He puts his arm around my shoulder. "You just said it yourself, who is to say what God is doing?"

"But there must be a reason. Why can't I see it? Why?"

"I don't know. I'm a doctor, not a mystic philosopher."

An involuntary chuckle escapes from the prison of my tears. He looks at me, his face close to mine. I look up into his eyes.

"You sound just like Dr. McCoy on the old *Star Trek*."

Something comes out of him, rippling through the brooding waters of his dark mood. A smile.

He smiles and I get tender. So tender. I know I'm not supposed to be doing this but maybe there's just something about guys in baby blue V-neck scrubs. I kiss him. On the neck. When nobody stops me I kiss him again, higher up—hmm, carotid artery: I can feel it pulsating—then higher: the chin, the cheek, then the lips. He kisses back. We kiss. It gets real.

It gets good.

And we are not ashamed.

Normally I'd go on a few dates with him, make him dinner, meet his folks. Who's got time for that?

Soon after I suggest we go visit his house.

Stan says no, he's got enough landlord problems.

"You don't take your forensic work home with you, do you?"

"I'm just absentminded about paying the bills."

There's a knock at the door, and two seconds later Antonia wants to know what on earth's going on, so I tell her, "Stan is coming home with us."

She says, "Yayy!"

"Hoo-hah," I say. "You've made a hit."

Dark. A nice manly chest. And not too hairy.

"This old thing?" he says. "I've had it for years."

Sex in the age of condoms: "Whatsamatter? Can't get it up?"

"Oh, I can get it up—I just can't get it *on*."

"Here, let me help." Mmmmmmmmm. Not bad for a white boy.

He says: "I've heard of small, but you have *no* breasts!"

"That's my *back*."

"I knew that."

"Ouch! Watch my wound."

"Sorry—"

Knock knock. It's Antonia. She's crying. We're making too much noise. She was sleeping next door in Rosita's bed, she woke up in a strange room and I wasn't there with her so she got scared. I try to calm her down and get her to go to sleep but she wakes right up and jumps into bed with us.

"So much for—"

Stan bursts out laughing, and hugs Antonia. I knew it already, but it's further proof of what a truly nice guy he is. She sits up and talks with us for nearly an hour and it takes us another hour to get her into a deep enough sleep so that we can carry her back to the other room and dare to try again.

I whisper, *"Ven, hagamos dulces recuerdos."*

"What's that?"

"Nothing. Let's make some memories."

The first time is awkward and unsatisfying. But the second time feels like the cold rock under the soil has come back to life, cracking open and filling the streets with waves of hot magma that melts everything in its path.

And the two become one.

Oh, what a wonderful statement.

Three A.M.? Four A.M. God, why do I always pray for special favors? Salvation isn't enough for me? I've been brought up to believe that's wrong. But is it? Or isn't it the way You made us?

*   *   *

Morning.

"Ready to face the world?"

"I'm up for anything that doesn't require *moving*. I need some painkillers, Doc."

"Believe it or not, right now, that would be the worst thing for you."

"Can I get a second opinion?"

"Sure, I've got to be on call in twenty-five minutes, but I'll come back later tonight to see how you're doing. Don't do anything strenuous, or exert yourself in any way."

"No problem."

Colomba lays out breakfast for six. I try to give her my last fifty dollars in American money for food and she says, "I loan it to you. You just do what you got to do. You'll pay me back."

"Thanks."

I call Wai-Wai. She tells me the chemical data printout Faith did for us helped her identify a number of compounds about 10^6 times faster than chance, but she says that I'm not going to like what she has to say.

"What?"

"That sludge has got a little bit of everything in there. It's a carbon-based nightmare."

"So?"

"So all the other chemicals—the trade names I couldn't identify? They're new experimental compounds for breaking down the others into less toxic by-products, for containing oil slicks, for neutralizing acids, for speeding up volatilization, for—Fil, he's going into the environmental protection business."

I get a good laugh out of that.

"I'm serious, Fil. Environmental cleanup is a growth industry."

"So he's going to make a profit by charging us to clean up the mess he's been making?"

"It looks that way. Fil, like it or not, this is a legitimate business. We can't touch it."

"Anything Morse finances comes from his other murderous enterprises. So much for 'legitimacy.'"

"Have it your way. Sorry. Whatever else he's doing, *this* project's legit."

"Shit."

It's the third day of the EPA's attempt to get on the Kim Tungsten site, but they're still being stonewalled. Gina says they should have the search warrant by tomorrow morning. She says she might even come out to serve it herself.

My car's finally ready, but first I drop over to see how Reggie Einhorn's doing and thank him. He answers the door and I almost let out a frightful yelp. He's positively gray, like a flagstone on a cloudy day.

I tell him, "You look awful."

"You don't look so good yourself," he says, pointing to my swollen and discolored flesh and day-old bandages. "Well, I guess we showed that punk who he was messing with, huh?" Reggie chuckles, but the chuckle turns into a phlegm-clogged choke and he has a two-minute, disgusting, coughing fit. "I'll be all right, just hoisted a few too many last night, celebrating my victory over the years. The guys down at Kelsey's are going to have my lead pipe bronzed. I tell you, it felt just like old times."

"Yeah, for me, too." A time I'd rather *not* relive. "That's a real regular crowd place, huh?"

"Sure is."

"I miss that. Since I left Ecuador I haven't really had that rock solid crowd to hang with. I've never been in one place long enough to make that many friends."

"Pretty girl like you? Come on. What's the matter? Won't let the guys beat you at arm wrestling?"

"I don't know. It happens. You keep in touch with all *your* friends?"

"I guess not," he says. "Maybe you're not enough of a cheap date?"

"Me? Are you kidding? I grew up thinking a good time was dancing on the corner with three girlfriends and a radio. I was happy if a guy would take me to the movies."

"Ah, the movies today ain't worth the price of a ticket. Nothin' but weirdo sex and buckets of blood, and I seen enough of both in the Pacific, young lady."

I nod. He goes on: "When Vera and me were dating we used to go to the movies all the time. Picture palaces, with uniformed ushers, a fifty-foot screen, and real stars like Gary Cooper, Randolph Scott and the Duke, larger than life. And they ain't come up with a new idea since. Just use the same old stuff over and over. Last few times I went, I left in the middle 'cause I already knew how it was gonna end."

I agree with him. "Yeah, I already know the rules for survival if I'm ever in a movie or a TV show."

"Hmm?"

I count them off on my fingers, one-by-one: "Don't go for your gun first in a Western of any kind. *Never* say, 'Goodbye, Mr. Bond,' with a thick foreign accent. Never, *ever* be an unfamiliar crew member on a *Star Trek* landing party—"

Reggie starts laughing and once again the laugh becomes a coughing fit that hurts *me* to watch it. He groans in pain as he recovers, rubbing his chest and biceps.

"You better take it easy," I say.

I've been meaning to ask him about his working for Morse, but I figure it's better just to chat for a while, not excite him too much.

"Tea?" I head into the kitchen.

"Hack! Ptoo! Sure, why not?" he calls from the other room.

I start the water running. Then I clang around for a pot to boil it in. I call back to him: "You know, I meant to thank you for what you did yesterday, I just didn't get a chance. You really helped me out when I needed it. Say, where'd you put that tea I brought you, Reggie? Reggie?"

A cold premonition and I bolt out of the kitchen, through the hall and into the living room. He's stretched out on his back, eyes looking up beyond the ceiling. He knocked over the end table with the ashtray and the ashes are scattered all over him.

"No. No. No!" I say to no one, feeling for a pulse. Nothing in the wrist, nothing in the neck. No breathing. No eye movement. No response. I start CPR, pumping away at his chest, one, two, three, four, five, hold his nose and breathe through his mouth. I see his chest rise, so his airway's clean. I repeat. Five pumps and one breath. His chest rises but I'm getting nothing else. Five pumps and a breath and I lunge for the phone, pull it off the table down next to me. Five pumps and a breath. Dial Colomba. Cram the receiver under my chin, five pumps and a breath.

"Hello?"

"Hello, Elvis? Call Stan's office, tell them to beep him, Reggie Einhorn's had a coronary! The number's in my purse. On the hospital bill! Yes! Bye!"

I keep it up for seven or eight minutes. Stan was already on his way up to the hospital. He spun around on the road, made an illegal U-turn across a highway divider and headed back. I have that effect on people.

Eight minutes of CPR and *zip*. Reggie's got dead eyes—opaque and white, if you've ever seen them. And still. He has slipped across the awful gap between person and corpse, gone down that one-way street towards the blind alleys of night. Fade to black. The end.

There's nothing left to do by the time Stan shows up. He calls the county, relays the correct technical information and waits for the ambulance. He says he's going to observe the autopsy. I go with him and wait outside for a full three hours.

It took me nearly four years to find someone who even feels like he could make me forget Antonia's father (that asshole), we have one night of terrific love and now this.

When Stan comes out, he snaps off his rubber gloves and stretches, then sits down next to me, still wearing his full-length OR gown.

"It was a clot, not an arrest."

"A clot . . ."

"There was nothing you could have done. If that helps any."

"It doesn't."

Blood clots. I know that was on the list of symptoms Gina gave me. But which one? Which workplace chemical did this to him?

"A clot: Dammit, Reggie was *murdered*. He and a thousand others like him."

"Filomena, there's been no murder."

"Sure there has. It just took him ten years to die."

"There was nothing you could have done."

"No. But I'm going to do something *now*."

12

Sure, it's a nice town. It's probably no crookeder than Los
Angeles. But you can only buy a piece of a big city. You can
buy a town this size all complete, with the original box and
tissue paper. That's the difference. And that makes me
want out.

—RAYMOND CHANDLER, *Farewell My Lovely*

Reggie Einhorn was laid to rest in Veterans Memorial Cemetery
within sight of a grave marked WEINSTEIN, the man who gave him
fifty more years of life, after a simple service attended only by
neighbors and co-workers. He had no more family.

Death is good-bye forever, and at least I got a chance to say
goodbye, forever, to the man who gave me a few more weeks of
life. As I watch them lowering his bright new coffin into the thick
cold clods of eternal earth, the thoughts fill my head: Jesus, and I
thought *I* had it bad. . . . At least I'm alive, I've still got a chance.

We're all doomed from birth, and the only thing that lives after
us is what we do while we're here.

When everybody's gone I take out the brown paper bag I've
been hiding under my arm and I buy Reggie a beer. Domestic. He
would have wanted it that way.

We walk home. I think about Reggie and the others like him,
like that independent garbage hauler Reggie told me about, the little guy trying to make an honest living by providing cheaper and
better service; but the story doesn't end with him prospering and
being respected for his labors. No, the story ends with him getting

threatening phone calls from gruff voices that tell him what clothes his daughter is wearing at the playground two blocks away, then dying from three slugs in the chest while trying to make sure the 911 operator gets the damn facts straight. What's wrong with this story?

As the sky turns red, and the night starts to fall, my putting Antonia to a prayerful rest is interrupted by a low muffled roar that shakes the whole house. I look out the window. A bright orange glow explodes across the horizon out over the wasteland that is Kim Tungsten.

The fire department arrives within minutes and chops the chain off the gate, the police arrive two minutes later to keep the crowd back, but half the neighborhood is already in, jogging after the trucks because the fire is at the other edge of the site. I walk fast. Police cars race past me, trying to contain the crowd, which is tough because most of them are running even with the fire trucks. Why aren't they setting up a perimeter, I wonder? Why are they so concerned with getting people *out* of here?

"Come on, Fil!" says Billy, gesturing for me to join him.

"I can't run that fast."

"Okay, I'll see you there," and he runs on ahead.

The police rapidly establish a semicircle around the fire engines and keep the crowd back. They call for backup, which arrives a few minutes later to seal the gate and drive on the site to ferry the rubberneckers back to safety. But by now it is clear that the local fire fighters do not have sufficient preparation or equipment to deal with hazardous chemicals and get the fire under control. I wonder half-curiously to myself if the water they're pumping to put it out is so full of inflammable toxics that the two just feed on each other, which would be a kind of poetic justice. Something is certainly wrong, because a young guy, obviously a rookie, sweating buckets in full fire-fighting gear, loses his cool and makes a frantic radio call for the Emergency Response Team. That's the EPA. That's what the regulations say he's supposed to do. But he's new and he obviously doesn't know he's not supposed to do what the regulations say because his boss starts shaking him down and I step close enough and shout, "Shouldn't you be fighting the fire?"

The Chief glares at me like he's going to remember my face for the next twenty to thirty years. Great. This draws attention and the cops whistle at me, waving me over to them: "Ma'am? Step this way, please. Ma'am? Would you step this way please?!" The fire is spreading to Morse's side of the fence, inaccessible from this side. I've got no choice but to cooperate with the authorities, who pack about sixteen of us into the back of a squad car and drive us back to Pleasant Valley Road.

We watch as the orange wound in the nighttime bleeds wider and wider in the distance. Then I break from my catatonia and realize—now's my chance! I race walk back to the house and get my car keys. The engine coughs and dies. It wheezes. It grinds. It starts. I let it warm up for a minute, against all instinct screaming at me from inside. While I'm sitting there counting backwards from twenty-five, Billy comes up and leans his head in the window.

"Where you going?"

"I thought they might not be watching the front of Morse's place as scrupulously as always."

"Can I go?"

Pause. I can't do *this* alone.

"Okay. Get in."

"*Yes!*" He hops in. "Gee, Aunt Filomena, you're the only person who ever takes me anywhere."

I could do without the "Aunt Filomena," but I let it go. The kid needs attention.

But it's no use. We drive over to Carthage and Morse's place is sealed tighter than ever, with a pair of security guards inside the fence and out, and enough illumination to blast any critter that comes within buckshot range. I make an illegal U-turn across two lanes of oncoming traffic and head back.

"What are you doing?" he asks.

"Going home."

"Why?"

"What do you think? I'm going to ram the gate?"

"Aww, *man*—"

"Sorry. That's life, Billy."

On the way back he asks, "What does 'scruplessly' mean?" I try to explain.

I park the car in the street. There's some excitement up ahead. The EPA's Environmental Response Team has arrived, and a dozen trained experts are arming themselves in shiny moonsuits. They don't do much for your figure, but even at this distance I think I spot a female form among them. The hottest thing in steel-toed boots. Gina.

I run up to her. "You're the On-Scene Coordinator? Took you long enough."

"I had to wait for my nails to dry."

"Got any more moonsuits?"

"No, but I've got some spare Tyveks and booties."

"Booties? Now, don't try to tell me your leathernecked male colleagues call these things 'booties'?"

"You want them or not?"

"Sure. Two pairs. One for him."

Billy says, "Hi."

"We've met," says Gina. "Here, these zoot suits are unisex."

A Tyvek is a plastic body coverall that feels like a mottled garbage bag. And it's pure white.

"Gee," I say, "you couldn't get these in Day-Glo orange?"

"The idea is to be seen."

"Yeah, well, I'll fix that."

Fully suited up, Gina commands her crew to head in, and the local cops try to stop them.

Gina says, "This is an *emergency* response, you idiots!"

"Gee, you have a knack with words," I tell her.

"And who are you?" says the cop.

"She's with me. Now move."

"I got orders—"

"And I've got federal authority, photographic and chemical evidence of PCBs and other toxics on this site. That fire ignites them and we'll all die a little sooner. Now you going to let us through or do I have to start taking down badge numbers?"

The guy hesitates, then submits. What the hell is going on here? We hang on to the back of the EPA's Emergency Response vehicle and Bill lets out a "Yahoooo!" like he's riding shotgun on a stage-coach in a John Ford movie. Okay, I'll admit my blood's rushing a bit, too. We get there and the fire has quadrupled in size, half of it over on Morse's side. For a moment I feel almost alive, like my presence matters, like I can *do* something.

At her command, they weaken the steel mesh with boltcutters, then one of Gina's boys commandeers a pump truck and drives it through the fence. The others follow, trying to re-establish a perimeter and contain the blaze.

It's hot as hell and we're in spill suits, which afford zero protection from flames while keeping in all the heat so you sweat like a pig. There's a tremendous explosion behind us as a fifty-five-gallon drum of something goes for it. I dive facedown into a puddle of mud. Shrapnel's flying. Everyone scatters like mad. Gina regroups her forces, directing them to a pile of barrels that is about to be engulfed.

"Now's our chance!" I tell Billy. "Follow me."

"Follow *you*?" he asks.

I'm rolling over in the mud, covering myself from head to toe. He gets the idea and jumps in, camouflaging the fluorescent white with good old-fashioned earth tones. We circle around the searing wall of flames with Gina's troops, step through the fence and take off into the woods. There's another tremendous explosion that sends some tall trees crashing to the ground in flames. We put that mess behind us.

But I'm blind in the dark after the flames. For a moment I panic. I've lost my bearings and we could be heading for a toxic sump, but when I see the red signs with bright white letters reading: RESTRICTED AREA, DO NOT ENTER WITHOUT PERMISSION, I know we're heading in the right direction. Not that I get a lot of comfort out of *that*.

A couple of hundred yards of trudging through the trees and we finally make out the silhouette of the big Morse plant. They've only got it illuminated from the front, and an eerie nimbus of cold tungsten arc glows around its edges. I tell Billy to slow down. The pain is returning to my chest. He asks me where we're headed. I get him to stop for a moment. We kneel down behind some barrels and I describe what I'm looking for. I tell him we're heading for the Billing Office, which is over the shop floor, which has a back entrance, but I only know how to get there from the front of the building.

Billy says half the football team's dads worked here, he knows the layout of the shop floor and which stairway to use. My, my. Good thing I brought him. I actually allow myself to relax and regroup for a second, thinking maybe we really do have a shot at this, that long shot I've been hoping for. I lean my head on a barrel before a line of trees goes up in flames, lighting up the night and I read the label on the barrel: DANGER: PROPELLENT STORAGE.

"Oh, shit!" I say, in as nice a way as possible, and we stumble to our feet and get away from there. Billy reaches out and stops me from braining myself on a rusty iron railing. We follow it to a long, narrow runway over the cooling pits to a ladder. It takes us up to another runway about fifty yards long over a low rooftop to the back wall of the plant.

Just then a dark bank of lights unexpectedly bursts into life, searing my eyes, lighting up the back of the plant and the surrounding acres. And as if that isn't enough, a big iron door opens about twenty feet to the right of where the runway butts the plant and three security guards carrying shotguns come out and take up positions along the outer wall.

This time I wait a few seconds before saying, "Oh, shit." For variety.

Billy looks at me and whispers: "Now what?"

"Forget it. We've gone as far as we can. Time to go back."

And he says, "No, it's *not*! If you get those guys down off of there. I'll handle the rest."

"You will?"

"Yes, dammit!"

"What the hell." I retreat down the ladder, across the runway over a pit of something I'd much rather not think about. Even covered in mud, I'm pretty easy to spot with these air raid beacons on me, and I draw their attention before I dive behind the barrels. Hmm. I haven't got any of those exploding bullets James Bond used in *Live and Let Die* that would come in so handy right now so I regress to the early bronze age, strip off the top half of my sweaty armor and start throwing stones. Two of the guards climb down a vertical ladder, drop to the ground and spread out. They've lost me, but they know where I should be, and the stone-throwing only fools them for a minute. So I find a length of rusty scrap metal and start pounding on the fifty-five-gallon drums of propellent. It makes a hell of a racket, and the two of them converge on me. I see Billy start for the runway, but that's all I see because two guys with guns and the criminal trespassing laws on their side are after me. They radio for backup. Have I said "Oh, shit" yet?

A year ago I would have run back to the fence, but my lungs are constricting around a dozen venomous sea urchins, and besides, I can't leave Billy in there. I figure maybe I can pass for an EPA Investigator come to warn them about the fire—if they catch me. But I'd prefer to avoid that, so I do the unexpected and slip the top of my camouflaged Tyvek back on and head away from the barrels *towards* the building, on the other side of the cooling pits and the low outbuilding. I hear a lot of movement coming towards me from the front of the structure. With no other thought in the world I grab the railing, climb over it and hang off the inside edge over the cooling pit. They run by above me in the direction of the barrels. I lift myself up—and I nearly fall in. I'm getting weak. Dizzy. Old. Yet some spontaneous irrational effort of mine gets a grip and I pull myself out. I duck under a ladder, drop to the ground, run the length of the low building, go in close to the loading dock and climb up. There's a line of drums outside a steel-shuttered entry-way, and I realize I'm standing at the gate to the shop floor, about twenty feet from where I want to be: the Billing Office. Of course there is the matter of the steel-shuttered door.

But I'm actually looking up at the second-floor window, contemplating how to climb up there on the barrels when a red pinpoint of light pierces the wall two feet in front of me: it swivels right into my face as I duck down and a high-powered bullet shatters the concrete, spattering me with splinters. If the material had been brick it would have cut my face open.

I dive down behind the barrels. The fuckers have goddamn laser sights and hollow-point magnums, judging from the damage. But I have something they don't count on: The will to live for another fifteen minutes. I slide down to the far end of the line of barrels, keeping low. My heart is pounding. I'm sweating buckets. I zip the Tyvek back up. I don't know why.

Ten feet back where I was standing some instants before a barrel ruptures as a high-powered bullet shatters through it, blowing a hole eight inches wide and loosing a gurgling of thick, viscous fluid. It's only now that it occurs to me how insane it is that they're shooting at me. Is this normal business practice on Long Island? Are these standard security procedures? But there is no time to analyze. Eight feet away a second barrel goes out with a blast of shrapnel and chemicals. They pause for dramatic effect. Then a third six feet away. They know I'm here, and they're systematically searching and destroying. *Shit* that makes me mad. To cheat death for so long and to die like this? A fourth barrel four feet away dies a glorious death. No, this is not the moment for anger. Think, Filomena, think. They're being systematic—*God*, that irks me!— but life and death are not systematic, they're chaotic. I wait. I figure. No. I don't figure. I abandon myself to the void. I cover my face and head for protection. A fifth barrel explodes two feet away. Razor-sharp fangs dip into my arms and elsewhere in a dozen places. Now. I dive back towards the first barrel into a puddle of ooze as the barrel I was pressed up against shatters into infinity.

I'm face down in a pool of something that could be toxic waste. But I'm alive. And I'm pissed. Not that that'll be any protection against what they've got, but who cares? I'm going to die anyway. I lie there, and listen. My ears are ringing with the silence. I can't hear their footsteps. But I see movement, and it sure isn't me so it must be the goddess Athena who springs to my feet with a roar that fells flaming trees half a mile away. I must be quite a sight, a half-mad furious female dripping with toxic waste, arms outstretched towards them like Frankenstein's monster: Unstoppable.

I curse them 'til the end of infinite and eternal time or at least for a solid minute until I realize I'm doing it in Spanish and switch to English. They step back, holding their guns up. I keep them at bay for longer than seems humanly possible before pain from a thousand shards of flame begins to eat at my body, and they realize that I'm only a woman.

One small woman.

They stop retreating. Their guns lower. They cock them. This is it.

Then Billy charges like a fullback right through them, knocking three of them to the ground. He spins around, kicks one of them in the head and pushes him off the loading dock. I grab the other's shotgun and try to slam the butt across his face, but it slips out of my hand. He tries to shoot me, but the viscous waste won't let either of us get a grip. Fuck this. I lunge for him, tackle him in the belly and push him, skidding on a sheen of toxic chemicals to the edge of the dock, where a horizontal iron railing delivers a solid shock to the middle of his back. He's down, in pain.

Somehow, Billy's next to me, his arms full of papers. We drop to the ground together and run. The reinforcements close in but they can't shoot because they're surrounding us, facing each other. We don't stop running. Billy dodges one, two, fakes to the left then plows into a third, clipping him low, and we're running back towards the fire. Now I know I'm crazy.

"What'd you do to that first guy?" I ask, between painful wheezes.

"Him? Oh, he was easy."

But the other pricks start shooting at us again. Billy picks up speed, zigzagging among the trees like a seventeen-year-old football player. But me, I'm getting the feeling I've swallowed a bottle of hydrochloric acid. Every cell is burning, every organ, every atom is dissolving away from my body on its own separate course. Everything's bright hot fire, but fuzzy. I think a tree falls on me and I go down on one knee. Billy turns back and makes the play, picks me up with his one good arm and runs with me for a good seventy-five yards as the crowd roars before I slip from his grasp and fall to the forest floor. I hear shots. I feel prodding. It's Billy, urging me to move. I try. He helps me to my feet but every way we turn the alleyway of trees leads to a slime-covered security guard wielding a shotgun. All angles are closed. Fence and flame, trapped between hell and safety. The pile of transformers has ignited; a wall of flaming PCBs blocks our path through the jagged, molten fence.

Another gunman. Red light blinds me. Another pellet of energy from God knows where falls into my reactor and I re-seize the initiative.

"Come on, Billy!"

"What? Where!"

I point the way and run. I don't know how thick the flaming wall of PCBs is. I'm going to have to hope. Gunshots. Jump. I clear the gap.

On the other side of the life/death barrier, I hit the ground and fall. Limp. Feet on fire.

I die.

A distant scream.

A noon whistle.

Lunchtime?

Out to.

Bright lights?

Nothing.

Streaking trails . . .

The city.

The window.

Upside down.

Red   blue   orange   all flashing.

And then

the

darkness

* * *

I'm trying to escape the darkness, slow-motion running through a thick, black, mucky swamp, sinking into deadly toxic waste that eats through my feet and chest like acid. Buried in the mud are razor-sharp objects that slice into my feet at every step, leaving them shredded, hanging on by ribbons. Sheets of broken glass.

Long, plastic hoses are attached to my body, flooding me with insecticides, and PCBs, and carbon tetrachloride, and lead, and all the various poisons I've been fighting, leaking into me. And the hoses start constricting around me until I can hardly breathe. Until I can't breathe. I manage to twist and find a slack spot so I can breathe again, but the hoses tighten and tighten again until I can't breathe. Again. This is it, I panic. This is it. No more breath.

Somewhere in the cold distance there is the sound of breaking glass.

And I slam into the hard darkness. I'm flat on my face, a great unseen weight pressing down on me. I'm alone, hugging my mother, the earth. Incredible, crushing weight. I push against it, but I can't break away. ¡No, mamí! Let me go! Please! Por favor, lo siento, mamí. I'm sorry, mamí, but please let me go. I promise I'll stop them. I'll stop them mamí. I'll try, I'll try, I'll try, but you've got to let me go on for a bit longer so I can do it . . . Yes . . . Gracias, mamí . . . Gracias . . . I promise I'll do everything I can to stop them . . .

I push away . . .

And I wake up to one more day of life.

"Jesus, Filomena, I told you not to exert yourself."

"Sorry, Doc. I saw my chance. I had to take it."

Another doctor pushes in beside Stan: "May we observe you? No one's ever run through a smoking cloud of PCBs before and lived to tell about it."

"Fuck off." I mean that in a nice way.

"Larry, why don't you leave us alone for a bit?" says Stan.

Larry goes, "Wohhh wohhh wohhhh!" and is gone.

"Filomena, this is not making me look good."

"Is that all you're concerned about?"

"No! And you know it! I'm concerned about *you*. You almost got yourself killed."

"Yeah. How about that."

"Now, we've determined that most of the pain that you felt was temporary, caused by the steel shards coated with toxic residue. They burned a lot, but almost all of those wounds are superficial. Much more serious are the burns on your feet and the damage to your lungs from smoke inhalation of God knows what chemicals and enough PCBs to—"

His voice trails off. He makes some vague gestures in the air with his hands.

"To what?"

"That's just it, Filomena. We have no data. No live human subjects exist that we can examine quantitatively. Running through a trough of flaming chemicals isn't considered a control experiment."

"So am I going to make you famous?"

"You're going to get me fired if you don't behave."

"Oh, come on . . ."

"I mean it!"

"Oh. Yes, sir."

"Now: I'm going to start you back on chemotherapy."

"Okay. Tomorrow."

"Why tomorrow?"

"Because I already feel enough like shit, okay? You got any painkillers? These burns are a real bitch."

"Filomena, it isn't ethical for me to attend you now that we're—"

"Fucking. The word you want is 'fucking.' "

"Must you speak that way?"

"I'll stop when you give me some painkillers."

He shakes his head. "Okay, okay."

Five minutes later he's back.

"I've got to go home," I say.

"Filomena, don't start that again—"

"My kid hasn't seen me in *two days*! Don't you know what that means? No, of course you don't. I'll stay in bed. I promise. As long as there's a phone."

"Why a phone?"

"To run a phone sex service. What do you think? To do some goddamn police work!"

"Keep your voice down! Please?"

I smile at him. "Close the door."

"Filomena—"

I grab his hand. I squeeze. "*Te deseo. Ahora.*" He's concerned. I pull him closer. It hurts. I hug him to me. I love it. "Close the door."

It locks from the inside.

We do it right there. Highly unethical. But the best medicine. With his help I have a shuddering orgasm that leaves me without feeling in my legs for a couple of minutes.

Or is that the painkillers?

Billy and Stan help carry me past Colomba's chicken coop and up the stairs to bed. Antonia clings to me like she almost forgot what I looked like. I sure like looking at her, too. I tell her Mommy has just a little more work to do, just a little, and that if she counts off five, hmm, make that seven days, then she'll have me for all time. So she counts to seven right away. I also tell her I'm not moving from our bed for three to five days. Stan will make sure of that.

"Boy, you really turned into the Toxic Avenger the other night," says Billy.

"Just what I've always wanted to be: A comic book superhero."

Colomba serves me breakfast in my sickbed. Toast, real coffee and two freshly laid chicken eggs, fried. Yum.

Stan, very severe, gives everyone in the house some last-minute instructions about what I'm not allowed to do, which is basically everything.

As soon as he's gone Billy and I get to work.

"Okay, what have you got?" I ask.

Billy that one-time wastrel has stolen half an armful of invoices from the billing office of Morse Techtonics *and* last year's Visitor's Log! He didn't even know about that! He just saw it and figured it might be useful. I pat him on the head and tell him, "See? There's something up there after all."

He smiles all awkward and shy like he's just been morphed into Tom Sawyer or something, but there's a tinge of pride in the smile, too. Real pride.

I flip through the log as fast as I can—it takes a couple of hours to decode all the hastily scribbled signatures—and I find enough public servants have been visiting Mr. Morse to fill the entire party ticket, and a few names that sound curiously reminiscent of some mid-level organized crime figures. I call Van Snyder. It sounds good to him so far, but of course it's not enough. Not yet.

We switch to the invoices. I call up the New York representative of Ergot Importers to ask about some model numbers. The guy can't seem to find the invoice. Imagine that. I call up the computer customizer. At least that's what the invoice says they are. They apologize for the shipping delay, which is odd, because I'm holding a copy of the bill of lading from the exporter, indicating that the shipment went out months ago. I call the exporter, and they find an original that verifies the shipping date.

And you know what's funny? I've called three different numbers in three different states and gotten three different people, but in the background a radio is playing *the same song at every one.*

WBIW. A local station.

13

All governments are brothers under the skin.   —MICHELET

Not that there's anything I can do with that information. Not yet. But at least Antonia's presence is no longer the only thing keeping me from slitting my throat. Now I have hope. Besides, it's pretty cute to watch a four-year-old attempt hip-hop steps, especially the head spins. She's got to watch less MTV.

She's an only child, so she wants to know all about family relations. I explain that Aunt Colomba is Daddy's sister, and that her three children, cousins Rosita, Elvis and Billy are brothers and sisters.

Antonia says, "I don't have a sister."

Oh, no: "Who talked to you about *that*?"

"Nobody."

"Uh-huh. Just like 'nobody' broke the jam jar this morning."

"That's right."

Bless her if that doesn't make me laugh. It hurts my stitches though.

Wai-Wai telephones to ask if I need cheering up. I tell her to come on over. Then I get a burst of inspiration, or anyway what passes for inspiration when you've been lying on your butt for three days. I call Gina and ask her to come. I figure between the two of them some sparks ought to fly and maybe we can get something done that'll lift me out of this funk hole.

Don't get me wrong. Stan's bedside visits are more than all right. But I can't kill this yearning.

I sleep and dream. I know it's a dream because of the upsidedown stuff. I'm gathering poisonous mushrooms, something you don't want to mess with, even in a dream. I'm making a soup. And I wake up thinking, What I wouldn't give for just *one* curaretipped blow dart.

Wai-Wai and Gina hit it off instantly. Colomba brings up some hot food, and soon we're all sitting around my sick bed, a network of subversive women, participating in the continuing chain of passing knowledge down from our foremothers to our children, working outside the system because the system has refused to recognize our problem.

"Oh, this is a hell of a case," says Gina. "Real charming. We found slop sinks that drain straight into the ground, and monitoring wells filled with crushed gravel to prevent us from taking samples: by the time you pull the sample up, half the stuff has volatilized."

"And what's left?" asks Wai-Wai.

"What's left? Carbon tetrachloride and trichloroethylene were the most commonly used solvents and cleaning agents in the onsite buildings. They were stored in drums and open evaporation pits that leached into the soil and groundwater."

Wai-Wai says, "Aside from volatilizing into the air—"

"Wait, there's more," says Gina. "Some of the longtime employees remember an explosion in warehouse six, seventeen years ago, but due to the classified nature of the incident, they do not know the details. Most of the witnesses are dead, prematurely, from chronic improper exposure to hazardous chemicals. We found one former employee who worked there when it was still Prosystems who believed that PCB-filled waste oil was dispersed by spreading it on the site's dirt roads."

"Back when Morse owned the site?" I ask.

"Yep."

"So is there any reason to believe that he's not doing the same at his new place?"

"Why not? But he's stopped us at the door so I can't go in there without a warrant. Even with a toxic disaster next door to worry about. Give me another day or two."

"But the Morse site looks so innocent, nice landfills with trees on top," says Wai-Wai.

"Ninety percent of Superfund sites are like that. That's part of the danger. They do not 'look' like toxic-waste dumps. The poison was dumped twenty years ago, and it's all underground with twenty-foot trees growing on top of it. But by the time you detect lead in the drinking water, the neighborhood kids have all got permanent brain damage."

Pause.

"*Madre de Dios,*" says Colomba.

"You said it, sister," I say.

"*¿Y para qué pagamos tantos impuestos?*"

"What did she say?" asks Gina.

"Gina, you work in New York City *and* Puerto Rico," I say. "It's about time you learned some Spanish besides '*buenos días*' and '*otra cerveza, por favor.*' She wants to know where all our taxes go."

"Oh, that. I've dug up some real classy info on that, too. Did you know that the town of East Carthage is a fiction? It does not exist in any common sense of the term. The site perimeter, one foot outside the fence, is incorporated as the town of East Carthage. It's an autonomous tax shelter, untouchable by your town authorities."

"They going to elect a president and start issuing their own money?" I ask.

"They have already, in a sense. They're immune from the town health agencies."

"Well, that explains a lot."

"Unfortunately, volatile poisons do not respect town limits."

"Tell me more about the chemistry of this site," says Wai-Wai.

"Well, for one, those open evaporation pits are a major threat to the aquifers."

"The what?" I ask.

"Nice, clean pockets of underground drinking water," says Wai-Wai.

Gina continues: "They also used to deliberately blow up transformers to test what to do in the event of an explosion. They learned a lot about building better transformers, but they scattered PCBs over the entire neighborhood. I mean, a few nanograms of PCBs in the water is enough to increase the risk of cancer by a factor of seventy."

"But aren't PCB concentrations usually higher in sediment and suspended matter than in the associated water column?" says Wai-Wai.

"Yes, because of the high soil adsorption constants for PCBs."

"What about low-level exposures due to bioaccumlation and slow excretion of PCBs?"

"There's a real lack of quantitative data concerning the pharmacokinetics of PCBs following inhalation and dermal exposure."

"Not anymore," I say, cynically.

"They're not entirely lacking," says Wai-Wai, pulling out a sheet of Antonia's drawing paper. She purloins a red crayon and draws two hexagons connected by a single bond. She makes the hexagons mirror images by assigning numbers and their primes to symmetrical angles, finishing up with two arms descending parallel to each other from the center of both hexagons. "These are the chlorides. There can be anywhere from zero to five of them. PCBs would tend to distribute to the liver and muscle tissue, because of their lipophilicity, then they'd be redistributed to the fat, skin and other fat-containing organs."

She turns to the rest of us: "That's why fattier fishes like bluefish tend to contain more PCBs. Stick to the lean bland ones, like flounder." Bluefish is local, plentiful in Long Island Sound.

"What about embryotoxicity and fetotoxicity?"

Gina says, "It's severe. Embryos, fetuses and neonates generally lack the hepatic microsomal enzyme systems that facilitate detoxification and excretion of PCBs."

"Have you done capillary column gas chromatography with electron capture detection?"

"Sure, there's been a significant increase in the use of mass spectrometry detectors, but most labs rely on electron capture detectors, which are more sensitive in electron ionization mode—"

"Of course. Two or three times as sensitive."

"Right."

And I lie back, just listening to the two of them speaking to each other, confident and comfortable dealing in complex technological terminology that I won't even attempt to reproduce, unmediated by performance for the benefit of male superiors, who still think of women as either helpless bimbos or frigid brains. Or superwomen.

Ouch. My butt hurts. No superwoman here.

Just watching them work: Slouched on twin beds, Wai-Wai on her stomach, raised up on her elbows, feet in the air reading off Gina's data reports, Gina sitting in faux–lotus position directly across from her, batting around more data between them than two chips in the old Unisystems 1200. It's like a pyjama party. Well, almost. I wonder, would men sit like this? Oh, why am I analyzing everything?

They must notice my eyes glazing over because Wai-Wai says, "Fil's getting tired. We better go."

"No, no," I say, waking up. They laugh.

"Okay, see you later. Take care." Wai-Wai bends over to shake Colomba's hand good-bye, but Colomba is cradling a sleeping Antonia. "See ya."

"Bye." Wai-Wai goes.

"Well, the same for me too—"

"Wait, Gina."

"Yes?"

"Come here. Sit down."

Gina sits next to me. Colomba's slipping Antonia into the other bed. I ask: "What about Morse?"

"Can't touch him yet, Fil. But we're going to hurt him. I've got Department of Justice authorization to relocate affected residents temporarily, provide alternate water supplies for the community, and begin excavation and pumping of hazardous substances for treatment and disposal throughout the entire Kim Tungsten site. That's going to block his takeover bid—and the bank loan defaults in three days. Oh yeah: We're going to mess him up bad."

"Thanks, Gina."

"Of course this is not what he deserves."

"How do you mean?"

"I mean, he deserves *worse*."

Colomba turns out the light over Antonia's bed and quietly says good night to us.

"Gina, did you ever have a case that just ate you up inside?"

"Sure. Lots of times."

"Like what?"

"Well—nah."

"No, tell me about it."

"Okay. It was out in Jersey. There was a public water supply contaminant: One substance. Now, that's pretty rare—"

"Especially for Jersey."

"Yeah, yeah. I mean, it was so bad the Health Department issued a public warning to boil the water. Well, one company was found using the one contaminant—they were dumping it in a seepage pit. They had actually tried to fix it. They spent eight hundred thousand dollars digging it up, aerating it, reburying it. It was naturally flushing to below fifty ppb. But once it's on the Superfund list, it can't get off. There's no bureaucratic mechanism for taking a site off the list. So many offenders try to block us, delay us or belittle me personally for being a woman, but not these guys: It was a black-owned business, the only one in the neighborhood that had provided steady employment for minorities. It wasn't a big place, maybe thirty or forty employees, but it was all they had. The two owners weren't worth more than a couple of hundred thousand. And one of them had a retarded daughter who was eating up every penny he was making in health-care costs.

"He opened up his entire financial record for me. And it was all there. He was telling the truth. But even after they spent eight hundred thousand dollars and almost completely eliminated the problem, the machine of governmental procedure forced me to seize their assets and push them into bankruptcy."

We sit there. I look over at Antonia. Sweet, innocent Antonia. Dreaming with the angels. Puchungo curled up next to her, purring.

A crisis of conscience in the profession.

Gina says, "Why didn't I just lose the file behind the radiator?"

I squeeze her hand. "Yeah. You probably should have, you just didn't know it at the time."

Gina nods. "You have days like that when you were a cop?"

"Constantly."

"What was the worst?'

"The worst? That's a tough one."

"All right. Just a representative sample."

I smile at her regulation metaphor.

"Okay. We were in the middle of the annual August crime wave, when two unlucky gents picked the wrong victim: He was carrying a gun and he shot them both in self-defense, killing one and leaving the other in a wheelchair. The community hailed him as a hero. This was at the height of the crack wars, and the citizens needed a guy like him to rally around. It didn't help any that the criminals were black and the victim was white. Now the two guys were low-level career criminals, with about twenty counts each of burglary, assault—meaning muggings—but no battery. No violence against them at all. That seemed pretty unusual, so I did a little checking, and it turned out that the 'victim' had been arrested a few times for spraying racist graffiti on buildings and for beating up immigrants, queers, and, one time, a black Good Humor man.

"So I ask around, real low-key, and find a couple of witnesses who say the two guys were just sitting on the front steps not bothering anybody at that moment, when this other guy walks up and shoots them both so quick and easy they thought it was a hit and laid low with their story for days. So now I've got a problem: our 'victim' is a racist pig who just murdered a black man. Racial tension was already pretty high because of the Bumpurs case. So I took it to my sergeant. He says, 'Put it back in the box, Fil.' The guy's a hero, and there's no way anyone's going to bring him up on murder charges during an election year. I ask him: 'So we let him go on being a hero?' He says: 'I guess so. . . . ' "

Pause.

"Why do people kill each other, Gina? Why? Just to show whose balls are bigger? Just to get more for themselves? Is that *it*?"

We listen to Antonia breathe.

"Good night, Fil. Catch you in the morning."

"Good night."

Not quite. A phone rings a little after 3 A.M. If this is another goddamn threat—it's Billy. He's been arrested. I ask him to hand the
phone over to a cop and the cop explains, "Traces of marijuana
were found on the floor of the vehicle."

"Traces? What the hell does 'traces' mean?" He describes it to
me. Turns out to be some flecks, like maybe .002 mg and a seed.

"*Whaaaat?* That can't be significant."

The cop asks me what I mean.

"I mean a few flecks and a seed are not enough to convict someone of possession. An amount that small could have come from
anywhere."

"You know something about the other drivers of the vehicle?"

Forget it. I limp out of bed, fire shooting through my feet, and
wake Colomba. She gets dressed and goes off to the police station.
What a night. Even the chickens are clucking. I watch her go and
then put the kettle on and sit down at the kitchen table to think.
I'm all the way up to "What kind of tea should I have?" when I hear
a clank outside, like a raccoon at the garbage can. I get up—
ouch!—and get the broom. And I hobble over towards the back
door just in time to see it kicked open with a loud splintering of
jambs, and two guys with Smith & Wessons come in. Hinge pins
clatter on the floor behind me.

"Well, well," says the one on the right. "Look who keeps late
hours."

I've never seen either one of them.

I warn them: "Careful, guys. Remember, the kitchen is the most
dangerous room in the house."

They look at each other and smirk. Back to me.

"Wrong. It's the bathroom," says the one on the right.

"Relax, babe, we're just here to scare you," says the idiot on
the left.

"All right. I'm scared. Now beat it."

"Why you fucking bitch!" He starts towards me.

"Easy, Joey," says the one on the right. Obviously the brains of the outfit. "We're just here to make sure Miss Buscarsela gets the message to stay out of other people's business."

"Fine. Message received. Now beat it."

The smirks again.

"No, we really gotta do this," says Joey, advancing.

Then the brains makes a mistake: "The kid's in the first bedroom at the top of the stairs." And I guess I go mad. Cursing a mother's curse as I lunge forward, I jab the idiot in the stomach with the broom then swing around and deliver a Bronx Bomber uppercut that deflects the brain's weapon up as it smacks him on the chin. A silenced bullet rips through the ceiling.

Joey's down and I follow through with a whack to his head that nearly knocks him out. The brain throws his weight against me— that's his second mistake—ripping open my stitches, and the pain sears through me, screaming intense nerve signals that I channel to anger and fear that leave my body through the swift ruthlessness of a fighting animal. I go for maximum damage, throwing him off me into the dishrack full of knives and glasses. It makes a lovely sound.

There is a moment of dreamlike clumsiness as pots are thrown, faces bashed and fingers mashed in cabinet doors and silverware drawers, and all the while guns are going off, one silenced, one loud.

I go for the quiet one first, clubbing the brain as hard as I can. The broom cracks in two on his head and a last-second instinct stops me from delivering a deadly stroke to a vital organ—as he goes down my aim shifts slightly and I impale him in the side with it. I hear screaming. I knock the gun out of the brain's hand and sweep it away into the hallway. Then I go after Joey, who's trying to stand up. I grab his gun hand and swing around and put a hold on him from behind, locking my fists around his gun. He stomps on my foot. "*Yow! shit!* That's supposed to be a woman's move, asshole!" I bring both fists up to his throat and dig my knee into his kidney, bringing him down hard, deliberately smacking his skull on the linoleum-covered cement.

But he's a tough sucker and he's still wriggling. He points the gun at me but I'm not there anymore, because somehow in my furiosity I'm biting down hard on his gun hand and pulling him to his feet by his hair and dragging him over to the stove where the flame has been making the kettle steam away like mad for I don't know how long. Joey's hand jerks involuntarily and harmlessly empties his gun into the clock over the stove. I give my teeth a rest. Now the brain is still moving so I kick the kettle at him. He curses me as the scalding water seeps through his clothes, but he stays down. The idiot figures it's his chance and he elbows me in the abdomen. Fortunately I've got some heavy bandages on there to keep me from exerting myself but it still hurts like a bandsaw cutting through me and I singe the guy's hair on the gas jet and warn him: "Don't do that again, *do you hear me?*"

He complains. I grab a can of soup from the counter and throw it on the burner two inches in front of his face. The label catches fire. The brain's starting to get up again but who cares?

"Not a good idea," I say. "One more inch and your partner takes home a flame-broiled face."

The brain says, "Jesus."

They must think they've taken on a she-devil. And tonight, they have. I'm holding the guy's face up to the can heating on the stove. It's starting to glow.

He manages to speak: "We'll both die."

I say, "No, *you'll* die. I'm already going to die. Haven't you idiots figured that out yet? Now: you ever even *hint* of doing *anything* to my little girl and I will *cut off your balls and feed them to you,* then I will *slit open your stomach and strangle you with your own intestines.* You got that? YOU GOT THAT?!!"

"Yeah! Yeah! Let go of me!"

"Good!" I throw on an insulated glove and knock the red-hot can off the stove. Then I let go of the idiot but I yank the heating iron from the stove because he swings the gun at my head and I have to brand his face with it.

"AAAAAAAAAAAAAAAAAAAAAAAHHHHHHHHH!"

"Come *on,*" says the brain, ducking out. "She's too crazy to hold."

"You got that right!" I curse them, brandishing the red-hot iron in front of me like a charm against vampires.

But I did it. I actually have put the fear of motherhood into these extremely seasoned tough guys.

Click!

I curse and turn. Antonia has just pulled the trigger on an empty chamber. I grab the gun from her. "Goddamn you don't you *ever* do that!" I slap her. Hard. And I immediately regret it, fall to my knees and hug Antonia tight like I'm never going to let go ever.

But of course I have to someday.

Contaminating my kid. It was bound to happen. How many times has she heard me say that I'd like to kill Morse? I've got to stop teaching her that crap.

There's blood on the floor. I'd better mop it up.

It's just that when I think of Morse, and what I'd like to do to him, I become a deranged animal. But as the waves of rage recede I remember my teaching, that violence is to be avoided at all costs, as a final resort when all other options have been exhausted. And I know the law on "self defense"—you have to have exhausted all other options. I know I haven't. I can still flee. No dishonor there. It's the law.

And yet . . .

I tell Antonia, "I'm sorry I'm sorry I'm sorry I love you I love you I love you I love you—" Words are not enough.

And I bargain with God. Oh, how I bargain. And when it's over, Antonia says to me, "You're not mad."

And I tell her, "No, I'm not mad."

I'm just pissed off.

My feet are bleeding and it feels like I'm walking on knives. I limp to the phone and pick it up. It's Colomba. She's gotten Billy out on bail, but he has to go back if the drug test turns out positive, which he says he'll pass with no problem. I murmur understanding. I don't tell her what happened to her kitchen. Somehow, I can't come up with the words. Maybe later.

Anyone who says the bathroom is the most dangerous room in the house doesn't know my house.

I sit there for a moment, then I call Gina. The sun's up, right?

Gina's voice: "Another damn phone call *for what?*"

"Did I wake you?"

I hear her fumbling for the clock. "No, I'm always awake at five A.M."

"Good. I'm in trouble."

"You sure are."

"Can you arrange a meeting with Morse?"

I need stitches re-sewn, fresh bandages, the works.

I call the hospital. "Stan, I've *got* to go out."

"Not without a wheelchair."

"Then *get* me a wheelchair."

14

A man with about as much mental agility as a lump of lead or a block of wood, a man whose utter stupidity is paralleled only by his immorality, can have lots of good, intelligent people at his beck and call, just because he happens to possess a large pile of gold coins.

—THOMAS MORE, *Utopia*

I commit several felonies today. First I break and enter Reggie Einhorn's place for something of his manufactured by the Colt Corporation of Hartford, Connecticut: "Only eight pieces," he told me. "Easy to break down . . ."

The EPA is all over Kim Tungsten Steel and Glass, and when the workers find out about the dangers they've been facing, they vote to go on strike for safer working conditions, shutting down production and forever killing Morse's takeover bid. Gina comes by in a company-issued van with wheelchair accommodations and U.S. government plates.

"Got an ejector seat?" I ask.

"Just about," says Gina, helping me fold up the wheelchair and throw it in the back.

"What are we going through all this for? I bet Morse's place isn't wheelchair accessible."

"Good. That's one more summons I can throw on him."

We climb in and she starts the van.

"You're really looking forward to this, aren't you?" I ask.

"I just want a level playing field for the final shoot-out."

We drive past the massive deployment of toxic avengers all over the Kim site. Gina's investigation team now believes that a propane leak caused the fire, which then spread to the toxic storage area. I wonder out loud if Gina really thinks they can clean up that mess.

"Well, flushing out twenty years of underground leaching isn't like mopping up spilled milk off your kitchen floor. It can be pretty hard to get the public to understand that. They always seem to think 'modern science' can fix everything in about a week. Sometimes I wish we could boil it all down to a nice, slick Madison Avenue sound bite, like: 'The EPA: Tough on dirt, gentle on your lawn.'"

"That's fine for the suburban market, but what about the inner cities?"

"Oh, I've got one for that, too: 'EPA: As nasty as the crap we clean up.'"

"Yeah, and maybe a radio jingle, like: 'What you gonna do/When your baby turns blue?'"

Gina laughs.

"They don't want science, they want magic," I say. "But you can't uncook an egg."

We're on the highway now, and a driver speeding along at about 90 mph comes up behind us and has to brake. Upset by this, he tailgates us for the next two miles, clearly expecting us to get out of his way. The middle lane is clear, but he flashes his lights as if to say: "You're in my way."

I got in Morse's way, and he killed me for it. And he's gonna pay for that.

Now the guy's honking at us. Gina finally signals and pulls right. The guy takes off again at 90 mph. Asshole.

"You know. I still remember all of Morse's license plate numbers? The stretch limo, the Mercedes and the Jaguar? It's been years."

"I know what you mean. I get the same way, waking up in the middle of the night with chemical shipment serial numbers coalescing in my brain."

"Sick, isn't it?"

"Uh-huh . . ."

We pull into Morse Techtonics and stop right in front of the door. No hunting for a parking space for us, not with these government plates. Gina makes a big show of operating the hydraulic lift so I can come down to earth in my wheelchair. She scorns the security guard's help and lifts me onto the curb, then opens the door for me so I can wheel myself in. I don't have to put on an act. I really am in considerable pain from my unplanned exertion last night. We sign the shiny new visitor's log, pass inspection with the handheld metal detector—my chair keeps setting it off, so the guard finally pats me down to make sure.

Gina punches the elevator button and we wait. Okay, I'll admit my heart is pounding and my palms are cold and clammy in this June heat. Right on time for our appointment.

Gina is told that Morse is in a meeting and will be with us in about an hour. She doesn't accept that. She flashes her U.S. Government Inspector's ID and announces that Mr. Morse will see us *now*. Then we go in and break up the meeting. I must say I'm quite a sight with my bandages, blisters and wheelchair. The meeting is definitely over. They all leave except Morse and some guy who works as a beer-hall bouncer in the off-season when he can't get work in his regular line tossing railroad ties.

Morse explains: "My lawyer's here because Miss Buscarsela gets a little—excited around me, as the record will indicate. So I need protection."

Because I have nothing left to lose.

Gina introduces herself and gets down to business: "I'm putting Kim Tungsten on the list of Superfund sites, and I'm initiating a full investigation of the acreage surrounding Morse Techtonics."

Morse is not fazed. "You can't do that. It doesn't belong on the Superfund list. Okay, it's not clean. No place is clean. Any industrial facility is dirty."

"Thanks for that bit of information," Gina responds. "I know that you're speculating on four hundred and fifty acres of undeveloped land just north of your fence. The land is worth real money if designated as clean, but is practically worthless if your site goes on the National Priorities List."

Morse smiles. "I think we're beginning to understand each other." He makes a gesture to the tie tosser, who reaches into his inner pocket. I cringe instinctively. Morse gets a chuckle out of that. What the hell, I reach under my blanket and start reassembling Reggie's Colt All-American. In separate pieces, the parts were small enough to fit snugly against the chair's metal framing and get through the security check.

The tie tosser takes out a cashier's check for $10,000 made out to CASH. He lays it horizontally across Morse's desk in front of Gina's eyes.

I say, "You call *that* a bribe? Don't insult us, Morse."

Morse, trying to get me: "So you *are* a whore, I just can't afford you."

Pause.

Me: "Right. So?"

Morse nods to the tie tosser, who produces another cashier's check with $25,000 cut across it in big red numbers.

Gina continues, "We've detected PCB concentrations in the soils ranging from less than one to thirty-three parts per billion at the common border between Kim Tungsten and Morse Techtonics. This is sixty times the proposed limit, and this contamination has leached into the groundwater. Gas chromatography–mass spectrometry procedures have recently been developed to determine milligram-per-kilogram levels of PCBs in women's breast milk. Some of the neighborhood children have already absorbed more PCBs than an adult worker breathing high concentrations of PCBs in the workplace for one year."

The tie tosser has one more check. $50,000. Tax free.

But not interest free.

Gina's answer: "One eight-month-old infant had gastritis, which progressed to hypertrophy and hyperplasia of the gastric mucosa, producing mucus-filled cysts that penetrated the surrounding tissue."

Morse waves the checks away, the tie tosser makes them disappear. No more Mr. Nice Guy. "All right, enough of this shit. We're not guilty of any environmental violations and you know it. It's just *her*, trying to get me. Al?"

The tie tosser produces another paper from his inner pocket. It's a summons. For me. I'm being sued for harassment. There's a twist.

I say, "You know, maybe you didn't hear what happened to those two goons you sent to scare me away last night."

"I don't have any idea what you're talking about."

"Yeah. Right. How did they know that Billy wasn't in the house? You know you really screwed up, sending them only ten minutes after Billy was arrested. But thanks to the call, I was up—and they weren't expecting *that*."

"Jesus, listen to these allegations!" says Morse. To his "lawyer": "You taking this down?"

"Yes, sir." He doesn't move.

Gina says, "If I may continue: The EPA's disposal rules for PCBs typically require that materials be disposed of in chemical-waste landfills or destroyed in high-temperature incinerators or high-efficiency boilers."

"You can't pin me with that," says Morse. "That site's been Kim Tungsten's since 1986."

"The disposal rules were published in the July 1984 Code of Federal Regulations, section forty, part seven sixty-one. You owned the site then."

"Don't try to hit me retroactively: I'll throw more lawyers in your face than you've ever seen."

"More than the Department of Justice?"

"Look, who knows what products that we use today, *legally*, twenty years from now you're gonna find out they're cancerous?"

"The penalties for improper disposal of radioactives like uranium hexafluoride are even more severe."

"We never used uranium hexafluoride."

"There was a release of uranium hexafluoride gas eleven months ago. It turned to a white powder and was found on your side of the property marker. This is documented. We also found carbon tetrachloride—"

"Hey, hey: People used to use carbon tet for home dry cleaning. I bet your mom used it to take spots out of the rug."

"Don't talk about my mother." Gina glares at him.

"I'm calling for judicial review of every one of the Agency's decisions."

"Delay all you want," says Gina. "The longer you delay, the worse the environmental damage, the more you'll have to pay in the end."

She gets him with the only thing he understands: Money.

"And what if I cooperate? After all, I provide a lot of jobs, and computers are a new, clean technology."

Gina smiles. "I think we're beginning to understand each other. But the colorless chemical by-products of your manufacture of adhesives and plastic computer casings are just as deadly as the black clouds of soot produced by the old, dirty industries."

Morse says, "I beg to differ—"

Gina: "Oh, stop pretending! You probably think the appearance of cooperation will help you delay long enough to disband Morse Techtonics and form some other corporation that'll be untouchable for another few years."

"Can't I?"

Gina's starting to loose her cool, it's my turn to take the relay. "Please leave us alone."

The tie tosser says, "Huh?"

"Get going."

It takes a moment, but Morse gives his approval and the big guy steps around the desk.

He brushes close to me. I can feel the floorboards bend under his weight.

Gina looks at me like she's not sure she should leave me, but I tell her, "Go ahead."

"Okay . . . I'll be right outside."

They both leave us. Morse is probably taping the whole conversation anyway. But I don't care.

I tell him, "I'm making a citizen's arrest."

"You can't do that."

I quote from the scripture. No, not that scripture. This one: " 'A private person may arrest or prevent escape in cases of murder, manslaughter one, robbery, rape or sodomy and in immediate flight therefrom.' I charge you with all of the above, but I'll settle for First Degree Murder."

"Who am I supposed to have killed?"

"Me."

He laughs. "Have fun making *that* stick."

"And what is this garbage?" I say, throwing the summons back across the desk at him. "Somebody's been harassing the hell out of me and it wasn't the county officials you've been corrupting because they're not smart enough to do it. No, this took planning. First the child abuse allegations—that was you all over, Sammy, hitting me where it hurts the most, then there was the guy with the wrench—you shouldn't work so cheap, Sammy—then last night—"

"You continue and I'll sue you for libel and I'll win."

"So you *are* taping the conversation, huh?"

Still doesn't faze him. "My lawyers will blow your brains out."

"Not before I blow out yours."

"Oh, good, here come the threats."

"Turn up the volume, I don't care."

"What was it you said to me? 'I'll cut off your dog's paws'? Was that really you?"

"No."

"Let me give you some advice—"

"No, don't. Your advice tends to stick in my throat. It's a real choke hazard."

"Just trying to do business."

"How much money are you worth, anyway, Sammy? How much?"

"Have you considered psychotherapy?"

"I know just *one* of your corporations is bringing in twenty percent a year on an eighty-four-million-dollar investment. That's an annual profit of sixteen to seventeen million dollars. That's not enough? Why the rest? Why?"

"There is no such thing as too much money. In fact, I'm thinking of shifting some of my interests to South America. There's tons of money to be made investing in Third World development."

"And I thought I warned you to stay the hell out of my hemisphere."

"Keep talking, babe, the tape's rolling."

"Oh shut the fuck up! And stop smiling at me."

"You got a short fuse, honey."

"Not as short as yours. *I* don't kill people that get in my way. That is, until today."

I throw aside the blanket and raise the Colt level with Morse's chest. No reason to take a chance on missing him just to splatter his head. His hand edges toward the desk panel.

"Don't *move*," I snap at him. "Touch that and I sneeze."

He stops. He waits. He says, "Just like old times, huh?"

I tell him, "You know, last night I hit my kid. Hard. I hurt her. If I can hurt the one person I love the most in all this world, *imagine* what I can do to the ones I *hate*."

He might be getting a little worried. "What do you want?" he asks.

"I want you to suffer. I want your lungs to burn up from inside, just like mine. But there's no time for that. So this will have to do."

"What?"

"I've forgiven a lot of criminals over the years. But a gleeful serial killer like *you*—"

"What's with you?"

"Sorry, I guess some people just die more gracefully than others."

"Wha—what are you talking about?"

"You mean, you don't know? And I thought you had feelers everywhere. You see? Even *I* thought you were omniscient. I'm dying, asshole! I'm dying of lung cancer thanks to you and your fucking methyl isocyanate."

"It'll never hold up in court."

I stand up out of the wheelchair and lean on his desk. The gun's about two feet from his heart. No problem there.

"Boy, you really are dumb, aren't you? Haven't you figured out yet that I'm here *because* it'll never hold up in court? And that in a few weeks I'll be beyond their reach anyway? Haven't you figured that out yet?"

This is turning into a replay of the scene we had several years ago. Only this time I'm not thinking of the future. I've got him.

"Okay," he says. "Okay. So maybe we can make a deal."

"You're forgetting one thing."

"Uh, what?"

"Morse, this is *me*. Remember? The woman you murdered."
Well, *finally* he's starting to look a little worried.

"Wait: I can explain that—"

"Explain *what*? I'm the star witness in the case against you. I
can't pin my murder on you, I can't pin criminal neglect of a thousand workers on you, I can't even pin the toxic dumping and cor-
ruption of local officials on you, but there is a *higher* court of law
that considers it a crime to inflict unnecessary anguish, and you
are guilty as hell, Sammy, and the judge is passing sentence." I lean
the gun closer.

"I've seen this act before. This is the part where you threaten
to—"

I smash him across the face with the gun. My feet twist on broken glass as I re-open my stitches again. I can feel warm, wet blood
leaking out through the bandages.

"*That's* for leaving my child motherless."

He'll carry *that* scar for a while.

When he recovers, I say, "You know, this is probably my last
chance to kill you. . . ."

"What do you want?" he asks.

"I want you to tremble and die." I press the barrel against his
bloody lips. His eyes flit up to meet mine. Oh yeah: he knows I'm
not going to miss at this distance. His eyes show it: He *knows* he is
about to die. That's the look I've been waiting for. My finger tight-
ens. My lips are starting to form the word, "asshole," but instead
his arm flails out in a final self-preservationist effort, knocking
some framed photos to the floor, cracking the glass.

And I stop.

One of the pictures shows a smiling, white-haired old woman
with her arms wrapped lovingly around Mr. Samuel F. Morse.

Only now do I draw back a bit and look at the other pictures
scattered across his desk. Family pictures.

"That your mother, Sam?"

Long pause.

"Yah." A puff of breath.

"What does she think of you?"

Longer pause.

I say: "She doesn't know, does she?"

He shakes his head once: No.

"She thinks you're the greatest, doesn't she?"

Yes.

"Ah, *shit*."

I can't kill somebody's kid.

And I strike a deal that makes me sick. "You leave me alone and I'll leave you alone."

"Okay."

"That means tearing up that summons, erasing the tapes and telling your 'lawyer' you cut yourself shaving."

"Okay." Barely audible.

"Okay?"

"Okay."

"That's better. And get your mother something special."

In the van, I just let it out: "He's covered a hundred different ways and he *knows* it! Dammit! *¡Carajo! ¡Maldito malu jillu! ¡Cay isma allcucuna!*" and I pound the dashboard in frustration.

Gina says, "Well, I'm glad to see you're not getting emotional about this."

"Take me home."

"Right."

Gina drives me back to Minoa, where I check into the Heartbreak Hotel and stay there in the bluest room for five days. Billy helps drive me up to the hospital twice a day for chemotherapy that makes me nauseous.

One morning Morse's picture is in the paper, and Antonia says to me, "He's bad."

I say, "That's right." But how did she know that? I didn't tell her anything.

No answer. Elsewhere in the paper, three pounds of heroin were seized in a Central Islip couple's basement, and gang members shot a sixteen-year-old girl in Mineola, mistakenly thinking that she was calling the police to rat on them. *Madre de Dios*. And a congressional panel probing a housing scandal involving the junior senator's Long Island office was indignant after the town official skipped out on his testimony and left them interviewing an empty chair.

Stan tries to be encouraging, saying that the dark blotches on my lungs don't appear to have advanced any, that I might be going into remission because of the chemotherapy and I'm beginning to accept it, but I'm still at about the lowest point in my life, alternating between being in a depressed stupor and angrily reprimanding myself for being in a depressed stupor, when I get a call. It's Kelly.

"You want to go the beach?"

"Sure, I need a break from all this riotous living."

Kelly drives down to pick us up. My feet are getting better. Stan said it was okay to walk, but I can't go in the water yet. Kelly is amazed that I still have to carry a whole bag for Antonia's snacks, beach toys, extra clothes in case of a bathroom accident.

"I always travel light," she says. "Carry-on is the only way to go. No hassles."

"Except you can't carry weapons in carry-on luggage."

"Uh, true . . . Fil, are you okay?"

"No, but I guess I will be, soon."

That stops conversation for a while. We go to the Old Town beach. It's got amusements for kids, and I push Antonia around on one of those small merry-go-round type things. Sheesh! Who needs drugs when you've got this thing? Leave *me* wasted. In fact, I have to get off and sit down and suppress the urge to retch again. This chemotherapy is really getting me down.

But Antonia's in a good mood. After she's tried all the rides, the swings, the slide, the rocking duck, we walk down the beach. She's just happy to be with me again.

I tell Kelly: "You know what I love about kids? They love you for who you are. No payoffs, suck-ups or sweetheart deals. They love you because you're Mommy."

Kelly nods.

I ask, "So how's your work going?"

She sighs. "I feel like I'm an assembly line worker in an information factory. And they keep lowering the admission standards. You know, ninety-eight used to have to be your average, not your body temperature."

I tell her, "It could be worse. My schoolteacher had to teach four grades at once and scrub the floor afterwards."

"Yeah, well we're coming back to that."

I stand and stare at the wide expanse of water that might as well be the ocean. "A one-room schoolhouse in the Andes. All they cared about was keeping us quiet, separating the boys from the girls, and putting us in alphabetical order for *everything*. Buscarsela. I was always second or third. I *never* had time to be ready. To think. I always screwed up. As you can see, it scarred me for life."

Kelly laughs. "I was always right in the middle, so average and boring. Even when we went in size order."

"That never worked for me either—a tall girl by *mestiza* standards. No, all we had were muddy boots, rubber stamp–wielding bureaucrats and hundred-year-old textbooks that tried to pound Colonial-style order into our little heads."

I swing Antonia through the air and let her down. We walk along the beach holding hands. "Oh, I'll be watching out for Antonia in school." From wherever I am . . . "I don't want her to have her sensibility crushed by standardized tests and fascist administrators."

"Mm-hmm."

"She's almost four now. That means I can't screw up anymore, 'cause she's old enough to remember it now."

"Is that why you're so upset about giving up?"

Silence is my answer.

After a while, I say, "It's clear in my head, I guess, but I don't know how to put it. That kind of thinking always loses something in translation."

"I've got news for you."

"What?"

"Plato had the same problem."

"He did?"

"Yes."

"My, my. Thank you, Kelly."

Kelly says, "I'm going to go in. Want to come?"

"I can't."

I sit and watch her swim while Antonia goes around collecting shells and throwing rocks into the water. She comes to me with something in her hands. It's a syringe covered with seaweed. I tell her it's garbage and throw it away.

"Here's a shell with some purple in it."

"Cool!"

That kid. She's sifting water with her hands, trying to bring it to the beach.

She observes, "We get it and we don't get it."

I just sit on the beach watching one medium flow into another.

If you stare long enough, things begin to come alive. You see more than just water, carbon, minerals, green stuff. You see yourself. It's what we're made of, too. In the same proportions the planet has.

There are always other ways of making the pieces fit.

I admire Kelly's swimming. If she were an animal, she'd be a dolphin—sleek, vivacious, flexible and full of youthful energy—and the most intelligent animal in the sea. She swims a few imaginary laps, then comes out, wet and glistening and brimming with the brightest eyes. We all sit holding hands until she dries off.

Kelly points to the horizon. "On a clear day you can see the Bridgeport stacks. That's nearly thirty miles away."

"You mean, on an unpolluted day you can see the source of all the pollution?"

"I guess that would be the cynic's way of putting it...."

I throw a rock and watch it splash.

Kelly says, "It took that rock four hundred years to cover that distance and now look what you've done. Shakespeare was alive when that rock was last out there."

"Sorry. Four hundred years?"

"Sure. During the Pleistocene ice age, the glaciers advanced this far, stopped here, melted and created Long Island. It's called a 'terminal moraine'."

"How do you know that? I thought you were a literature student."

"Eighth grade earth science. Required on Long Island."

"Oh."

She picks up a wet rock.

Antonia says, "They're so pretty."

Kelly says, "That's quartz, baby, commonest rock on earth. They were smoothed by the glaciers over ten thousand years ago."

"Ten thousand *years* ago!" says Antonia, astonished, as if no number could possibly be that big.

"This granite came all the way down from New Hampshire."

"Wow. How long did it take?"

"Well, they move slower than an inch a year, if I remember Mr. Lattimer's lectures properly."

"I'm sure you do."

"See those dunes? That cove was created in 1930 when they dug up the beach sand and shipped it to New York City to mix into the concrete for the Empire State Building. There's a piece of this beach in the Empire State Building."

"Really."

"And the sand and gravel deposits left by the glaciers created the underground springs, which is why we have such good drinking water."

"Until now."

"Hmm."

"I mean, my fate is sealed. But what about Antonia? And Billy? And you? You ever get the feeling God is going to show up one day like a parent in a teenager's bedroom and say, 'Will you *look* at this mess? You are grounded, young humanity.'"

" 'No more space flight until you straighten this place up.' "

"Exactly." We get up and start walking some more.

"Personally, I'd like to keelhaul the frigging lot of them," says Kelly.

"No, don't do that. Nail some of the suckers to the mast."

Kelly laughs. "Yes, but you have to remember to blunt the points first. When you nail someone to the mast, you don't want to split the mast."

"Boy, Kelly. Isn't that the stereotype? That all you old North Shore WASPs know all about sailing?"

"I guess. Funny. When you're a WASP, you don't really think of yourself as belonging to an ethnicity."

"You're as ethnic as I am, Kelly."

"Yeah, I guess so. Say, you know what we're near?" she says, pointing up the dunes to the tree-covered hills.

"No, what?" All I see are some enormous faraway mansions overlooking the water. I'm not picky. I'd take any one of them.

"That's the old Shore Oaks place."

"Ohh . . ." I wouldn't say I'd forgotten it, I just haven't thought about it in a while.

I've never seen it from this angle.

"Too bad it burnt down. We used to have a lot of fun there."

"You did?"

"Sure. When I was fifteen, sixteen, we all used to sneak onto the grounds at night from the communal beach to party and make out."

"Hmm. That ain't in no town files."

"Of course not. We saw plenty that ain't in no town files."

"Like what?"

"Like mafiosos holding meetings in the library."

"*What?*"

"The place was a cash drop, too."

"And all the local rich kids saw what was happening?"

"Sure."

"And never told anyone?"

"And risk losing the best place for secret screwing on the island?"

"Thanks: Morse and his thugs can't kill a dozen prominent children of the local elite, can he?"

"I'm not sure I—"

"*When* did it burn down? Exactly?"

"Eight years ago. July."

"Let's go."

"Fil—where are you going?"

"There's a pay phone back at the public beach."

15

Revenge is sweet, but not fattening.   —ALFRED HITCHCOCK

I call Van Snyder. Collect. The Precinct switchboard operator starts to give me shit, but I shut him up good.

Van says, "Hello?"

"Jack in, old boy, find out if there are any unsolved disappearances from July, eight years ago."

"That's quite a job, babe. Got any search fields at all?"

"Start with New York and New Jersey."

"Thanks, I considered that in my first statement."

"Then may I suggest you try major mob underbosses and their favorite union heads, ward officers and delivery boys—you know, big enough to count. I bet *that's* not too big of a list."

"No—it's not. What you on to, girl?"

"I don't know. Just a hunch."

"What kind of hunch?"

"Just a feeling, Van."

"Of *what?*"

"That I might be able to bring you a murder."

"Hot damn, just what I need: Another murder."

"A big one, Van. A real big one."

Pause.

"That's quite a hunch, girl."

"Yeah, it is."

Pause.

"Van, I've got an *instinct* about this."

"Oh that's just great. I can't justify an investigation based on a hunch or a feeling, but an *instinct*—well, that changes everything."

"You know what I mean."

"Yeah. You know, the use of reason over 'instinct' is supposed to be one of those things that makes us better than animals."

I snarl my most feral growl at him. Kelly looks around to make sure nobody else heard it.

"Trust me, Van."

"Yeah, yeah."

"So?"

"Give me a couple of days."

"No." And we have our usual exchange where he tells me it's impossible and I end up talking him into doing it by tomorrow morning.

"Where you gonna be?"

"I don't know," I say. "I'll call you." I hang up the phone and tell Kelly, "Thanks. I think you may have saved my life."

"How?"

"By giving me hope."

Kelly drives me to the university library and goes with me to ask to see the Shore Oaks blueprints again. Prunella's not there. It's the creep who didn't like Antonia.

He says, "Again? You must be mistaken. We don't have any such blueprints."

Kelly begins to protest but I shut her up and take her out of there. "It doesn't matter," I explain. "Now I *know* we're on to something."

Kelly smiles. "Neat."

" 'Neat?' " I laugh. It's time to go back to Minoa.

Kelly says, "Wait."

"Yes?"

"In case I haven't said it—Filomena, I—I learned a lot from you. Good luck. Go with God."

"Thanks. You, too." We hug. Close. Tight. Together.

It takes Van eight straight hours to check up, sniff out, chase down and squeeze blood from, but he gets it: Three guys who weren't "made" themselves but who worked for the mob on Long Island. He gets their sheets, with the town names. Two of them—Paulie "The Greek" Kratides and Alan Goldstein—are concentrated in Queens and Nassau, but one has got a little more time in Suffolk: Abe Slaney. A Chicago-based grifter who headed east when the wind shifted.

Van says, "It's time to play that hunch."

It's time to see Kate again. I call her office to ask if Gates is in. When I'm told, "He'll be in a meeting until three o'clock," I say good and go in to see Kate. I tell her what we need, which involves inventing a bit of "evidence," loudly and publicly, and then planting it where it will make the most noise.

At a quarter after three, Phil Gates and his clone Frank Schmidt come back from their meeting and find me leaning over Kate's shoulder at her computer design console.

"There's no more traces because of the fire," I tell her. "Only police photos. The message makes no sense. He was on his back, and therefore writing 'upside down' relative to the lighting in the photo, which actually highlights the features from below."

"Well, what I can try to do is scan in the image, then manipulate it once it's on screen to light it from 'above.'"

Gates says, "May I ask what *you're* doing here?"

I flash my badge (I get it right this time): "Official police business. Ms. Minola has consented to help us with a crucial piece of evidence in a murder case. I'm sure you won't mind."

And I've just committed another felony. They're starting to add up.

I give Kate the photo. She turns it into megabytes in about five minutes. Her disk is pretty full, so it's bulky and slow, but it works. Katherina inverts the image, then gets to work on the patterns of light, telling the computer what to do to reverse the values, pixel by pixel. It takes twenty minutes before we can start to make it out. It's still a messy pattern, a scrawl, but suddenly the name "DiMaggio" forms out of the random fragments before our eyes.

"Goddamn, will you look at that?"

"Now what did you say this photo was?"

"It was found scratched into a piece of green felt at the Shore Oaks estate," I say.

"Why wasn't it destroyed in the fire?"

"I don't know."

"And where is the original? Since you can't use *this* as evidence," she says, pointing to the computer screen.

"Nobody knows. It disappeared when they were cleaning the place out. Maybe it's in your plant."

Katherina chuckles.

"Or something else that was saved from the fire."

I get the image to Van Snyder, who has the story printed in the local papers. Then we sit and wait. For two nights we stake out the storage closet on South Campus holding the Shore Oaks grandfather clock. Nothing. Then, on the third night . . .

A shape comes creeping through the storage drums, gingerly keeping a penlight aimed at the ground directly in front of him. He knows right where to go, though he trips noisily on a box and curses. He waits. Several minutes go by. When he's sure all is still, he takes out some keys—*keys*—I can hear them jingling, and opens the door to the inner closet. He goes right up to the slightly scorched grandfather clock and opens the pendulum chamber. Nothing. His breathing gets a little frantic. He searches, then seems to think of giving up, like it's all too improbable. Then he discovers the second drawer under the pendulum and forgets himself: "Aha!" he exclaims in triumph, holding up the tattered fragment of dirty green felt. I can see it from here. It says, in big letters, FREEZE, SUCKER.

"That's it," says Van Snyder, at regular volume, and the lights go on, and Frank Schmidt stands wide-eyed and open-mouthed, trying to cover himself up like a teenage Portnoy caught with a slice of liver.

"You still going to take all the flak for your boss?" says Van.

Schmidt's still clutching the message. I ask Van, "You put that in there?"

"Shucks, yes, ma'am."

"You scamp."

Gates's defense is that the mob started meeting at Shore Oaks with Vaughan Carter back in the fifties, but that plea has more holes in it than the junior senator's memory. New York looks down rather harshly on misuse of state property. Of course, Gates isn't guilty of murder, just guilty of being a shithead. Schmidt was just his gofer. Gates knew what Old Man Carter had been up to and saw no reason to discontinue the tradition, taking his cut like a good little boy. And when the fly went foul all he wanted to do was protect all his nice images and endowments, so he withheld evidence from investigators relating to a mob murder. That doesn't go over well at all.

And of course all those mob sitdowns were about splitting the "rights" to poison the territory with their illegal toxic waste dumping. How's *that* for a PR nightmare, Mr. Gates? I give odds he'll last about two seconds before he tells them everything he knows.

Now here's the funny part. Morse has *nothing* to do with that eight-year-old mob murder whatsoever. He's completely clean in that regard. But when Van initiates a full-scale investigation of the site, something funny happens.

The police start sifting through the ashes at Shore Oaks. They find the charred remains of $50,000 in cash—or rather, in ash—and they're well on their way to finding more. I turn in those text fragments I found at the site. I don't know if they'll do any good, but they sure help slow things down. Morse is screaming for them to finish and get out, but sifting eight-year-old ashes for possible clues to a murder takes a couple of weeks and you know what? The bank pulls out of Morse's Shore Oaks deal too, and then his whole empire starts coming apart at the seams.

It appears that Mr. Samuel Morse was leveraged to the eyebrows, and the two deals that have just been killed cut the rope from under him, leaving him dangling. Creditors start lining up to take shots at him, and the biggest blow of all lands three days after the cops seal off Shore Oaks: Unisystems sues Morse for $300 million for "massive fraud." It seems that he had an elaborate scam going that I stumbled onto but couldn't do anything about. Unisystems would lend him money so he could get the computers "customized" for a special foreign market. He would send them copies of the customs invoices with the computers' serial numbers on them, plus the exporter's bills of lading and the importer's receipts as proof of sale. Satisfied, the company would lend him another $10 million and it would all go 'round again. But the fancy, customized computers were never shipped, because they never existed. Morse sent off-the-rack stuff and pocketed the difference. And you don't fuck with Unisystems, even if your name is Morse. It makes the front page of *The New York Times.*

The auditors say they can't imagine how he kept it up this long (nearly five years). The townspeople refuse to believe it—not the man who endowed the Little League team! And they defend him! Wait, there's more: Morse says the Feds can't touch him because so many little people depend on him for their incomes. So the Feds move in to seize his assets and prevent him from closing down: his one insurance policy with the county was the number of jobs he provided. Now he's got nothing, and suddenly all kinds of slime starts to ooze out. Rather than spend a few thousand dollars per load disposing of chemical waste properly, he spent a few hundred and had the mob-controlled carters dump it in the regular landfills, where it leached into the groundwater. Multiply that by a few thousand shipments and you get profit in the millions. But now the water in Old Town is threatened, and *that* turns the county irrevocably against him. They move in like sharks on a dead hippo. *Everyone* wants a piece of him and there's enough to go around.

Some serious probing begins, and a few days later Morse turns up on the front page of *Newsday:* Remember that incredible deal Morse swung, buying up farmland and reselling it for condo development at a huge profit? Well, it turns out the owner of the farmland had been trying *for years* to get the property rezoned, but the local politicians always blocked it. The owner finally gave up, sold it cheap to Morse, who paid off all the necessary people and got his highly profitable rezoning in a *snap.* The investigation eventually implicates several town and county officials, but nothing much happens to them. Something tells me Morse will survive this, too. His kind always does.

And some state officials apparently got "cut-rate" computer services from him, like a mainframe Unisystems 9000 for five dollars. Could this *possibly* have been in exchange for some services? Van tells me the fools made the mistake of shredding only the incriminating documents: That's how he knew they were incriminating. Won't they ever learn?

One thing after another hits, as if by divine intervention. Having tried to work a deal with the Feds, Morse has gone to see all of his old county clients and asked them to discuss all their old deals while he was wired for sound. I figure he's got a few weeks to live if he keeps this up.

And a line of women make the front page of *Newsday* (again) speaking out at a town meeting, mad as hell, asking, Why is there so much breast cancer on Long Island, and, Is it true that it might be the contaminated groundwater?

Gina digs up the tidbit that Morse's mob friends used to get rid of PCB-contaminated waste oil for him by carting it into New York City and selling it to fuel oil distributors, who sold it to furnace owners who unknowingly exposed the entire Metropolitan area to toxic fumes for five years—all during the time I was there trying to raise Antonia in a drug-free apartment. And lest we become complacent, the state government admits that they may have caught Morse, but they are generally powerless against this type of environmental crime.

One good thing comes in the mail:

Dear Ms. Buscarsela [Hey: They got my name right this time.]

Recently you were notified of the existence of a report of suspected child abuse or maltreatment under the above registry number. The original notification explained that the matter was under investigation.

We can now inform you that as a result of the assessment made by the local Child Protective Service, no credible evidence was found to believe that the child(ren) has been abused or maltreated. The report has, therefore, been considered 'unfounded.'

In accordance with the law, all information that in any way would identify persons named in this report has been expunged (erased) from the New York State Child Abuse and Maltreatment register. The local Child Protective Service has also been notified to expunge all such identifying information from the local child abuse and maltreatment register.

> *Sincerely,*
> *Director of State Operations*
> *New York State Department of Social Services*

Hot damn! Morse is dead in the water and I'm off the hook! Call up the Devil and see if he wants to borrow my snow boots!

I'm sending a telegram to Ecuador, packing our bags and going back home. Colomba lends me the money for the tickets. I call Stan.

"Don't go," he says. "You need therapy. It'll lengthen your life."

"Longer life of this quality I don't need. You dig?"

"Yeah. When are you leaving?"

"Not for a couple of days."

"Let's get together. Let's talk."

"Okay, sure."

I read in the paper all about how the Feds are dismantling Morse's empire. Who would have thought his empire was made of glass? Three hundred million dollars owed and zero assets! How is that possible? He owned everything! Swimming pool construction, yacht sales, computers, trash hauling, restaurants, housing developments, condos, research parks, doctor's offices, medical labs.

Medical labs? I read and reread the paragraph. A Fairhaven Town commercial medical lab called Prolex owned and operated by a Morse subsidiary of a Morse subsidiary did throat cultures, tissue analysis, pathology—*biopsies.*

I call Stan back and they tell me he's on call. I tell them to page him then, this is a life-or-death emergency. They find him. I ask, "What lab did my biopsy sample go to?"

"I don't know, wherever the staff sent it."

"Could you check?"

"Sure, but why?"

"Just check."

After a while he comes back: "Prolex."

"Wait for me. I'll be right over."

Stan gets another in-house sample from my chest and analyzes it himself (against his ethics, of course).

The verdict: "It's benign. We can remove it and with treatment and maintenance you should be okay. They deliberately falsified lab results! That's an outrage! That's a crime!"

"Yeah . . ."

"But I need to tell you, it's not over. There's the potential for more tumor growth," he cautions me. "You'll have to keep an eye on this for the rest of your life."

"Which could be?"

"Oh, thirty or forty years, I should hope."

I hold Antonia to me and thank God, from one end of my soul to the other: *"Gracias a Dios."*

"Well, I like to think I had something to do with it. Filomena, I—I realize we come from—very different backgrounds. After all, *Scientific American* was bathroom reading in my parents' house. But won't you reconsider?"

"Reconsider what?"

"Staying here. With me."

"I don't know. It wouldn't be good for your career to be living with a convicted felon. In fact, I'd better blow before they get me. Now that Morse is going down I doubt our deal's still in effect."

"What deal?"

"Oh, nothing."

"But you need treatment, operations, constant monitoring—"

"We've got doctors in Ecuador, too, you know. Listen, you," I say pulling him towards me. "You've got the means. I'll write when I get there, and you can come visit me any time you want. Sound good?"

"I guess it'll have to do."

"That's not an answer."

"Okay: It sounds good."

We kiss. He says, "It'll be at least five weeks before I can take any time off. I'll have to start planning now."

"Well plan, boy, plan." We kiss again. "We'll have more to say to each other in five weeks, anyway. What am I going to do here, sit around and watch TV?"

"Why Ecuador?"

"God answered my prayers, and I have to live up to that now. What else can I do? Sit around and rub Morse's nose in broken glass?" We kiss. A long, good-bye kiss.

I leave the room floating on air. Life! Life! Thank you, Lord, thank you. For the good and the bad. For giving Antonia a mother. Together you and I have really accomplished something here this day.

And God? Thank you for the joys of sex, too. One of your better ideas.

But I stop. The cops have brought in a middle-aged man who looks too weak and distracted to need the two armed guards who are watching his flanks. Never be indifferent when other people need you. I go up and ask the cops what's going on. They say they just pulled the guy off a bridge. No job, a failing marriage, he decided on suicide. Now they have to bring him in for psychiatric observation.

"You mind?"

"Go ahead."

I walk over to the guy and tell him, "I just got over lung cancer. Everyone told me I was dead. But I kept fighting. Now look at me. Doc says I could go on for another thirty, forty years. You hear that? Don't ever give up. Never."

He smiles. "Thanks."

"It's nothing. I owe this place one."

I take Antonia outside and breathe deeply.

"Smell that, Toni? —Clean air, blue sky, green trees? That's life, Toni, life. *Es tan preciosa como lo eres tú.*" It's as precious as you are.

As for the mortal fears—well, I guess I'll always have them.

Colomba calls a cab for us, and Billy says he's applying to the University at Running River, thanks to me building up his self-esteem a bit. "Good." I recommend Kelly Hughes's intro course to women in literature: "Guaranteed to shake up your perception of reality." And he hers.

We all kiss and hug and say good-bye and then we're off, driving past the long lines at the lottery store. One step ahead of the Feds.

I haven't seen the Andes in the longest time. The mountain air will do me good.

I'm sure someone in Ecuador needs my help.

Acknowledgments

Thanks to Alison Hess and Virginia Capon of the U.S. EPA for their war stories; to my agent, Nancy K. Yost, for being in my corner; to my editor at Dutton NAL, Audrey LaFehr, for not losing the manuscript under her ever-shifting pile of work; and to associate editor, Genny Ostertag, for always getting the answers, even long after sundown. Go home!